D0916917

And This Is the Light

Lea Goldberg

AND THIS IS THE LIGHT

TRANSLATED BY
Barbara Harshav

EDITED WITH AN INTRODUCTION
AND AFTERWORD BY
Nili Scharf Gold

The Toby Press

And This Is the Light

First English Language Edition 2011

The Toby Press LLC
POB 8531, New Milford, CT 06776-8531, USA
& POB 2455, London W1A 5WY, England
www.tobypress.com

Originally published in Hebrew as *Vehu Ha'Or*
by Sifriat Poalim, 1946, 1994
© Hakibbutz Hameuchad Publishing House, 2005

The right of Lea Goldberg to be identified as the author
of this work has been asserted by her in accordance
with the Copyright, Designs & Patents Act 1988

Translation © 2011, *The* Toby Press
Introduction and Afterword © 2011, Nili Scharf Gold

Published by arrangement with The Institute
for the Translation of Hebrew Literature

ISBN 978 159 264 229 8, *hardcover original*

A CIP catalogue record for this title is
available from the British Library

Printed and bound in the United States

Contents

Nili Scharf Gold

Introduction

One of the first novels published in Hebrew by a woman was Lea Goldberg's 1946 masterpiece *Vehu Ha'Or* (*And This Is the Light*), long considered to be the poet's only novel.[1] Its psychological, semiautobiographical qualities, its fragmentary form and episodic texture – precursors of later sensibilities in Hebrew literature – were foreign to its contemporary literary landscape and not welcomed by readers focused on the national-historical events of the period. Additionally, the novel's seeming uncertainty that Zionism would succeed might have contributed to its cold reception.[2]

1. Lea Goldberg, *Vehu Ha'Or* [*It Is the Light*] (1946; Tel Aviv, 1994). The title *Vehu Ha'Or* is a quotation from a poem by Moses ibn Ezra, translated by Raymond Scheindlin in *Prooftexts* 17, 1997, pp. 260–265. This translation is used within the novel, as well as in the novel's epigraph. Goldberg uses Ibn Ezra's Hebrew phrase *vehu ha'or* as the novel's title; it is translated by Scheindlin as "It is the light"; it is translated as "And this is the light" in the novel's title.

2. Additionally, Tamar Hess suggests that the existential anxiety of Hebrew readers made them unable to tolerate a narrative that underscored the vulnerability of Zionism by portraying it as an abstract idea that cannot be realized. Tamar

The status of Lea Goldberg in the canon of Modern Hebrew Literature, however, has changed dramatically since then. Renewed critical appreciation for and interest in this great, prolific author began in 1994, near the 25th anniversary of her untimely death and around the time a comprehensive conference was held dedicated to her work (the papers presented were published in 2000). This previously marginalized member of the "Moderna" poets' group (Natan Alterman and Avraham Shlonsky were its center) has since been reread in light of increased Israeli awareness of women's writings. Other important strides made in understanding Goldberg's work have been extremely recent. A complete edition of her personal diaries, which had been partially studied over the years, was finally published in full in 2005. In 2010, an earlier novel she wrote, entitled *Losses*, was posthumously published. Written in the mid-1930s (before *And This Is the Light*), it was permanently shelved by its author, and lay in the archive for decades.[3] Finally, the 100th anniversary of her birth has been celebrated in an international and interdisciplinary conference organized by the Hebrew University in Jerusalem and Tel Aviv University in May 2011.

These new events notwithstanding, Goldberg's novel *And This Is the Light* remains somewhat marginalized. Even though it was reissued in 1994, not a single paper focused exclusively on it in the aforementioned 2000 publication. Instead, the attention to Goldberg's prose has been concentrated on her scholarship; her lyrical, epistolary composition *Letters from an Imaginary Journey*; and her

---

Hess, "The Punishment of Those Who Have Imagination: On *And This Is the Light*, Reception, Zionism and Gender," *Literature and Society in Modern Hebrew Culture: Papers in Honor of Gershon Shaked*, Judith Bar-El, Yigal Schwartz and Tamar S. Hess, eds., Keter and Hakibbutz Hameuchad, 2000, pp. 274–288.

3. Giddon Ticotsky, who edited *Losses*, intimates in his Afterword that it was Goldberg's extraordinary attempt to write a socio-historical novel in the nineteenth-century European, and specifically Russian, tradition. It is all the more impressive because she was writing this novel in 1930s Palestine within a society that was "completely invested in local collective values." See the "Afterword" in Lea Goldberg's *Losses* (Tel Aviv: Sifriat Poalim, 2010), p. 343.

memoirs.[4] Against this background of continuous critical neglect, the appearance of an English translation of *And This Is the Light* is especially exciting. With the representative collection of Goldberg's poetry and drama also at his or her disposal,[5] the English reader can now gain a fuller understanding of one of the most multifaceted and fascinating pillars of Hebrew literature.

Lea Goldberg was born in Koenigsberg in 1911 and grew up in Kovna, Lithuania. Her family escaped to Russia during the First World War and crossed the border back into Lithuania with great hardship. Goldberg attended the Hebrew Gymnasium in Kovna and wrote Hebrew poetry as a teenager. She received her doctorate in Semitic languages from the Universities of Berlin and Bonn in 1933. That year, her poems first appeared in print in Hebrew-language journals. In 1935 she immigrated to Palestine, where Shlonsky surprised her with a published copy of her first book of poems. The poet lived in Tel Aviv where she was a central figure in its flourishing literary scene. She ultimately published ten volumes of poetry in addition to plays, iconic children's literature, literary criticism and translations of European classics from seven different languages. Many of her poems have been put to music and continue to be an integral part of the Israeli song canon. In 1952 she moved to Jerusalem, where she later founded and chaired the Department of Comparative Literature at the Hebrew University of Jerusalem. Goldberg also inspired and influenced a generation of younger poets like Yehuda Amichai, Dan Pagis and Tuvia Ruebner. She continued her literary, scholarly and pedagogical activities until her death in 1970. Her work lives on. Her poems are still studied in schools, her children's books are still bestsellers, and her poems are still being made into popular new songs.

---

4. Criticism has particularly focused on the book dedicated to her encounter with the rather unknown poet whom she admired, Avraham Ben-Yitzhak, in which she constructs a spiritual portrait of him.

5. *Lea Goldberg: Selected Poetry and Drama*, Rachel Tzvia Back, trans., The Toby Press, 2005. This volume also includes T. Carmi's translation of *The Lady of the Castle*, originally published in 1974.

Indeed, despite the long period of scholarly neglect, Goldberg has always been widely read and loved for her high aestheticism, musicality, and unique merging of intellect and humanity. She promoted the beauty of everyday life and had the courage to be sentimental during a time when most Hebrew literature was devoted to nationalistic themes. At the heart of Goldberg's poetry there has always been a duality between the "simple," almost folk language and subject matter and the complex elements she integrated into the intimate immediacy of her poems. Her translator into English, Rachel Back, notes the tension between form and content, saying, "Like Dickinson, Goldberg subtly subverts the very forms in which she is writing by unexpected rhymes, word connections…and startling imagery."[6]

But this is not the only duality that permeates Goldberg's oeuvre. In her only published play, *The Lady of the Castle* (recently republished by Toby Press), she is torn between the refined European culture she yearns for and the positive solution of Zionism; an ambivalence toward both underlies the entire play. And most relevantly to this discussion, the tension between reality and the distortion of it pervades all her prose. This theme is forcefully reflected in the madness that suffuses *And This Is the Light*.[7]

The translation in front of us faithfully captures this tension together with Goldberg's elastic and vivid, yet sparse, prose. The novel's fluidity and its lively, believable dialogues are testament to Goldberg's Hebrew: in the 1940s when the novel was written, modern Hebrew was far less equipped to capture contemporary everyday life than it is today. When one compares Goldberg's prose to other works of fiction written in Hebrew in the 1940s, one cannot help but admire her linguistic and stylistic achievements: whereas the language of her contemporaries is often reminiscent of that of the *Mishna*,[8]

---

6. *Ibid.*, pp. 18–19.
7. Adi Zemach, "Into Reality: On the Prose of Lea Goldberg" in *Pegishot im Meshoreret*, ed. Ruth Kartun-Blum and Anat Weissman, Sifriat Poalim, 2000.
8. *Mishna*: the first written compilation of precepts passed down by oral tradition, collected in the third century c.e. by Rabbi Judah HaNasi.

Goldberg's Hebrew style remains definitively modern, and sounds alive even today. The fact that there is no trace of archaic language in this translation is due not only to Harshav's effort to bring to the English reader a work that is accessible and readable, but to the clarity and simple elegance of the original. Goldberg's style is lyrical and poetic, while remaining light, simple, and at times, conversational and humorous. Harshav preserves the musical cadence Goldberg built from her short sentences. Significantly, the translation also retains Goldberg's artistic eye, which combines that of both a painter and a writer.[9] In describing a scene, she captures not only the physical and tactile details, but the entire atmosphere – you can all but picture yourself in the space. Nothing escapes her eye.

In the following quote, the underwater atmosphere of a room is almost tangible even though it's in the attic.

> A green carpet covered the floor; comfortable green silk armchairs and a small crooked sofa surrounded a round table. On the wallpaper were pictures of orange leaves long as seaweed, and heavy greenish drapes decorated the windows. "Aquarium," Giltman had called that room. (p. 113)

Harshav also manages to retain another signature of Goldberg's style: the controlled yet loaded way she describes the most delicate movements of the soul, even at the height of emotional turmoil. The split-second when the young woman in love realizes that the heart of her beloved belongs to another woman exemplifies this style beautifully. By using the flaming, radiant red of the other woman's clothes, Goldberg avoids slipping into sentimentalism and yet is able to show the inner shift in mood of the betrayed woman with unmatched precision.

---

9. Goldberg did, in fact, paint. Her works were seen especially in her later years and in the papers she left behind.

Nora couldn't see anything but a red coat and a red hat and some sparkling and radiant freshness in her fair face beneath the beautiful flame of the hat...in that half minute, the happy fear that had stirred in her at the sound of his voice was snuffed out completely... (p. 96)

Goldberg also uses her incisive grasp of detail to depict more comedic situations. Through rhythmical repetitions of phrases, she imitates a town's provincial small talk with accuracy and understated mockery: "'You're going the day after tomorrow?' 'Yes, I'm going the day after tomorrow'... 'And you're not sorry to leave the family?' 'Yes, I'm sorry to leave the family.'" (p. 195)

While Harshav's translation of the novel feels authentic and alive, it is important for the English reader not to lose sight of the unique role that the Hebrew language plays for its heroine and, significantly, for its author. As the analyses that follow in the Afterword will argue, the Hebrew language is an active force in the novel.

Without further ado, here is *And This Is the Light*, the only novel Goldberg chose to publish – fragmented, poetic and achingly, undeniably human.

NILI SCHARF GOLD is Associate Professor of Modern Hebrew Literature at the University of Pennsylvania, where she has been teaching since 2000. Born in Haifa, Israel, she studied Hebrew literature at the Hebrew University of Jerusalem and later earned her PhD from the Jewish Theological Seminary of America. Dr. Gold combines psychoanalytic, biographical and cultural-historical approaches in her study of literature. Her most recent book is *Yehuda Amichai: The Making of Israel's National Poet*.

It is the light that goes on glowing through my youth,
And glows yet brighter as I grow old.

— RABBI MOSES IBN EZRA
(Translated by Raymond Scheindlin)

Chapter One

The Train Returns Home

At the second stop after the border, a Jew got into the compartment where Nora was sitting. He was about fifty-five years old, had a big grayish beard, and wore a squashed hat with a narrow brim. He was of average height, and his potbelly poked out between the sides of his long, threadbare coat. His smug expression marked him as one of those small traders who does lots of deals in the little towns on the German border, and this time he'd had a good season, but he didn't intend to flaunt his success. He put his small, worn-out valise under the bench, sighed a short polite sigh, sat down, at first on the edge of the seat, surveyed the rest of the passengers in the compartment with the fluency of a man of experience, and when he had convinced himself that they weren't really dangerous, he sat back comfortably and easily, sucked his fat lips flickering between the mustache and the beard, and spat a lush gob of saliva onto the floor.

I'm back in my native land. At home. A thought of derision went through Nora's heart, whose bitterness wasn't yet mature. Nora was twenty years old.

And as if to confirm her thoughts, the international train started creeping slowly on the tracks, as if it too admitted: I'm home, in my native land, no rush!

Through the half-open window, which bore the tremors of the electric light inside the compartment and the shadows of the trees outside it, rose the smell of the Lithuanian forests – a dank, mossy, peaty smell, and the distant fragrance of pine; a smell of damp fallen leaves of red-leaved box trees and the golden oak – and here, very close, the heartbreakingly thin white trunks raced by the train, the trunks of a birch grove in the dark of a starry August night.

Home, Nora dozed off in a hesitant warmth.

Her neck, long and tilted and very white, moved a little in the sweater's warm gray collar.

The Swedish doctor sitting opposite her leaned his elbow on the little shelf under the window, smiled at her and looked back and forth between her face and her reflection shaking in the black window pane. He smiled at her tilted neck and at the tiny embarrassed movement of her thin shoulders, and at that great seriousness and that extreme resolve that was for some reason in her brown eyes and which are so touching in the faces of the weak and very young.

And Nora suddenly felt the stare of her temporary companion – as if she had been touched – who stopped his conversation a moment; inadvertently, she felt embarrassed and wanted to shield her eyes from him, and as she did, her look wandered to the bearded Jew, now leaning back, with his jutting belly, rolling and crushing a thin cigarette in his nicotine-stained fingers.

He cleared his throat, proclaiming his existence in the compartment, and addressed Nora as if to demonstrate his awareness of her presence alone and thoroughly dismissing the "goy" sitting across from her.

"Ah, excuse me, where are you going?"

Casually and not strictly following the rules of courtesy, Nora dropped the name of the capital and addressed the Swede. "In another hour and a half, hour and a quarter, we'll be there."

He hadn't yet wiped the smile off his face, but there was now something pleasant, free, that made the conversation simple and very nice. "Impatient, aren't you?"

"My mother's waiting for me," answered Nora, and blushed. For some reason, she thought she had to explain and apologize. "She's busy all year long. And now they extended her vacation. She teaches handicrafts."

The image of the mother now hovered, especially soft, in her mind's eye. In the window pane her face appeared bending above her, from her childhood, standing over her bed to wish her good night.

"An only child?" the Swede smiled from a great distance of maturity.

"And where are you coming from?" the bearded man suddenly blurted out.

"Berlin," answered Nora, who didn't feel she had to tell him that, when the school year ended, she had spent two weeks in a small fishing village in western Prussia.

"Berlin?" the Jew repeated and sucked on his cigarette. "And what were you doing in Berlin?"

"Studying."

"Ach," the bearded man dismissed her. "Why do they, girls, study there, of all places? You don't have high schools and universities here?"

Nora shrugged, both amused and annoyed. There was something too close and known in that comic mask, asking questions.

"When I was your age," the Swede wanted to continue the conversation, "and just like you, returning home for vacation, and the train approached the big forest near our village…"

But here the Jew sliced through vigorously. "And what's your name?"

God almighty! Nora sighed to herself and said aloud, "Krieger."

"Krieger, Krieger," the Jew chewed her answer. "So, Krieger…" And he sank deep into thought.

From now on, there was no escape. The interrogation had clearly begun.

Something upset Nora's equilibrium, and the little bit of humor that had been in her so far gave out. It was all, as she had guessed from the start, because the bearded man leaned his head to one shoulder, shut his left eye halfway, and asked shrewdly, "Which Kriegers?"

"You certainly don't know my family," Nora muttered with a trace of hope.

"Ach," he stuck out his bottom lip. "I know all the Kriegers, every one of them!"

"But my family isn't from here," Nora defended herself.

"Doesn't matter," scoffed the Jew. "So, where are they from? Africa? All the Kriegers come from one place. To me she tells tales. Krieger from the owners of the brewery, eh?"

"No. I told you, you don't know them!" Nora shifted impatiently in her seat and her hand began nervously unraveling the tail end of some thread in her dress.

"So?" He didn't relent. "So, the dentist Krieger! He's not your father? Or some relative? Really, not a relative?"

"Really," said Nora almost weeping. "I don't have any relatives."

"But attorney Krieger must be your brother, eh? I know him, attorney Krieger, the only Jewish officer in the army? He had a little sister, of course he did! You never saw him? He's not in your family either? So, what Kriegers are you from?"

Nora didn't answer and turned back to the Swede. And he, who apparently grasped the content of the bearded man's questions, since they were said in slightly Germanized Yiddish, smiled at Nora compassionately, and in his narrow gray eyes behind the heavy glasses, twinkled a tiny, unambiguous glimmer. And Nora smiled back with perfect understanding. And at that moment, she was seared by that deep and burning shame, a strong shame for all three of them. And it was as if she stood on display naked before the two of them: the Jew and the Gentile. Damn them, why can't I just be me, me without being affiliated with one of those two strangers?

Helplessly, she lowered her head, and she didn't think she could raise it again ever.

"Will you allow me to lower the window completely?" said the Swede, who didn't sense her shame. "Or might you be afraid of the wind? There's a smell of water coming from there. I'm willing to swear there's a river here among the trees, or a pond. How forested this country is!"

And since the Swede talked again, so did the Jew. "Well, I don't know your relatives, you said. But I must know your parents." And crushing the cigarette butt with a yellow shoe, he said, "What does your father do? What business is he in? Exporting geese, eh?"

Nora was silent.

"Krieger and Company," the bearded man went on. "Exporter of geese. A fine Jew. An honest Jew. I know him well, eh?"

One more question and he'd know, thought Nora. Know the truth!

In a rage, she turned back to the Jew, and before her brain could choose what came out of her mouth, she blurted out, "I don't have a father! My father's dead! You hear, dead!"

Her voice was choked. Across from her, the face of the pesky Jew twisted in amazement and fear, and he shut up all at once, offended, submissive, in great pity. And from a great distance, from the foreign eyes of the Swede – blurred and shocked – a wise and mature look, a look of polite compassion, flickered at her. But it didn't matter.

What did I do? What did I do? Good God, what did I do? She kept thinking those same words. She no longer hid from herself that that lie, an accidental lie as it were, that escaped from her mouth inadvertently out of shame and anger, had something murderous in it. Out of the *hidden wish* in her heart, something she had never been willing to admit even to herself, and now, since the words had been said, she could no longer ignore it: that damned desire for freedom! And the horror was in another awareness, an incidental awareness, as it were, telling her that, indeed, the lie contained a refuge and a way out and great convenience for the future: the words that slipped out of her mouth now couldn't be futile and anomalous. She knew she would go on using them, taking advantage of them, enjoying them, as a person enjoys a stolen fortune not to be given back.

The rattle of the tracks shattered the silence. She was cold. Papa! She pictured a festive street in her hometown. A crowd. Joyous masses at display windows and Christmas trees. Masses, joyous and dangerous masses. The father ties her hood tight. Holds her up to the window. She's a little ashamed. She's eight years old. You don't carry big girls. Cold. Silver and gold birds in the branches of the fir tree. And the father's blue eyes laughing. What to buy you, little girl?

(Not to think, not to think. That stranger, the Swede, he's a doctor. Our foolish attitude toward mental illnesses. What's he looking at, for God's sake? No. He's not looking at all. Never mind.)

In the room, there was a green carpet. The one that's now upstairs, in Mama's room. Cold. It was cold then, too. I was doing homework. Suddenly the door opens and he stands on the threshold. At the moment not really expected from the sanitarium in Switzerland. Melted snow in his yellowish beard. His hair wasn't gray yet. His face was so fresh, and his lips were laughing: I'm right on time, my little girl's home!

Now of all times I remembered all that, God almighty! I had forgotten all the good. Rightfully, rightfully, rightfully. I wanted to hate. I believed that hatred frees. I remembered, I remembered that night. In the gigantic, unheated apartment. Waking with a start. A stranger's voice. The little girl is scared. A knife bared above her head. A scream. Or perhaps it was a razor, or some sharp kitchen utensil. Fear and other days. Long white corridors of a mental hospital. A man's hysterical weeping, and the broken mother…and the playground and the children: Krieger's father from third grade! He's crazy! Don't think. That Swede. And I, what did I say?

Nora's temple was leaning on the cold black window pane. (The Swede didn't pull it down and it was cold even so.) The beating of her heart and the clatter of the tracks came together in one, inseparable beat. She thought to the rhythm of the hurtling of the wheels, maybe, maybe I'll see him in the very next days. The train is returning home.

She thought, but I resolved to be different, to be quiet, to be quiet, to be free, to be different. I resolved.

How much time had passed? How much time? Why are they silent? Why? Here, the bearded man's back. He got up and stood at the door. What does he care. A broad back, and nevertheless, like a cripple. The train creeps slowly –

And she didn't know and didn't understand how and why – maybe it was the smell of the trees that came from outside? – but all of a sudden she remembered yesterday morning with a sense of relief. I walked on a forest path, in a bathing suit, to the sea, among young pines. The rain was warm and fell on my shoulders and my neck. And I was free.

And from the distance, from another time, Aunt Lisa's voice rang in her ears. "She can't think of anything but herself." And the mother's pleading voice: "She's young!"

When was that? Yesterday it rained. A doe ran toward me in the forest. I settled my account with the past. I'm free.

She felt a little relief. The dark forests hummed behind the window. The light bulb moved in the glass. A distant, fragrant, autumn land, a soaked, black land was there, behind the traveling, dark window pane. Everything goes backward there.

The silence in the compartment probably didn't suit the pesky Jew; he stayed in the doorway for a while and went out into the corridor.

The Swede watched him with a long, meaningful look. Then he nodded slowly and said apologetically, "That's how it is with pesky people." He held out an open silver case to Nora. Nora hesitated slightly and then took a cigarette. As he lit the match and put it to her lips, the Swede said as if to himself, "My father died when I was four years old. I don't remember his face."

Nora knew those words had a special generosity and that she didn't deserve it. To her amazement, she felt tears forming in her eyes.

"The smoke," she wanted to explain. "The smoke always gets in my eyes. I'm not used to smoking. I started only this year."

"Your mother won't be too happy about that new learning you've gotten at the university!" laughed the Swede. "I started smoking when I was eleven. My uncle found me one day hiding, in the well-known place…"

He told about the childhood experience, his furious uncle, his punishment, and Nora listened with half an ear, happy as he was at the quick flow of his speech, and already saw herself in a different light in her hometown –

Tomorrow, I'll walk in the streets, the main boulevard. Who's that walking there? Across the street? Why, that's Nora Krieger. Is it really Nora Krieger? I haven't seen her for a year. Of course, of course, she's studying abroad. Look at her, she got so beautiful, even her walk is different – Nora Krieger. Who? Who's she? That girl who got a prize for some scientific essay? A seminar paper. Something about ancient Egypt. So young! And Lucy Kurtz will come and Hannah Milner, and Mama and Lisa. They're waiting, of course, and getting excited and going out of the railroad station – and in the street, someone will be standing, and will ask: Who's that walking on the boulevard? Nora Krieger. I seem to have heard the name. Nora Krieger.

And once again the tracks were humming, and the express train passed by small stations, and the tracks sang: "No-ra Krie-ger, No-ra Krie-ger." And the cigarette smoke twined and stuck to the window pane, until a great light was seen, striking the windows of the train straight on. The Swede glanced at his watch. "I think you've arrived. Shall I take down your suitcase?"

He stood up and took down her things and she got up and muttered thanks, and looked up to his big hands, easily holding her heavy suitcase.

The bearded Jew came back into the compartment, took the worn-out suitcase, sighed, and said, not to Nora and not to the Swede, but to a third person, who was invisible, "Well, we're here."

Among the tracks, on the broad asphalt in the dim electric light, a few figures scurried about. They grabbed suitcases. They called porters, they waved handkerchiefs, moved around more than necessary, preened excitedly, as if they wanted to hide behind exaggerated activity.

A railroad station at night – young people bustling, tears rising in the throat, the nocturnal smile on the chapped lips and a long interrupted yearning, and a world beyond the tracks.

Those lost figures. The faces of the two women were lifted to the standing train – with hope, desire, supplication and fear – as if she might not come. They were the most lost of all here, more helpless than anyone, those two female figures. They were the only ones there who didn't run, didn't carry suitcases, didn't wave handkerchiefs, and desired only with their eyes, only by *standing*. From that lost standing, Nora recognized them from afar, and her head began moving toward them in the train window. In its pallor, its satisfied smile, her mother's face beamed, and the slightly stooped narrow shoulders of Aunt Lisa, her father's sister, the shoulders that expressed a constant willingness to accept a yoke, to sacrifice herself, were miserable, as always, and for some reason, stirred pity and affection and a touch of anger.

At last they saw her, and with a strange movement of joy, timidity and helplessness, the two of them lifted their arms to her, as if they immediately wanted to pull through the window – her, her suitcase, and all her words and stories about her year, a year away from home.

It wasn't long before she was standing next to them. On her face, fresh from the night's chill, the warmth of their kisses rained down. Both of them spoke all at once, brief, fragmentary, cracked words, empty of content and full of joy. And she gave them hasty, impetuous, unthinking answers.

"Mama, it's so late, and you're—"

But when she tried to look directly into the mother's brown eyes, something strange suddenly went through them, a kind of fear and worry and shame all together, and the mother lowered her eyes.

"What happened?" asked Nora, bothered by the evasive look.

The mother was apprehensive and smiled.

"Why are we standing here? Why are we standing here? It's late, isn't it, she's tired, isn't she!" murmured Aunt Lisa and turned her back to them. And her ringing voice, the voice of a girl, which didn't suit her long, miserable, ageless face, rang out through the railroad station.

"Porter! Taxi! Taxi!"

And in the sound of her hasty, small steps on the emptying pavement there was something desperate and ridiculous.

"I traveled in a compartment with a Swedish doctor," said Nora to the mother, and looked with a sudden longing to where the train had just stood. "He was very nice…" she tried to go on and broke off.

"You've gotten older and thinner," answered the mother irrelevantly.

It was soon clear that there were no more cabs in the railroad station and the porter lifted the suitcases onto a broad, comfortable carriage harnessed to a gray horse. The three women landed on the soft seat. The small suitcase rocked at their feet.

"How was the trip?" asked the mother for the third time since they met.

Nora told about the trip, about the examination of her belongings at the border station and mentioned again the Swede who had happened to share the compartment with her, and didn't mention the Jew.

"And I forgot to tell you," the mother cut through in the middle of the paragraph, and Aunt Lisa jumped ahead on the soft seat, her lips moving like the lips of a prompter worried that the actor will forget his lines.

"I forgot to tell you that you can't sleep at home tonight. They're painting the apartment. A mess. You'll have to sleep at the Bergmans tonight. Yes. There."

"And tomorrow," whispered Lisa's voice.

"Tomorrow," the mother continued, "we'll go to the forest, to a summer cottage, for two weeks. I'm off work now. I did write you. And it won't hurt you either. Yes. Home, in any event, is…a mess."

Her voice, straining to be joyous, dropped. And if Nora weren't so steeped at that time in the rustlings of her own heart and her homecoming, she would have recognized immediately how forced and artificial the cheer was in that beloved voice.

She replied politely and affectionately that she didn't care at all, that it didn't matter to her, and that she'd sleep "soundly" anywhere after such a trip. Only seeing the Bergmans – but she didn't finish, not wanting to offend the mother. And they, the two of them, sighed with relief and fell silent, and she didn't sense that silence at all.

How small the houses had become during that year! And the trees had grown marvelously tall. And that starry sky above. Real nights still exist in small towns. And it's good. That street is good, too. Because I'm only a guest. Because I'll leave here again. And everything that was – was.

For a brief moment, she lifted her head and chose, as in her childhood, one star to accompany her on the way. But she took her mind off it and the star was lost among the hosts of others.

And even though she always considered her soul and feelings carefully, there was now a special magic to that connection between the place and memories, something that gave her both importance and maturity, and sweet was the knowledge that here – in this place, on this road – when we were children, we used to go down to the valley behind the railroad station. How we walked here, a big gang of "Indians," armed with bows and twigs, with black bread and bottles of lemonade for the road, the boys and girls bringing up the rear. How long ago that was! The carriage rocked like a cradle. And here's the big rickety building. Papa built it before the war. Somewhere is a sign saying: "Architect. Krieger." When I was little, I thought it was beautiful; God almighty, how ugly it is! It used to be a theater. Here we'd hold the "traditional" Hanukkah parties of the Gymnasium. December evenings, chilly December evenings, and deep snow. And the eternal danger that always lay in wait for me in those days, catching the flu, was also "traditional." Please don't let the mercury rise in the thermometer! I can get over a sore throat in one night –

And the next day, a strange racket in her ears and the fever rising. The soft fluff a little heavy on her neck. And Mama's sad voice: "I said they don't take care of the children! If only they had at least heated the auditorium!" And that pleasure-pain of an illness that isn't dangerous and is exhausting. And a book, the thick book of Dickens, its pages yellow and worn from so much reading, and the names of the chapters in it so long and comforting, unlike the exciting plot. How good when the mercury rose to thirty-nine! And the memory of the small offenses from the party that vanished and the hardships of David Copperfield became one episode. Dickens's thick, beloved books are now resting on the bookshelves of the public library – once upon a time there was a little girl, as in a fairy tale – good God, where did that leap come from? And her father built that building, too. They're like scattered tombstones here in the city, those buildings. And they're not beautiful. I don't like that style from the turn of the century. I don't want to think about those buildings.

And that alley goes up to the mountainous park and the hills around it. Here, on that hill, she'd help Olia graze the goat. She was nine years old. The goat would consume the grass of the hill. The little girls lay stretched out on their backs among the high, lush stalks. The summer sky overhead, and the clouds above them moving slowly. When she was five years old, her father taught her to love those clouds. He told her about them as though they were strange and beautiful creatures from the Scriptures: Jethro's flock. And the light sinking on the treetop – the burning bush that isn't consumed. She always remembered those words, and her soul was elegiac in the bosom of nature even in her childhood. Sometimes, she'd think she was also a very marvelous creature, big and wise and knowing the secret of the grass and the trees.

"Listen, Olia, I hear the grass growing."

Olia twisted her mouth in scorn, just like a grown-up, and declared, "That's impressive."

Childhood street. Night. Why are the two of them silent? The carriage driver yawns. He's tired, too. I want to sleep.

The carriage turns left. Her street.

"Mama, are all the people asleep already in our capital city?"

The mother laughs. "Look at her, that night owl from the big city!"

And the leaves of the glorious chestnut tree across from the painted fence of the pleasant and quiet courtyard hadn't started falling yet.

In the Bergman house, they were expecting Nora. Everything there was as it had always been, even though supper was so late, and despite the year that had passed since she had last been there.

As always, fat old Bergman met her and her mother with his usual words, probably from all his life: "Good evening, ladies, come into my arms." And as always, after an answer that didn't come, he concluded, "You don't want to, no need. I'll find someone nicer than you."

And he laughed a laugh of fat pleasure, and withdrew to his armchair and sank into it, and would doze off and not open his eyes until food entered his mouth.

And Shoshanna Bergman, his wife, also chubby and short, her very black hair surrounding her round and aging face just like a wig, kissed Nora on both cheeks and hugged her for a long time in her warm arms. A tear even sparkled in her eyes: she always cried easily.

On the table, as always, a big copper samovar hummed and sputtered, called by the members of the household "papouchka," because it had a potbelly like the head of the family. And as on every day, so this evening, too, Shoshanna Bergman would pour tea into tall glasses and keep filling Nora's plate with pastries, and would take care to blurt out from time to time, "Eat, eat." And suddenly she would look at her in a different way, and would sigh and ask with great concern, "You *really* study there?" For, from the experience of her two sons who had been sent abroad to study, she knew you didn't "really" study there, and those studies were nothing but a delusion. And looking for a long time at Nora, who as usual blushed to tears and tried to mutter "yes," she suddenly nodded and drawled out in a voice melting with pleasure, "Well, yes, you're studious here too." And Mrs. Krieger, who sat wearily, and leaned her head on the back of her big beautiful hand with her own special grace, glanced gratefully at Shoshanna Bergman and smiled at Nora. And Lisa chewed a hard apple and didn't say a word.

And as always, so this evening too, the presence of the two Bergman sons was indicated only by a photograph, that enlarged photograph, hanging on the wall between two plaster bowls crowned with the cheap, colored reproductions of Raphael's angels, and everybody tried not to look at the photograph since the older one, Boris, a handsome fellow, clever and jolly, had been in prison for two years for communism; the younger one, Marek, a degenerate Tarzan, was probably playing cards at some "club" in town. The two well-groomed boys looked out of the photograph very calmly, riding next to one another on rocking horses.

The conversation ebbed. Sometimes, Shoshanna Bergman would glance into Mrs. Krieger's face with compassionate curiosity. Until finally, she nodded and said, "No, no!"

"What no?" asked Nora with the indifference of the slumber that descended on her and not noticing at all that no one answered.

And at that very moment, the door opened and Marek, the lost son, returned home.

"Ah, Nora!" he said and smiled, like someone recalling a very funny tale, and concluding in his father's voice – "Come into my arms!" – he tossed his coat into his mother's arms as she stood next to him and waited for that, just like a coat-check girl, and without paying any attention to her, he came to Nora, grabbed her like an older brother and said in his mother's voice, although apparently not meaning to imitate her, "You're *really* studying there? Eh?" And with a wink, "Or have you finally found something more interesting?"

"Idiot!" said Nora and thrust out her lower lip with disgust, and that too was as in the past.

"Nora!" scolded the mother.

"Children!" pleaded Shoshanna Bergman, who had meanwhile managed to give her son's coat to the servant.

"I want to sleep," said Nora. "It's late."

"Well?" the elder Bergman suddenly stirred from his doze. "If *that one*'s arrived," and he pointed at Marek, "it means it's very late."

The mother and Lisa got up to go.

"I'll be here tomorrow morning," said the mother, and they went, leaving her alone among those antiques in the Bergman house.

That night, a childhood nightmare returned to her. The same dream, without any change at all, just as she had dreamed it four times, always after an interval of many years. The first time, it came when she was still a baby, at the end of the first year of the Great War.

Things were clear and took place in the light of day. A clean and very spacious yard in their house in one of the cities where they wandered during the war. Antonina, the maid, goes out to bring wood for heating. She goes to the woodshed, chooses a few pieces, and among that wood is a dumpy Russian beggar woman. A small dark kerchief is on her head, and her arms and legs are amputated. She's short and smooth as a thick log. Nora, the four-year-old, walks behind Antonina and shouts, "Let go of the woman, Antonina, let go of the woman!" But Antonina's steps are even and calm. She goes inside. In the big living room she unloads the bundle of wood with the woman rolled up in it, then she calmly feeds it into the gaping maw of the stove. Her coarse, calm hands reach for matches in the big pocket of her apron. "Don't light it, don't light it!" Nora pleads. "Don't you see, that's the woman sitting in the little cart at the corner! She begs for alms 'for Jesus the Savior'!" And the little woman among the wood slowly nods her wrinkled head and her thin black mouth stretches into a smile of mute agreement, pitiful to the point of tears. The tears choke Nora. She feels her legs die beneath her. Then Antonina puts the lighted match to the dry wood, and it all goes up in flames.

At that moment in the dream, Nora awoke this time too, as in all previous times. Her heart was cold with absurd and endless terror; her legs seemed to be separated from her body, as if they were completely paralyzed. As soon as she woke up, it still seemed, as in childhood, that that wasn't a dream, but a *memory*, and that that whole incident was a reality from back then, but she couldn't remember when.

Afterward, her thoughts cleared up a little and she was amazed at the strange recurrence of the dream. But the silly physical fear still lived in her, fear of the cold heart, the cowardice of the paralyzed legs, the tried remedy against bad dreams, the known remedy from childhood that could be effective this time too: with every effort of the will to turn over onto the other side, and that – she believed – couldn't let the dream continue.

Her eyes got accustomed to the dark. Now the face of the little mirror hanging on the opposite wall would emerge.

In the dark of the narrow little room, the smooth surface of the mirror gleamed, magician and foe, and there was no refuge from it. Nor was there any refuge from this wakefulness in the middle of the night, just as there had been no refuge from the dream before.

That miserable room in the Bergman house, after the train ride, persisted in not wanting to be a room like any other. Nora felt the narrow bed under her body, the dents in it, the wrinkles in the sheet – that was just how she lay in that place, in that bed, in those days, when she had the German measles. That was –

The year nineteen hundred nineteen. We were a convoy of refugees coming back to the homeland. Through fire and cold and lice.

The first isolation in childhood. That silly event: the border guard of the small country, ignorant peasants in army uniforms, staring at the father's yellow shoes. They said they were a clear sign, those shoes, that he was a Bolshevik spy. Then they locked him up in an empty barn. And day after day, for ten straight days, they executed him, as it were. For ten days in a row, that game went on. And the man was broken, then, for the first time, Nora heard him weeping in a thin, female, sobbing voice. And the desperate pleas in the mother's voice: "For the child's sake, I beg you, for the child's sake..." And some strange woman, who knew how to preserve a polished appearance even in that shabby and exhausted convoy: "Isn't he ashamed, a man crying!" and a scornful laugh – and when they came back, they put him in prison. From there, the only road was to that hospital.

A two-week trip – it is strange, but beautiful fields were also engraved forever in memories. Blue flowers in the high corn, and that dull golden light of early September. And a tiny green frog sitting on the well one morning, after a rain, and the sky was gray and soft, and the greenery was glowing and deep.

They say they were hungry on the trip. She remembers, too: she didn't eat for whole days. But the hunger wasn't oppressive. There was water to drink, and for some reason, she made do with that. She still remembered only the first encounter with white bread and the happiness about it. There was nothing offensive about it. It was good in that warm, whitewashed peasant hut. The yellow straw on the floor, and the pink immortal flowers on the yellow fluff between the two window panes. And the clean white walls, no chill and no lice. The white bread was the first harbinger of real peace, of that "after the war" that had been promised her throughout her childhood. The peasants smiled goodheartedly. People didn't scare her anymore. That was the first time they weren't awful, after two weeks of wandering on the road.

And there was everything that very evening: the mother went to try something with the sentries guarding the father in the barn, with that clear-eyed, pink-cheeked officer who told with pleasant innocence how he had executed ten officers and soldiers of the Red Army: "One shot, Ma'am, and he falls like a bag of straw!" Nora remained alone at the crossroads among fields – to watch the pile of belongings. She sat on the bundles. Alone. In the field. At the crossroads. It grew dark. It was cold. Her hands and legs were frozen. Armed soldiers passed by. They didn't touch her. Hours passed. It was absolutely clear: never would her parents come back. She would freeze here at night. And a little self-pity: she was only eight years old, too young to die! But fear froze everything.

And only when the mother returned did a cracked, brief weeping burst out of her mouth. But afterward, there was the warm nice hut and the white bread.

When they returned to their hometown, it was night. The father was in prison; the mother's friend, the fat Shoshanna Bergman, was nice to people, smiled and wept and hugged her with warm arms. Afterward, they put her in this bed. The flowers on the wallpaper turned into wild animals, swooped down on her at night. From the little mirror on the wall, pale and contorted faces burst out, and her father's voice pleading in her ears, "Let go of her, let go of her, don't you see, the child is a pile of nerves!" Then she fell asleep and dreamed of the beggar woman burned in the oven. Here she dreamed, in this bed. The next morning the doctor came and diagnosed German measles.

When she recovered from the illness, thin and pale, all her dresses were too short; it was clear to her at long last that this was that "after the war" she had been promised for five years. But they didn't buy her the big doll. They wanted to reward her with an orange. The shining beautiful fruit, which had also become legendary during the war, was placed on the heavy, brown buffet in the dining room of that apartment. "Eat, eat," Shoshanna Bergman coaxed her. She grabbed the orange in both hands and sank her teeth in its peel. They, the grown-ups, looked at her and laughed. "She doesn't know how to eat an orange!" laughed Marek. Even Mama laughed. Nora put the orange back on the buffet and refused to eat it. Shook her head without a word, lest she burst into tears in front of them. Only the next day, when there were no people in the room, did she eat it. And by then she didn't care what it tasted like. That was the beginning of life "after the war." And that was how everything that came after was: school, that city, life at home.

Very slowly, Nora pictured to herself the years that had passed since the last time she had dreamed that dream. And suddenly she was afraid that her year, too, the year abroad, which she had fled to with the mighty desire for freedom in her, that year too, would end up wiped out and canceled because of those memories.

Suddenly, she pictured the strong, square image of that clean-shaven Prussian professor of history, who would sometimes show a dry excitement and prove the "deep logic of human history." Deep logic! Her face twisted with hatred. Deep logic, when a man's fate is determined because of yellow shoes. If that's the logic of life, go believe in the logic of history!

But suddenly, she sat up in bed and whispered, "I'll be very happy, just to spite them!"

And she unconsciously shook her head slowly, as if denying her own words.

Afterward, she lay down again. Her head was heavy. She leaned on her elbow. A wet pre-dawn light flowed in through the crack in the shutters, and the little mirror on the wall returned a chilled silver to it. Nora's head landed on the pillow, and she slept.

A few minutes before eight in the morning, Mrs. Krieger entered Nora's room and stood near the door. Nora was asleep. The light from the dining room next door and a leap of day that burst through the crack in the shutter crossed over the sleeping girl's bed, illuminating her light fair hair scattered over the pillow, half her forehead and part of her face. The end of her nose gleamed, and her lips were opened and a little puffed. That made her face look like a little girl's, and she was calm and relaxed.

The mother stood hesitantly. Then she turned her back on the sleeping girl and tiptoed out very carefully. She still tiptoed in the dining room and didn't dare walk freely until she came to the kitchen. There, Shoshanna Bergman, her hair wispy and gleaming from the heat of the stove, wearing a fuzzy red housedress, was frying black bread in butter in a big skillet – Nora's favorite breakfast.

"Well?" she said to Mrs. Krieger, who stood aside, embarrassed and helpless.

"She's still sleeping," she said, and remembering Nora's sleeping face, she added apparently irrelevantly, "She's so young!"

"We all were young!" sighed Shoshanna Bergman and turned the bread in the skillet with the end of a long kitchen knife.

And since Mrs. Krieger didn't answer and went on standing

hesitantly, Shoshanna Bergman turned her full face to her and said reproachfully, "You spoil her too much, Esther. Think how that will end."

"And your Marek?" Esther had a fleeting malicious thought, but she repressed it along with the sigh connected with the thought, and without a word, she tiptoed back to Nora's room.

At that time, probably by order of her mistress, the maid began opening the shutters of that room from outside. The light streamed in all at once, struck Nora's eyelids, and she woke up.

When she opened her eyes, she immediately saw the mother standing near the door, and immediately smelled the toasted bread. Everything was for her sake: mother and bread. A good awakening, as in her childhood after a long illness.

"Good morning," said the mother in a slightly emotional voice, as she approached the bed and sat down in the Viennese chair next to it.

They smiled at one another.

"How did you sleep?" asked the mother and somewhat nervously straightened the blanket on Nora's bed.

"Excellent. Thanks."

And at that moment, Nora really didn't remember her dream or being awake at night. But suddenly something moved in the mother's face. Nora saw a little bit of gray in her short, fashionably cut hair, over her very white temple with its thin blue veins. She's getting old, she thought with a slight pain. But no, that's not it. Not that. And suddenly she remembered her dream, and she saw precisely some strange line, going down from the mother's soft lips to her chin, a kind of bitter wrinkle cutting the face with a cut that wasn't in it before. And it was absolutely clear to her that something had happened. Why didn't I see anything yesterday?

"I was afraid to wake you," said the mother. "You were so tired last night."

There was already something strange in her voice, as if she said those words to postpone other things.

"No, I slept enough," answered Nora. "In general, the trip was so good. A Swedish doctor shared my compartment on the train."

"Yes, you told me that last night," said the mother.

And they fell silent. Words suddenly ran out and Nora didn't know where to find other ones, since she did have to find some, because only conversation could put off, or even wipe out, wipe out completely, the thing that had happened. And now there wasn't a shadow of a doubt that something had indeed happened.

Her eyes left the mother's face and ran over the big bookshelf opposite the bed (next to that mirror) and for the twelfth time they read the gold title on the backs of the dozen volumes of Brahm's *Lives of Animals, Lives of Animals* –

"I wanted to tell you," she suddenly heard the mother's voice and her eyes returned to her face. The face was pale, announcing both a decision and an apology. And both of them, mother and daughter, knew at that moment that nothing would help and that what was said couldn't be taken back. There was a pause after the opening words. The mother shifted, almost gluing the chair to the bed. She smiled nervously and then pursed her lips a lot, and her face became severe, as if she were about to scold.

"When you weren't here, some things happened with us."

"Papa?" asked Nora in a frightened whisper.

The mother confirmed it only with her eyes. And silence once again. And Nora had to ask, "What? He came back? And the attacks?"

She wanted to add something, to say what she had prepared to say, about that perverse attitude to mental illness. The barbaric, stupid attitude, as that doctor in Berlin had said to her, "It's really like a chronic abdominal illness and there's no difference." Yes, that's what the doctor had said, and she would also say so. But the mother slowly shook her head and her face suddenly became alien and cold.

"That, too," she said in an opaque voice. "But I don't know your attitude to me. I couldn't tell you before. In writing? I couldn't. So, yes, I separated from…I divorced him."

The mother's face was tense. A chill lay on it like a rind over great suffering. It was almost dead.

"You did well!" Nora blurted out with sudden confidence, and since no other word came to her. "Very well."

"Thank God!" burst out of the mother's mouth. A damp flash sparkled in her eyes. And both of them were relieved.

"And now?"

"Nothing. Understand, he's still here. At home. That's why you slept here last night, even though he's very quiet now. You know, quiet and sober, and full of understanding and humor, as he is on such days," she said with restrained bitterness, and Nora slowly nodded, knowingly. "But if you came…and so you came back to us, and here you are – surprises."

Shuffling house slippers were heard, and old Bergman stood in the door, wrapped in a worn-out, wrinkled dressing gown, "that had known better days."

"Good morning, ladies, come into my arms!" And just like last night, he concluded to himself in a lush voice, "You don't want to, you don't have to, I'll find someone nicer than you."

"Well, come on, come on, old fool! Don't bother them!" His wife's voice was heard from the kitchen, and despite the nickname "old fool," there was an ineradicable trace of submissive admiration in that voice.

All those were conventions, but in addition to those conventions, Nora felt – even though she was a bit stunned from the conversation with the mother – that Shoshanna Bergman certainly knew what was being said here at this moment, and that if she had free time now, she was probably standing and listening behind the door. And it was bitter for her that she was once again being put, in spite of herself, into the loathsome common pot of their life.

Between one thing and another, the time wasn't right for such soul-searching. Bergman obeyed and took off. Once again, they were left alone, facing one another. She and her mother. But the foolish old man's outburst broke the mood of closeness and understanding between them. They couldn't go on from where they had stopped. Nora lay and listened to the Bergmans' big apartment waking up. In the dining room, certainly not far from the table, the paddling of the old man's soft shoes, the rustling of a newspaper. Far from that, Marek was walking around. He was also in house slippers, pushing some objects on his way and whistling some popular tune. In the kitchen, the maid was chopping meat or grating vegetables, and that even and muted sound disturbed and prevailed over all the other sounds in the house.

"What time is it?" asked Nora to break the silence.

"Eight-twenty," answered the mother, and some vague fear was in her voice; Nora felt that the question about the time wasn't proper and that, no matter what, she had to talk about "that issue," otherwise there was no point and no value to those encouraging words she had said. She sat up in bed and touched the mother's hand with one finger.

"And there, up there," she said at last, and the two of them understood that she meant their apartment on the second floor in that courtyard. "With him? Lisa's there?"

"Yes."

"And she?"

"She helped me, she gave me extraordinary help. I don't know what I would have done without her."

And those words, the mother's words, were steeped in gratitude, and yet behind them flickered something like a restraint about a vague insult.

Nora imagined all the details of the situation. Lisa was *his sister*, and no doubt: with her unbounded goodheartedness, her objectivity, as it were, to both sides, she did everything she could to help her sister-in-law. And she does everything wholeheartedly, but – as always – perhaps too wholeheartedly. Somewhere, behind her good deeds, truly good, lurked the feeling of pleasure at self-sacrifice, of being a sacrificial lamb, somewhere that strange desire would surface to both emphasize and blur the fact that she sacrificed her life for others, and that the debt of the others grew larger from one day to the next, and would never be paid, and she gave up repayment in advance – gave it up lovingly, submissively, almost appreciatively. All that Nora knew, and she said aloud, "Sacrifice and Christian ethics?" She couldn't repress the bit of a sneer.

The mother glanced at her in surprise, almost amazed. "You've grown up during the year." But her voice was immediately serious and scolding. "You mustn't say such things."

"But Mama," Nora was embarrassed. And she said, almost pleading, "You yourself said I've grown up. And I see everything. I also love Lisa. But I'm not a baby anymore."

For a moment, a smile lighted up the mother's lips and made her face very soft. But she sighed immediately and admitted, "Yes. Sometimes it's hard to be with a person who's immeasurably better than us."

"I don't like saints," decreed Nora unreservedly, and didn't feel how she contradicted her earlier declaration of love for Lisa.

The mother didn't respond, and Nora said, "And how is he now?"

"I told you, quite good. After months of dread, you know, of course…now he agreed to move to an apartment out of town. There's a Christian family there. Nice, honest people. Very honest. Yes, wonderful people. And the house is lovely. In a garden. And there are pear trees there. Really. A very lovely house," the mother exaggerated her praise of the place as if she were asking forgiveness. "And I had no other way. It wasn't about the apartment. In general. You know it's beyond a person's strength. And if I didn't do that, he wanted to go on living at home…yes, at home."

Nora knew and understood. And that wasn't the right time to preach morality about the attitude to that illness. At any rate, she, who said what she said yesterday on the train, she wasn't authorized to judge others harshly anymore.

"You did well," she repeated her earlier words, unable to find other words with any weight. And after a brief hesitation and blushing, she added, "If you had asked me, I would have advised you to do that. In fact, nothing has changed, and no one has to bear the burden of life and take on more than necessary."

She was talking about herself. She wanted expiation for herself. She knew that was the situation. But maybe, maybe this was the other way out, the way to liberation.

"Get dressed!" said the mother. "We have to travel today."

Nora got up, thrust her feet into dark blue slippers, and wrapped herself in a dressing gown without putting her arms in the sleeves. She picked up a towel.

When she turned back to the mother, Mrs. Krieger was weeping. Silently. Unmoving. But big tears flowed from her eyes nonstop, and she didn't cover her face.

Chapter Two

The Forest

The small ferry shuttling back and forth a few times a day between the city and summer resort on the river was packed.

Today was Friday and the merchants and their wives, the shopkeepers and their apprentices, left the city for the weekend and headed to the wooden houses and huts nestling among the pines across the river.

Nora and her mother barely found a seat on one of the long benches on the deck. The mother, wearing a silver-gray summer dress, sat in touching modest glory, leaning back against the white railing of the boat. Her hands on her knees were clasped, big and aristocratic, and one ring, old and dark, crowned one of the long fingers. (The wedding ring was no longer on her hand. How come I didn't notice that this morning?) Her nut-brown eyes, studded with small golden spots inside, were calm again. Nora looked at her from the side, from the space of separation still between them, and was a little proud of the way the mother looked and acted, as if all that were her handiwork.

The mother told Nora the details of her life here during that year.

"The girls learn whatever they learn," she said. "Sometimes their work is nice, even artistic work. I still love my work and think it's important. Just imagine, they're poor girls, from the lower classes, and when they finish school, they know a trade. But sometimes I'm tired. Simply, slowly getting old. Well, and Lisa, from morning to night, she's always in her office. Always taking care of all those stupid things. But she'll never get promoted; she's too honest and she's not pushy. Yes. And Aunt Zlata is very sick, I wrote you—"

The mother sighed. But because the conversation revolved around Aunt Zlata, Nora stopped paying attention. She was sick of that aunt. She had never grasped how the mother could have maintained close relations with that provincial and narrow-minded woman only because she was her brother's widow. Nora's eyes moved over the crowd and sought acquaintances, but a wall of broad behinds, fat bellies, well-endowed breasts and blowing beards, hid the rest of the passengers from her. Behind all their voices, behind the gurgling laughter of the men, the moans of the women and the shrieks of the children, rose a popular tune from last year, probably played by a small garbled orchestra, hiding somewhere on the stern of the boat.

Nora turned her head around, leaned on the railing and looked at the flowing water. The water was green and deep, and the river was very broad in that place. Beyond it was the bank with its oaks and pines, suffused with lushness, and here and there the cattails stuck up through the greenery with their velvet-brown heads. The heavy boat sailed lightly, and passed fields whose stalks were mostly harvested by now, and piles of yellow-green hay in meadows, whose good smell rose and even reached that happy ferry and mingled marvelously with the smell of sausage and duck fat eaten by the broad-hipped women and their pale children, and with the smell of wicker baskets and sheepskin and sour cheese wafting from a few peasants sitting close to Nora, who were returning to their villages after market day, with the basket empty and some copper and silver coins jingling in their pockets. Overhead, above the boat, was a high August sky, thin and distant blue, and a few grayish clouds stood motionless in it, like big tired birds frozen in flight. The banks passed. And there was already a lot of gold in the trees, and the clover was dark purple, and potato fields were black and pocked and desolate.

"I'm going to walk on the deck a little," Nora said to her mother and stood up.

A crush. Bodies. Elbows. Sweaty faces. A pungent, sticky smell of sweaty armpits. Bare arms. Freckles. I sit amid my people.

"Damn him, may he join his father's father's father!" one of the clumsy, furious women above Nora's ear cursed. "My Hershele ate his apple, says the damn gentile. My Hershele of all people, I beg him from morning to night to taste a little food, him of all people…"

"But Ma'am," said a tall thin Jew with a short beard sticking up and shaking nervously, "why get so excited? So, he ate it – good health to him."

Nora wanted to squeeze through and pass between the voices and the bodies, but she got caught in the crowd, who were buying lush yellow pears from a peasant sitting on the floor.

"Here she is! My word! Nora Krieger! In person!" shouted somebody behind her back. Nora turned her face around.

Two students she knew from the past were holding out their hands to her at the same time. Nora returned their handshakes and smiled. She really was sincerely glad to see them, even though this time too, as with all meetings with them, it was never really clear to her why they pretended to be such "jolly fellows" when in fact they were not jolly at all.

"Here she is! Here she is!" the one named Giltman cheered, and gave her a long handshake.

"My God! My God!"

"And we, my lady, we swore, just this very moment we vowed a true vow by all that's holy to us and to the Pope in Rome, that you were still abroad, studying the science of Persia! Oh, yes!"

"But he was right, the American, wasn't he!"

"Oh, yes!"

Nora laughed and pushed and was pushed, and pressed and was squashed by the crowd and was amazed at the manners of the two, and her head was spinning. "Who? God in heaven? What are you chattering about? Why 'Oh, yes!'?"

"It's our fault, my lady, it's our fault, we've betrayed, and so on...but some American here is looking for you."

"Where – here?"

"On deck. On this splendid 'steamer'! He came in a splendid auto just as the boat was leaving, oh, yes! And he asks the whole honorable crowd and investigates and demands: Where is Mrs. Krieger and her daughter Nora, and where is Nora Krieger and her mother Mrs. Krieger! That's it..."

"Dammit!" Nora got angry and grabbed Giltman's arm, which served as a shield against the basket of a skinny Jew who was passing by just then. (You couldn't stand in one place. And even those who imagined they were standing were slowly moved forward by a wave of people.) "Speak in a human language! What are you jabbering?"

"No, my lady, please forgive us, we aren't jabbering. A minute ago, here, on this deck, he spoke to us, your faithful servants...oh, yes! Look, Giltman, she looks well. Here, my fair lady, et cetera. You didn't even say hello to us properly."

"Fine, but...he made us swear, us..."

"Oh, yes! The American made us swear by the hinds and wildcats, he made us swear to reveal your hiding place. Pleaded with us..."

"Stop!" Nora wanted to thwart them. "In what language?"

"In seven tongues: English, Yiddish, Russian, and even Hebrew. Oh, yes."

"What is this game you're playing? Anyway, what did you tell him?"

"It's not a game! We said you weren't on this planet at all."

"And he?"

"He said, 'Oh, no, oh, no! I know for sure; she told me, Miss Lisa Krieger in the office!' And now if you don't believe us, come and we'll take you to him, he's standing next to the band, still standing and begging the ladies and gentlemen."

They pulled her behind them, working their elbows diligently and parting the crowd like the Red Sea. Nora was drawn, not knowing the object of this game, or what surprise was in store for her on the stern of the boat. Her two escorts pushed her and others, and chattered nonstop, and she chattered and laughed and for some reason was also a little excited.

"Here he is!" Giltman suddenly shouted.

Next to the horn player in the band, who had just finished his piece and was wiping the shining brass with a filthy rag, stood a tall man in a very light gray suit. The man was thin, slightly bent, his hair dark with gray strands here and there. You couldn't tell his age at first glance and that was surprising, and he looked somewhat vague, but there was definitely something sad and hesitant about him at that moment.

Nora's two escorts pushed her to him, while they themselves stood off to the side like badly behaved babies. Some shadow of fear passed over Giltman's face. He rounded his lips to declare Nora's arrival with some clownish bombast usual for him, but there was something in the stranger's face that stopped him, and his voice came out thin, like the voice of a rooster who only yesterday had been a chick. "Here's…Nora Krieger."

Nora looked at the stranger with amazement. His whole figure told her that this wasn't a joke and nobody was making fun of her, but there was probably some mistake here. She stood hesitantly, stood for the twinkling of an eye, but it felt as if she had been standing like that for a very long time and all eyes were fixed on her. She turned around to ask for help from the students, but they had taken off in the meantime and she had to glance at the face of the stranger, and then something flickered in his expression, something known but not grasped. And at that moment, he stretched his hand out to her and smiled as if both apologizing and glad at the same time.

"Oh, yes, of course, Nora Krieger."

The voice was a little surprising – low, muffled, a bit too drawn out, the accent was foreign, and Nora knew for certain that she had never heard that voice before in her life, for if she had – she wouldn't have forgotten it. Nevertheless, she held out her hand, and then some change took place in the man's face and she was very frightened and blurted out, "But, but – Albert Arin."

Meanwhile, Arin's face held no solution since it neither affirmed nor completely denied the romantic feeling. His presence here, on this deck, was a fact. And yet, in some sense, he was still – abstract.

Now they were sitting comfortably, all three of them, Arin, Nora and her mother, on a long bench near the bow of the ship. For, in the meantime, the ship had dropped anchor at the first stop on the shore and most of the crowd got off for vacation spots in the forest. The deck was suddenly spacious. The band wasn't playing anymore, and as the trip continued, the pine smell from the forested shore grew more pungent.

The three of them were still very excited, and the mother showered Arin with questions: When did he leave California? When did he arrive? Why hadn't he written during the years or answered their letters? And does he know that Olga wrote from Detroit that a rumor of his death had reached them? And they didn't want to believe it and hoped, nevertheless. And here – and had he really come last night from Berlin? Nora had also come last night from Berlin. And why didn't he write a letter or send a telegram and tell them? And how had he found Lisa's office this morning? Yes, yes, sometimes he had written her at that address, and she was still there. And how had he managed to catch the boat? And where was he headed now, and did he have any future plans? Albert, Albert, there was no way she would have recognized him, no way, if he hadn't said his name – twenty-three years –

"Twenty-five, Esther…"

The low, slow voice was close to the ear. Here, he was actually sitting here. Sitting and talking. And for some reason, there was distress in Nora's heart. A feeling of surprise attacked her too strongly, and only behind the amazement, something crept up, a kind of joy at meeting and expectation of a wonderful continuation. She thrust out her lower lip a little, and moved her head back, leaned it on the railing and looked at the guest out of the corner of her eye.

He didn't look at all like the Arin in the two photos he had sent her in the letter. And nevertheless, after a few moments, even the voice was no longer a partition between them and she was quite sure that *this*, this was the face of the man she had never seen in her life, whom she had invented only from his letters. So it was no wonder she knew him!

In the mother's eyes, too, Arin's face was a kind of very blurred photo, a photo of a living and real expression from her past. And her life, that life, whose whole essence was real in her eyes and even more physical than the present, was now dimming like twilight before her eyes.

"Twenty-five years!" Her words rose like an echo of her thoughts. She thought, twenty-five years! Jacob and Albert and I. So young. A year after we got married. The apartment was new. Pink wallpaper in the living room. That was considered good taste back then. Jacob was sure Albert would be sentenced to hard labor. His poor wife! So pale. Shapeless. Her dresses hung on her like a skeleton. Like a sack. And only the chest stuck out. She was nursing then, the poor woman. And that arrest. It was spring. Yes, of course, it was spring. I had a purple straw hat and a scarf and violets in my lapel. Two officers turned their heads. Yes, we were so happy compared to Albert and his wife. It was spring. We thought they came for no special reason, to stay with us, when we moved to that city. It was spring. Jacob said the whole business of the expropriation was stupid. Five and a half rubles in the post office. The Russian Revolution. And for that – to Siberia. I had a gray spring coat with a wide collar. Yes. New. Who believed he would escape to America? And I had violets, Jacob said –

In the syntax of her thoughts, which had been accustomed for so many years now not to rely on her husband's words, old phrases just popped up: Jacob was sure…twenty-five years. She was no longer thinking of Albert Arin, she was thinking of herself, her youth, her handsome, brilliant, healthy husband.

And only rarely did her eyes return to the silent face of the guest. What is he thinking now? What is he remembering? He is surely also reciting to himself: twenty-five years.

Twenty-five years – thought Nora – a quarter century. I wasn't even born. They were unimaginably young. They probably think they were happy then. They always think that after many years. They don't remember the hell in the heart of a young person. But that's their past. That doesn't concern me. They didn't have a war like that in their youth.

For her, Arin's real reality began later. She was fourteen when she got the first letter from him. And a Hanukkah present. From someone almost anonymous: Papa's friend. But the legend of Arin came before. The letters that arrived from him, which he wrote to his parents right after the war, when she was eight years old. And the stories, those stories of that adventurer…yellowish paper, like ivory, and a verse in Yiddish, stuck in her memory like the opening of a song:

> *Es iz geven amol a tsayt, az ich bin geven farlibt in Shpanish.*
> (Once upon a time, I was loved in Spanish.)

And a song in a foreign language:

> *Siempre vago per il mondo*
> *Siempre voy adelante*

What a soft word: *adelante*!

He was in Mexico, Guatemala, Honduras, and then in California. The epic of Arin: Siberian episode, wanderings in the homeland of the Incas. She had never believed her parents that he was exiled to the Yucatan for some trivial matter, because his revolutionary activity was unwise. Not him, not someone like him. The correspondence of her early youth, that was some journey *for her,* what an odyssey! She would always remember with open-eyed clarity, almost by touch, the yellowish paper of his letters, and the firm's header at the top of the page. At first the firm's header was also wondrous. A strange overseas address. Like an oath. But when she learned English, the words were translated simply: "Cigarettes and Tobacco Company." Offensive, awful reality: her Odysseus a shopkeeper! That was a harsh blow, a slap in the face. In the city of shopkeepers, among the sons of shopkeepers, she had found refuge with someone amazing, completely different. And all of a sudden – suddenly here he is, too, the adult friend, who writes letters *like that* to her, as to a grown-up friend – a store for cigarettes and tobacco! Why, why did Albert Arin have a store? To this day, something inside gnawed at her, something that forced her on those nights to say a fervent prayer to the God of all girls who have no god, to that hidden force, whose name is "if only" – if only he was a day laborer, a sewer cleaner – anything. But a shopkeeper, her Spanish poet, the wanderer – *Siempre vago* –

"Quite simply," Arin wanted to explain to Esther Krieger a tenth of the reason for his surprising appearance, "something like missing the old homeland and old friends. And because you live here, and not in the city where I grew up, I was too impatient to wait until I'd be 'rich Uncle Sam,' and I set out as I am."

"And your business?"

"The store?" He raised his head a little, rolled his neck back and laughed a jolly, mischievous laugh, as if he had just heard a good joke and he had to reply with an even better one. "My store has departed from this life. End of the store. I sold it and am squandering the money I got over here."

Nora suddenly felt relieved. As if something was lifted, an obstacle cleared away, a hard question somebody was supposed to ask her during an exam, deleted. She was relieved, and didn't know if it was because of the liquidation of that store, or because of the good ring of the laughter. But now, in her eyes, Arin was at long last a real reality that wasn't burdensome.

"I always wondered – who are you?" At last she addressed him and blushed.

He smiled, took a while to answer, looked at the strange childish way she blushed: the redness flooding from the end of the nostrils to the cheeks and the earlobes. And when her whole face was red, he seemed to recall that he was embarrassing her and looked straight into her eyes looking at him – bravely and loyally despite the embarrassment – and declared, "This is who I am. A Jew with gray in his hair. And you, Nora? I remember your letters very well. Are you still 'wasting away in the provinces,' young lady?"

Nora shook her head, wanting to shake the red flame off her cheeks.

"No. I'm at school in Berlin now."

Her answer was whispered, and he didn't seem to hear it at all, and when he started talking again in the muffled, low voice, she didn't know if he was answering her question or saying it in a contemplative voice, simply, "And I, if I had had a choice, I would have rowed day and night on this river."

That's how they always are – thought Nora – all those who grabbed handfuls of life and saw a whole world, they advise us to be satisfied with this river.

And he said, "Look at that beautiful shore."

And on the shore, the pine trees thinned out. Then a yellow sandbank appeared. Beyond it, beyond a turgid strait, appeared – their backs to the crowd – rows and rows of small huts with sloping roofs. Latrines of the summer resorts. Who knows why the owners of the resorts had built them just at that place where the boat docked.

"The resort house," a big wooden, two-story house, was still new. Its construction had been finished only at the beginning of that summer. The walls of the room still smelled of wooden boards and carpenter's glue. Here and there, drops of resin gleamed clear as amber. The forest was both outside and inside.

The furnishings were bare, random, meager – two iron beds, a big brown, clumsy armoire, a rickety table, two chairs and a wardrobe. But within an hour, the two women had settled into the room and it was changed beyond recognition. A few small things, trivial objects, were scattered casually in it. Some vase was presented, a cloth was spread, an embroidered rustic towel was hung in one of the corners, a small perfume bottle, and even a brush and comb on the wardrobe gave everything a homey charm. That was Esther Krieger's motherly, feminine hand.

It was four-thirty in the afternoon. The mother had already finished hanging up her things in the armoire, lay down on the bed and was absentmindedly leafing through some book.

Nora was kneeling at the drawer of the lower closet and putting her shoes in it. The wind came from the open window, drifted over her bent neck, played with her hair and blew the smell of pine into it. And because her face bent over the drawer was hidden from the mother, it was easy for Nora to talk to her.

"Isn't it strange, Mama, that he came straight to the boat?"

It was good that, between their conversation that morning and now, there had been the "event." It didn't matter what resulted from it. Every incident was now a separation they both needed, and from now on, it was possible, as it were, to start living.

"Has he changed a lot, Mama?"

The mother closed her book, put it on the bed, and looked at Nora's back. She thought some unimportant thought and said, "I don't know." Then she picked up the book again, but didn't open it, and repeated, "I don't know."

Nora shut the drawer. She got up, went and sat down on the high windowsill. Her feet didn't reach the floor and were hanging and swinging in the air. There was some feeling of childish freedom and playfulness in that movement. Half her body was outside; below was a forest, trees, hammocks.

"You'll fall!" warned the mother as she would have warned her daughter in childhood, and laughed.

"But isn't that strange, Mama?" Nora repeated. "Here he comes!"

Under the window of the room stood Arin. He was whistling the first bars of some song.

"I'm going to rest," said the mother. "Go without me."

Nora ran down the stairs. Her heart was pounding from running and from some excitement even she wasn't aware of. Arin was waiting for her in the doorway. Now he wore a white shirt with an open collar, loose pants that reached his knees knickerbockers-style, tennis shoes and long socks. His face was fresh and younger than on the boat.

Nora wanted to say something, maybe to ask him if he had had time to rest or to comment casually that he looked like a tourist now, or perhaps to tell him that her mother apologized, she was tired and couldn't join their stroll. But she thought too long about which one of those things to say, and in the end, she felt she had somehow missed the right moment to say one of those things, and she smiled in embarrassment and didn't utter a word.

She waited in vain for Arin to get her out of her embarrassment and say something. He was silent and didn't see her timorous smile, as if that silence was self-evident.

But since they had started walking side by side, and were passing the hammocks hanging between the trees, passing the summer tourists lying on blankets spread over pine needles, passing the sounds of words and laughter and scratchy gramophone records rising from one of the distant summer resorts – the tension ebbed, and the silence wasn't heavy, and the embarrassment simply vanished. They walked very close to one another, like people who are long accustomed to walking like that.

There was some hidden border in the forest, where the kingdom of man ended. As in all summer resorts, here too everything was clumped together in one place, according to an unwritten law – here and no further. And beyond that was space. Nora felt that the trees here stood differently, and that they were different.

A narrow path stretched between ancient pine trees whose

trunks turned red and whose crests were dizzyingly high. Their growth wasn't cramped and the sunlight laid spots of light between them.

The day was clear, one of those calm days in late August, when thin sticky spider webs rise in the air. One of them came down on Nora's face and stuck to her eyelids.

"Wait," said Arin. He took a handkerchief out of his pocket and carefully removed the sticky silver thread from her eyelashes. And when they went on, he suddenly asked, "Can you sing?"

"A little," said Nora and looked at him inquiringly.

"Here," he said and started humming some old tune, a Russian ballad Nora had picked up in her childhood from the mother and Lisa, and it always reminded her of Mama's black hat, the one with the thin polka-dotted veil, in the style of the beginning of the war, and some rustling silk dress and the smell of mothballs. But Arin, apparently, connected the song with this forest, with outings in his youth, with that wind and those spider webs.

Only now did Nora dare look at his face. The face was harsh even now; only at the edge of his humming lips was there something like a smile. And strangely, that smile didn't soften the face.

"What is this, mockery?" thought Nora. And for a brief moment she felt a kind of fear. "Is he mocking me?" But she calmed down again immediately and realized that somehow he was making fun of that ballad, and maybe the memories of his youth.

"Mama used to sing that when I was little," she blurted out in a hesitant voice and looked at him apprehensively, lest she had said something dumb. But he nodded as if he agreed, understood, and now his face did become softer, and the smile was full and revealed very straight and strong teeth. He went on humming and walking, and here and there, a blurred and unintelligible word of the old song came out of his mouth, as if he had taken it out of a dusty box of memory.

As they walked along like that, Nora understood, as it were, the secret of her excitement as she came down the stairs to him: she was afraid he would ask her a lot of questions about the father, the mother, the family. And she was relieved that he clearly didn't want to ask and interrogate, and she was grateful he didn't use that walk and their first acquaintance to get some kind of confession out of her. But something was bothering her nevertheless: why doesn't he ask anything about her?

Suddenly he stopped humming and asked, "Why is your name Nora?"

"At that time, Lisa was reading Ibsen," Nora explained briefly and blushed. She remembered how her classmates teased her because of that name.

"Ah, Lisa!" said Arin and smiled.

They climbed a low hill and came to a small, bare clearing where all the ground was ancient yellow from last year's pine needles. Behind her was a grove of young trees, and a few boxwoods already had the red flame of autumn. One uprooted tree, apparently broken in a storm, was lying flat here.

"Shall we sit?" suggested Arin. And without waiting for her answer, he sat down. Nora chose a place where the trunk was bare of bark, and was smooth and comfortable – at some distance from Arin.

Here the wind blew stronger. Nora lowered her eyes and looked at her bare arms. The wind caressed them and slowly moved the soft, thin, almost invisible down on her arm. Something was magnifying the shape of things, and she thought of sheaves swaying in the wind, the corn bending over in the summer.

"So?" said Arin.

Nora shrugged, helplessly. He bent over, picked up a connected pair of pine needles, separated them in his fingers into the shape of a Roman numeral five, looked at them for a bit and said, "Say something."

"What?"

"What do you like to remember?" he asked as if he were thinking of something else. "Say something about this summer."

Nora didn't know why her mouth opened or why she said what she said. "This summer was very hot in Berlin," she sighed. "The humidity was stifling in the city. That humidity and the steaming asphalt and the gasoline – awful! My friend Antonia, she's a Christian German. She studies archaeology, like me. Yes. What was I saying? Yes, Antonia, she's a redhead. Her hair is like copper. Not gold, copper. That's not important. Once we decided to leave the city on the first morning train. At three-thirty. In fact, in the middle of the night. At sunrise, there were three of us – she and I and Rüdiger, our friend, a musician. Before dawn, we got to the station. We were going to Grinau, a suburb of Berlin. The city train was still empty. Almost no passengers. And the few there were – waiters returning from work in the cafés where they were used to a 'long night' (that's what they call it there), and the same sort of girls…worn-out coats over polished black suits. You understand? Waiters. And all the faces were sleepy. And a smell of tobacco and smoke. All through the train, a smell of clothes that absorbed smoke during the night. And two workers. Gloomy, as if they were angry at all of us. On Sunday. I don't know where they were going. But they clearly weren't unemployed. The unemployed look different. It's easy to spot them. It was a little uncomfortable to be among those who get up early. Because we got up early for leisure, for no good reason. But it's nice nevertheless. And from the train window, as we approached Grinau, we saw the sun rise. There was fog and it was red on top of the gray. A red ball. Without rays. Awful. By Grinau we were left alone. We got off. The sun almost couldn't be seen behind the fog. The suburb had its own special charm. But not a single person. Antonia led the way. Her reddish mane was very beautiful. We went out to the field. And there was sand and railroad tracks there. We walked along the tracks, and the fog grew denser. Just like a screen over everything. And all of a sudden, on the sand, next to the track, we saw such a multitude of red poppies. Wild flowers. And nothing else. Only those red flames and the fog. There was nothing in the world but those two colors. Red and gray. Only those two…"

"Yes?"

"That's all. Afterward, we went back to Berlin."

Arin was silent. And Nora lowered her head. Very slowly her

eyes filled with tears. Why did I tell all that? What demon pulled my tongue? Now he'll think I'm a fool and boasting of some special relation to nature. All that pretension, and anyway…but I didn't even know I'd tell that…

Arin was silent. At last Nora swallowed the hard lump in her throat and asked without lifting her head, "That's really dumb, isn't it?"

"What?" he asked as if returning from some other world. There was a kind of distant amazement in his voice, something completely disconnected from reality.

He wasn't listening at all, thought Nora. And that thought was both consoling and insulting at the same time – he was thinking about something completely different.

She raised her eyes and saw that his face was tense, as if he were listening to some faraway note. He wasn't looking at her at all.

"Horses' hooves," he declared at last.

"Yes," said Nora. "There on the road behind the grove." Her voice was still choked.

I was talking into empty space, she thought.

He stood up, nodded.

"Red and gray," he suddenly blurted out. "Only two colors. Red and gray."

A wave of warmth flooded Nora's breast and passed. Suddenly, she was relieved. She stood up too, and Arin looked at her closely and nodded in agreement.

"That's what I imagined," he said. "Yes. From your letters. But the story was even more beautiful. Because it was as if it were–" He broke off and sucked his lips.

"Irrelevant?" concluded Nora, and the two of them suddenly laughed out loud. He tapped her shoulder very lightly and said, "Relevant to another matter."

And when they turned to the road where the horses' hooves were heard, and two riders, a man and a woman in green tunics, were there, he looked at her again and asked with the cunning of a lad who trips up his teacher, "But the matter, what really is the matter?"

He doesn't talk much, Nora thought that night. But his silence isn't the silence of someone who doesn't know how to talk. Something happened in his life. A long time ago he used to walk on the banks of the Amazon or the Mississippi, I don't know. And then he sold cigarettes and tobacco. And when we had a war here, there was nothing there. He didn't see people swollen with hunger. And so what? What do I know about him? Suddenly his face was the face of a lad. But he is old, he could be my father. Could be my father, my father…

It was dark. A chirping was heard outside. Then it was stopped by the footsteps of a single person pacing, back and forth, back and forth, in the next room.

The squeak of the mother's bed: she was probably turning onto her side. And a sigh was heard and returned Nora to other thoughts she didn't want to think. It was a deep night, and she had to fall asleep. And she fell asleep. And in a dream, somebody stood and asked her, "But what is the matter, what really is the matter?"

On Saturday afternoon, there was a sudden downpour.

Most of the guests at the resort house had already finished their dinner and each one went off to his room. On the big verandah, only Nora and her mother remained. The mother was glancing at a newspaper and Nora, who had taken time to eat, was slightly bent over her plate and paying attention to a big and very ripe raspberry in her spoon. Inside the full red berry a tiny white worm was making its way among the pips of the raspberry to the dark hollow in it. Nora watched the worm crawling and suddenly a mighty thunderclap was heard.

"Oh, Jesus-Maria!" groaned the maid, Tekla, who was clearing the dishes off the long table.

The mother jumped up and dropped the newspaper, and Nora leaped up behind her.

And right after the boom, a terrifying rain poured onto the foundations of the forest. Big drops dripped through the cracks of the wooden roof of the verandah onto the table, the floor, and the heads of the two women.

Both of them ran upstairs to their room on the second floor. The mother hurried to the half-closed window, and was about to shut it.

"Mama, please, there's no need!" pleaded Nora gaily, hugging the mother's waist and dancing around her.

The mother smiled, pulled out of the hug, and opened the window wide. A smell of rainy forest, intoxicatingly sharp, a smell of burned pine and soaked earth, filled the room.

The two women undressed and lay on their beds. For a while, the sound of the resort house proprietress giving orders came from downstairs, along with the rustle of Tekla's quick steps, as she cleared the table and moved the chairs. And then those sounds fell silent too and only the mighty stream of the downpour was heard. No more thunder. The rain wasn't at all like the annoying rains of August. It had the strength of early spring. Through the open window were waving pine branches and the sharp, scared tip, thin as a cross on a church, of the single fir tree growing at the side of the house.

The two women were silent a while, listening. Nora's head was fresh, as if that downpour outside washed it out, too. Between the roots of her hair, she still felt the chill of the drops that had dampened the verandah.

"And what did you do in your fishing village when it rained?" asked the mother.

"There," answered Nora and laughed a short, happy laugh, "I was very busy. We cooked by ourselves. We'd crouch on the floor, Irena and I, and we'd peel potatoes (every single day we ate potatoes), and Hermann would sit on a tall chair and read us chapters from Jean Paul, with an awful pathos."

The mother sighed with fond mockery. "I can imagine the taste of your meals!" And after a short silence, "But where did Albert disappear to? Such a rain!"

"Tekla said it pleased the gentleman from America to go walking at six in the morning and it did not please him to say when he would return."

"Pleased him. Pleased him to come here and tour the area, fine, good. Such a rain. Of all days. And Lisa's supposed to come this afternoon."

"But it's a wonderful rain!"

The mother yawned. She turned her face to the wall and shut her eyes.

Nora lay stretched out and listened to the streaming of the rain and the creaking of the waving trees. Arin had been out walking since morning. What does he want here? Why did she tell him all that nonsense yesterday? But it was good. Rain. The hammocks downstairs would be wet and wouldn't dry out for at least two days. What a fragrance of a forest, good God!

Unwittingly she fell asleep.

When she opened her eyes, there was no more rain. In the open window was a backdrop of washed, blue sky, with the fresh green of the trees on it.

The mother was already dressed, standing at the little mirror on the wardrobe and fastening the collar of her jacket with a big coral pin. Slowly, lazily, Nora lowered her bare feet off the bed and thrust them into the blue house slippers. She sat sleepily, disheveled; the afternoon sleep had dispelled the freshness, something strange and heavy was cast into her, that disturbing heaviness liable to grow and become irritation and make her quarrel and argue with people for no reason, and not accept apologies.

"Why this sourness all of a sudden?" asked the mother, giving her a fleeting glance.

Nora was silent.

"Listen," said the mother, and turned her face to the door.

On the stairs was the hasty patter of a woman's footsteps.

"Lisa," said Nora. It was strange that that sound of feet climbing the stairs wasn't wiped out over the year by other sounds.

And when Lisa came in and sat down in the room on the chair in her own special way, "half-Turkish," with one leg folded under her and the other hanging in the air, a very childish way of sitting, which didn't fit the gray in her thin hair, it was like a prophecy that was fulfilled: the heaviness of habit in the way the three of them walked, an unavoidable shared fate, or whatever you call it…

A gray pall of weariness seemed cast over Lisa's face. Her lips smiled, but her sickly eyes were half-covered with heavy eyelids. Reddish, slightly swollen, as if they were worn out with constant weeping at night. Her expression had always been like that; Nora remembered it like that from her earliest childhood.

"Hello? Hello! Nora, show your face in the light of day! You've grown up, gotten tall, thin. It's rained! Well, have you had time to rest? It's good in the forest. It's raining! A summer rain. Maybe the last one. Did you sleep after lunch? Me? I'm not very tired. No. God forbid. Thank you very much. You got tanned at the seashore, Nora. But you're still thinner than you were."

Later on, when Nora dressed hastily in the presence of the two women, Lisa was telling how last night she helped the father move to his new apartment. How she settled him in his room, and what wash she took to the laundry. She went into great detail about the laundry, listed and detailed and lingered, as if there was salvation in laundry. And another pair of shoes had to be bought for him, and meanwhile, the old ones had to be mended.

Nora sat on the bed. It took her too long to fasten the two buttons of her sandal – her head down. No need to look. No need. When I was little, she'd sit for whole nights at my bed when I was sick. She could even tell stories. And she'd also help with arithmetic lessons, she and not Mama.

She raised her eyes. Saw the two of them. Something healthy was in the mother's face, had remained in spite of everything. A trace of that peasant blood flowing in her veins. Her ancestors were peasants, among the very few Jews of Belarus. They were still living on their land a generation ago. Sturdy Jews, easy with people, and not clumsy. Grandfather had nimble hands. He could make a table, plant a tree and trim it. But Nora knew that her own blood was conquered by the paternal base, and that she, like Lisa, was a scion of the Krieger family, great-grandchildren of rabbis and cantors. She didn't want to be like Lisa. But Lisa was good, really. Lisa took care of the father; Lisa worried about the welfare and health of people. And Nora didn't want to be so good, and didn't want to be loaded with worries about others, and didn't want her eyelids to be red, and didn't want all her loved ones to suffer pangs of regret, guilt mixed with pity – she didn't want all that, and at the same time, her heart attacked her for that lack of desire…because of Lisa.

"Aunt Zlata is very sick, I saw her this morning. She gets sicker from one day to the next. By the way, Nora, you hurt her very much: she thinks you should have visited her on her sickbed as soon as you came."

Nora dropped her head; you would have visited her sickbed, I know, I know.

The mother shrugged and blushed a little: her brother's widow was always full of grudges and complaints, even when she was silent and didn't say what was in her heart. After all, she could have understood. Now it's a good idea to change the subject of conversation.

"Go ask if Albert's come back yet, Nora. No, wait, your hair isn't combed yet."

Nora got up and silently combed her hair at the small mirror on the wardrobe.

There was a long, unnecessary silence. Then Lisa said, holding her breath, "Oh, Albert! And I completely forgot he's here. Really, isn't it strange that he came? I saw him only for a minute in my office. Hurrying so much. How is he?"

A lie, Nora sensed immediately. It wasn't clear why Lisa hesitated to ask. But now she was absolutely sure she had wanted to ask about Arin as soon as she had come into the room. Why do they always dissimulate? Always, always, all of them, when there was really no need!

The mother said, half in jest, half resentful, "Albert picked up his feet and escaped. Ever since this morning, he's gone off. If not for the suitcases he left in his room, I'd worry that he'd gone back to America."

"But what does he say in general?"

"Nothing, you can't get a word out of him. If I didn't know he was widowed, I'd ask how his wife was."

"He doesn't have to account to anyone!" Nora suddenly burst out.

The mother looked at her in amazement and grief. "Silent, silent, and then…as if I, of all people…" she said with a dismissive gesture. "Well, let's go down and have some tea."

As they went downstairs, Lisa's face grew gloomy and she said, "But in this rain, he went for a walk. He might catch cold!"

"Who?" the mother was amazed.

"Albert."

Nora bit her bottom lip. God in heaven, why does she have to worry about the health of the whole world!

On the verandah, the summer lodgers were drinking tea.

And the maidens go to draw water and there is no well in the village. And they go out of the village to draw, on the highway, toward the desert, and the drawers of water see a well and a big stone on the mouth of the well. One of the maidens tells the man coming toward her, Please roll that stone off the mouth of the well, for our flocks are thirsty. And the one coming toward her says, I won't roll it off, for the stone is very big. And the maiden raises her voice and weeps. And the man coming toward her says, Why do you weep? And the maiden replies, Because the stone is very big.

On the verandah, the summer lodgers were drinking tea.

Arin was there, too, and Nora's two guests, Giltman and Dina Globus. Dina Globus had been Nora's classmate in the Gymnasium. She had a gold tooth in the middle of her mouth and no other distinguishing features.

Lisa hurried to greet Arin. Giltman and Dina Globus swooped down on Nora. Nora didn't hear what Arin told Lisa and the mother.

The mother sat her guests at the tea table: Lisa between Arin and herself, Nora between Giltman and Dina Globus. The summer lodgers were drinking tea. The copper samovar steamed, and the wind blew its smoke to the rain-wet trees. Men with shining faces slurped the tea and wiped the sweat off their brow with handkerchiefs. Potbellied women drank their tea with thin, hasty sips, and would take compacts out of their purses or their bosoms and powder their noses, some openly and some in secret. The proprietress of the resort house, a tall, thin, erect woman, with a tanned face and a boyish haircut, supervised the cups and plates. Her face was serious and scolding, and her coarse voice imposed discipline on everyone. The guests were a bit apprehensive in her presence and didn't make much noise.

Only at one end of the long table did a woman's voice break out now and then and declare in a throaty Russian, "Mrs. Aronson said, but Mrs. Aronson said!"

Dina Globus said to Nora, "I saw Marek yesterday. I met Marek Bergman last night. He told me you came."

Nora said, "Yes, the day before yesterday."

Dina Globus said, "Marek told me you came. Anyway, I'm here at the summer resort with some friends. I said I'd come see you. Marek, they say, is playing cards in the club."

Giltman said, "And losing."

Lisa sighed. Arin was silent. The mother offered Dina Globus some raspberry jam.

Dina Globus said, "In our resort house, there's currant jam."

The mother asked, "Red?"

Dina Globus replied, "Of course."

Lisa remarked, "There's also black."

Giltman said, "Black smells like fleas."

Nora said, "And I like black."

Giltman said, "And I blondes."

Dina Globus laughed long and loud. The mother and Lisa laughed a bit for the sake of courtesy, not for Giltman but for Dina Globus. Arin smoked a cigarette.

Dina Globus finished laughing with a shriek and said, "They say that in Germany there is no currant jam."

Nora said, "I don't know. Apparently not."

Dina Globus said, "They say there's no white cheese there either."

Nora said, "There is, but a different kind."

Dina Globus said, "I was told there isn't. And no 'rosemary' sausage either. And the butter is fake. And everything's expensive."

Giltman winked at Nora. "And they don't have trees like this there either. Or a forest like this. And altogether…"

Arin said, "There really isn't a forest like this there. I've walked since dawn in the villages around and along the river."

Lisa asked, "And in the rain?"

Arin said, "A peasant woman took me into her house. I ate bread that was so black and milk that was–"

"So white," the mother concluded.

Arin laughed, "I swear, Esther, you're right!"

Dina Globus said, "They say there's no black bread abroad either."

Nora said, "Yes."

Dina Globus finished her tea and said, "Thank you very much. Now I have to go. I promised them a game of croquet. So long, Nora. You still have to tell me everything about your life abroad. It's so interesting! So long!"

She got up, shook hands with Giltman, with Nora, with Mrs. Krieger, parted from Lisa and Arin with a nod, and left.

Arin puffed on his cigarette a long time and pensively watched Dina Globus go. Dina Globus went down from the verandah and turned left, to the summer resorts. Arin said, "Why is her name Globus?"

Giltman laughed. "Her arms embrace the world."

Lisa sighed.

Nora thought, Why is her name Globus? And why do you have a name like Nora? Lisa was reading Ibsen. Dina was reading Globus.

Nora said, "Why is your name Albert Arin?"

Arin thought a moment and replied seriously, "My name, in fact, is Aharon. I don't remember now when they started calling me Albert. Long, long ago. But it was when I was in the Gymnasium."

Nora thought, Aharon Arin. She pronounced both words emphasizing the penultimate syllable, then played with them emphasizing the last one: A-*ha*-ron A-rin. A-ha-*ron* A-*rin*. She thought, Albert Arin. Nora Arin. Lisa Arin. Esther Arin. Nora Arin.

She caught herself in the thought and blushed.

The mother said, "Have we finished?"

Lisa said, "If Albert isn't tired from the long walk, I'd suggest wandering a little in the forest."

Albert wasn't tired.

They walked – the mother, Arin, and Lisa in the lead, Nora and Giltman behind them.

Nora stared at the three backs. Funny. A funny trio. Lisa's slender shoulders and thin, pitter-patter walk. Arin's big, long-legged steps. He's trying to slow them down to match the strides of the two women. And the mother's light, rhythmic walk, carrying her strong, full, soft body with such simple grace.

And when her look had to return to her companion, walking next to her and pouring a wealth of jokes, stories and wisdom into her ears, she was annoyed and wanted to avert her eyes. But suddenly, when she surveyed him from the side, she understood what in his face repelled her so much: the lines of the skull surfacing too clearly under his expression. As if that face carried something of death. So far, just a hint. Still fighting with it, a negligible fight. The irony in his eyes and his voice was still fighting. But the forehead was already turned to stone and dead. Suddenly, Nora compared her picture of this Giltman himself, in a few years, after he finished law school and became a successful attorney, and married a plump woman with money, how he'd then stride self-importantly on the main avenue of the city, his briefcase under his arm, and display in public the dead skull, stretched under the skin of his face, and other attorneys, also successful, would walk smugly with him, and they would also show their dead heads.

At that moment, Giltman was concluding one of his witty sentences. "…and I told them, this is all about lineage. Don't hurry, our Jewish women find themselves mates by lineage and not by titles."

And with a wink at Arin, he added, "Listen, Nora. Who is that mysterious Jew anyway?"

But meanwhile, the whole group had reached the riverbank, and because they were all sitting together, Nora didn't have to answer.

The bench was made of birch wood and was hidden among bushes. The ground behind it was covered with a curly carpet of berry leaves, some black and some red from the autumn withering, and some still green and firm and gleaming, as if they were covered with fresh lacquer.

Arin took out his cigarette case and offered it to the women. The mother refused with a smile and a shake of her head. Lisa took one and immediately started smoking, hastily and nervously, hurried like her walking. After some hesitation, Nora also reached out, took a cigarette, brought her face close to the flame and started smoking, glancing sideways at the mother, who hadn't yet seen her doing that.

The mother said, "That's something new. From when?"

"About a year ago."

Arin smoked slowly, pensively, his eyes held by the river before them.

The mother addressed Giltman. "It's nice here, isn't it? What's new in town?"

Giltman shrugged and declared contemptuously, "News of our metropolis! Who are we and what are we to those from the big world!" And he immediately turned to Nora and in his eyes were dismissal and ardor and cunning all at the same time. "But you heard, Nora, Ella Katz, who was in your class, is engaged to Doctor Dobrik!"

"She was a year ahead of me."

"Yes, yes. Katz and Company. Wholesale fabrics."

"That one!" The mother was amazed. "And I heard the whole deal was called off!"

"Of course, of course, we all heard!" cheered Giltman, as if an obstacle had been removed from his path at long last. "That's what makes it spicy and pungent." He smiled at Arin. "Theory of virtues and such. The thing was canceled first, that is, the deal, as the lady says. For, after the matchmaking and all the other negotiations, he, Doctor Dobrik, found out that the maiden, well, how to put it? That is, what happened happened, and that virgin bride is no longer a virgin for all intents and purposes..."

He waited a little and looked to see the impact of his words.

"Oh," muttered Mrs. Krieger, blushing like a girl and sneaking a glance at Nora.

Giltman went on, addressing only Arin now. There was the touch of the coquette in his voice now which Nora didn't grasp.

"So, the matter was canceled, as the lady said, but not completely. More negotiations began. The Doctor claims damaged goods, broken vessel, even for free I don't want it! To make a long story short, they haggled for two months and ended by offering him two thousand dollars more. The Doctor demanded three thousand, but they were forced to agree to two and a half thousand. They reached a compromise, as they say. And now the wedding will be celebrated splendidly and gold-bordered invitations have already been sent. And the whole town is full of the honor of Ella Katz and Doctor Dobrik. Isn't that great?"

And he gave his whole audience a very significant glance.

The women were silent and embarrassed; they weren't used to talking about such things in that company. But Arin burst out laughing. At first he laughed loud and clear, then his laugh stopped and returned in waves, tears filled his eyes, and between one fit of laughing and another, he blurted out, "Brilliant! Brilliant! Terrific! That's brilliant!"

Very slowly, the mother and Lisa started laughing with him. And then Giltman also started laughing. The lines of his skull were even more prominent when he laughed. And for some reason, Nora was uncomfortable. She bent her head down and didn't laugh.

"The face of our town," said Giltman, suddenly cutting off his laugh. "Here's what you're missing, Nora, in your foreign country."

"That's the way," grumbled Nora. "Nothing's new."

Arin wiped his face, glanced at Nora and let his eyes linger on her a long time.

She got up and stood, leaning on a tree, and hissed between her teeth, "Disgusting!"

"Well, well," declared Giltman. "Don't get excited, mimosa!"

He got up too. "I have to go. I promised Dina Globus to go back to town with her. Goodbye, people."

Arin shook his hand. "I won't forget your anecdote."

"I just pass on facts as they are!" He licked his lower lip, shook his head and set off. His back going away was like the back of a man hurrying to bring tidings.

"So," Arin followed him with a look that grew narrow. "And now we're back in the forest."

The mother and Lisa looked at him in amazement. But Nora nodded in agreement, smiled and sat down next to him. Now she knew that she and that man shared a bridge.

"Mosquitoes," said the mother, and tried to kill a big mosquito sitting on her arm with a nimble gesture.

"Remember, Liseke," said Arin. "Once we were together in the forest, about a year before I was arrested. With Jacob. I don't remember a thing except mosquitoes. And also that we dragged a samovar with us and heated it with pine cones, and we also made a bonfire of pine cones to drive away the mosquitoes. It was an awful smoke. But so fragrant. The smell was good. Remember?"

Lisa blushed and her face was younger and prettier.

"You've all got a talent: blushing!" remarked Arin before she opened her mouth. "All three of you."

That increased the fire in Lisa's face, and she spoke insecurely. "No, that is, yes. I do remember the outing. I don't remember the mosquitoes. But the outing – of course! It was Friday evening and I wanted very much to go out but didn't dare ask. Sima also went, you remember, the Bundist teacher."

"No, her I don't remember."

"And I came back from the Gymnasium, and the family would soon go into the house. And you know, I'm the one who did all the housework. And you were all standing in the door, and Jacob said he wouldn't eat at home. And suddenly you said, Come on with us, Liseke, leave this kitchen! And Jacob also said I should go...and I went."

Even now, when Lisa told that simple story, her look was radiant because of unbounded gratitude, and Nora's heart shriveled inside her with pity and shame, as if a door of some paupers who always wanted to hide their poverty from her was inadvertently opened.

Arin lowered his head and muttered warmly, "Well, fine, Liseke. There's something to remember!" Then he pulled himself together and laughed. "But those mosquitoes I won't forget."

"One's standing on your forehead to remind you," said the mother, and smacked his forehead.

The smack worked. Mrs. Krieger proudly held out her hand to show the red spot on it. Arin wiped his forehead.

"May his name be wiped out, that bloodsucker!"

"So let's go or they'll eat us alive."

Lisa said, "I have to go back to town tonight."

And there was evening and lights of the boat on the face of the river.

And there was evening and the shaking lantern of the fishing boat – on the face of the water.

Young maidens lying on their bed. Young maidens clear-sighted. And they hear, they hear the voice of the flowing river.

And all the rivers go to the sea and the sea is not full.

Nora and Arin walked Lisa to the boat back to the city. And when they walked from the ferry station to the resort house, the forest had already gone dark. Their feet slipped on the damp pine needles. Nora's steps were hesitant and Arin held onto her arm.

"Has everything changed a lot?" Nora asked Arin.

From the movement of his arm, she sensed that he was shrugging.

"No. Lisa, for example, hasn't changed at all. She was always like that. Even though, back then, she was just a fifteen-year-old Gymnasium student."

Nora, who didn't know her aunt's exact age, did the math: fifteen and twenty-five – forty!

Arin, who understood the meaning of her silence for some reason, suddenly laughed, "No, that's not extreme old age. For me and people my age, a woman of forty is quite young. Hard to believe, eh?"

"No, but…"

"Here's a bench," said Arin. "Let's sit a while. Aren't you cold?"

"No." Nora fastened a button on her coat and sat down.

"It's not a matter of age," said Arin. "Lisa was like that even back in those days. And your mother was always young."

"And how was Mama?"

In the dark, Nora didn't see Arin's face, but she sensed in his voice that he was smiling. "She was very happy in those days, with your father. So happy that, between her and everybody else, there was a kind of space. And I was scared, when I came here, that everything had fallen apart. And now I see her. How did she manage to keep that perfection of hers in spite of everything? I don't get it. But her charm of hers, her softness…and you, do you have eyes to see her?"

"I don't know. Sometimes. I think – yes."

After a long silence, Nora asked, her voice scared and a little teasing, "And I? Am I very much like Lisa?"

She felt the night's chill. She shivered. Arin, who had previously been sitting at a little distance from Nora, moved to her and his face was now very close. Nora could now almost distinguish its details and saw the flash of laughter in his eyes. "How did you come up with that?"

"Who am I like?"

"Like a little girl who's too serious for her own good. Your mother's laugh and her eyes. Your father's forehead. But in general, if you want to know, you've got your own face. But what made you think you were like Lisa?"

With an effort, Nora whispered, "Because…because I'm…not pretty."

Arin looked at her a moment and asked, "How do you know that?"

"The mirror," replied Nora tersely and waited a little while, and because he didn't say anything, she whispered again, "When I was little, I'd jump and play with children, and Lisa would always say, 'Look, she moves so heavily!' 'Look, so clumsy!' She wanted to teach me modesty, I know, but nevertheless…"

"Like that!" grumbled Arin angrily. "And after you grew up, you didn't hear the opposite?"

"I don't know. I didn't believe it."

"All that is nonsense!" he said emphatically. "A lack of confidence for no reason. If you pass by the mirror someday, don't think too much, you'll see the face of a young person there, the face of a girl. And I would advise you very strongly to smile at her. It's worth it, really. By the way, why don't you laugh? Why do you laugh so little?"

"Sometimes I laugh," said Nora, embarrassed. "But–"

"But what?"

"I always remember so many things. My generation here – my childhood started with the war. And afterward – but then, you know."

Arin took her hand in his right hand, and with his left hand he touched the back of her hand gently.

"Fine, little girl, I do know. And what I don't know I can imagine. It's not so simple. Clearly. But one thing I do want to tell you: don't be a person who always exaggerates how much he's suffered, especially to yourself. Understand," squeezing her hand hard, "I don't have the right to preach morality to human beings. I don't. I'm not preaching morality. But there's nothing worse than a person who pities himself."

Nora slowly shook her head.

"No, I don't pity. But I," she whispered excitedly, "I'm scared. When I was abroad, I thought I wouldn't be scared anymore, that it was over. But here, at home, I'm scared."

"Of what?"

Her voice was low and tormented. She said, "Of madness."

"Nonsense!" Arin exclaimed in a loud voice and dropped Nora's hand. "You mustn't even think such thoughts. That episode is over and done with. I know you're brave. That's obvious."

A group of strollers passed by them. Splinters of conversation and fragments of song:

"But I told you, a person can go crazy because of sixty-six…"

Was macht der Mayer auf Hymmalaya–

"Ow, you stepped on my foot! On the blister!"

"Professor Doctor Friedrich Wilhelm von Mayer."

A big dog following that group lagged behind them and stopped at the bench facing Nora and Arin, raised his sharp muzzle to them, his eyes glowing in the dark. Nora stretched out her hand and patted the strange dog's head gently.

Arin said, "I don't like them, that nation."

"What nation?"

"Dogs."

"But they're so wise!"

"They're petit-bourgeois sycophants, basically corrupt petit bourgeois. Class conscious and law-abiding. Look, look at him, that gentleman, how he's wagging his tail now. If you only saw how his fellow dogs greeted me back in those days, when I was a peddler, or an icon seller in Mexico, how they'd attack me when I'd walk along torn and tattered. You think that flatterer, when I'm dressed as a fine lord, makes me forget their contemptible behavior from those days? There are things a person doesn't forget!" he said with sudden anger and total seriousness. "Go, get out of here, dammit!"

"Hector! Hector!"

The dog ran.

Nora was silent a while and then said apologetically, "I wanted to ask something else…"

"Please, ask," Arin sighed. Nora thought he was a little upset.

"But don't get angry. I wanted to ask: why did you have a store?"

Arin looked at her in amazement and for a moment he seemed to be considering something. Then he burst out laughing. "That's it? But Nora! If you only heard how you asked the question!"

"Why?"

"Your voice was as if you were asking: why were you a pimp? Or something like that. Nora, that's great!" he went on laughing. But when he looked at her and saw that she was embarrassed and sad, he stifled his laugh and said, "Why did I have a store? Why was I a shopkeeper? I don't know. Apparently because I didn't succeed in all the other things I tried. By the way, if it's any comfort to you, I didn't succeed as a shopkeeper either."

Nora finally smiled weakly.

"Yes, as long as my wife worked, we could make a living. But I, well, it's not interesting, Nora. But I think I'm beginning to understand something now, Nora."

It was nice to hear him repeat her name. His eyes were fixed on her face. They were watching her and thinking of her. After a short pause, he said, "So, at the time you created a romantic image for yourself, a Childe Harold, a hero of the prairies and the pampas, an Odysseus, eh?"

He waited for her answer. Nora lowered her head and muttered, "Y…yes."

Arin put his hand on her shoulder.

"I'm very sorry, Nora. But you have to get rid of that image forever. I had a cigarette and tobacco store, and that awful stain can never be erased. And maybe it would have been better if I hadn't come here, eh?"

"No, no!" Nora blurted out.

He smiled. "Don't be in a hurry to deliver a verdict. Why are you shaking?"

"Cold."

"So let's go."

They walked carefully on the pine needles. Arin's arm clasped Nora's shoulders. She felt good and very comfortable. Behind the trees, the moon rose. Arin looked at Nora's chestnut hair gleaming above her forehead, so pale in that light. And Nora walked and was suddenly sure that everything would be good, that there was nothing to worry about, that he would take care of her.

What a musical night!

Perhaps the nightingales are singing joyfully in the depths of the forest.

The moon stands in the sky. What a musical night!

But I can't fall asleep. I can't. I won't, I don't –

May she not open her eyes, may she not see me sitting in the window. Only in my nightgown.

What a musical night –

The maw of the gramophones gaped in all the summer colonies. Death to nightingales! The moon stands over the forest. Yossele Rosenblatt pours out his feelings in a melody of the Days of Awe. His neighbor is Marlene Dietrich. For the tenth time: *Ich bin von Kopf bis Fuss.*

Death to nightingales!

"May I ask Madame to dance?"

Titina, O Titina

Titina, O Titina

The cantors, cabaret singers, jazz musicians, what a night!

You mustn't even think of that, little girl, little girl, because I was an icon peddler in Mexico, you're brave.

The moon stands over the forest.

The electric light is lit on the verandah. The proprietress of the resort house went to the city. No authority, no reverence, no fear. The big samovar. Spoons bang on glasses.

"Tekla, bring tea!"

"*Es iz geven amol a tsayt, az ich bin geven farlibt in Shpanish.*"

Barefoot Tekla, light-footed Tekla, fat-thighed Tekla, Tekla, bring tea –

"On the contrary, one plays *romma*."

"*Romma*, rummy, please."

"Tekla, cards!"

"Didn't you hear, didn't you hear yet? Can it be? Can it be? Can it be? Two and a half thousand. Two and a half thousand. Dollars, dollars, not pounds."

"Queen of spades."

"Please, Ma'am, I said the queen of spades!"

"Obvious. He's an American. They've all got a fortune, money, hundreds, fame."

"Obvious."

"And that's why she divorced her husband. Didn't you hear yet? Shoshanna Bergman told me. Fat Shoshanna, Shoshanna Bergman, the wife of the crazy Bergman, Shoshanna. Honest, honest."

"And he's running after the daughter! After the daughter!"

"King, a tenth, and alt!"

"Not the daughter, the sister-in-law…and I thought–"

"Naïveté, sir, naïveté, I said! Tekla, where's the jam?"

What a musical night.

Es iz geven amol a tsayt –

When my head is full of dew, my locks are droplets of night. Because his hand was on my shoulder, because he is so mature. Because I, I, I will see him tomorrow. A serious little girl, even too serious. Maybe you'll pass by the mirror. I suggest you smile. I'll laugh out loud, I'll laugh loud. The moon stands facing the forest.

Because

    that

       guy

          was her fiancé

             a long time ago.

"How low, how low to leave a sick husband in the arms of his poor sister and run away to America, just because he's got money, fortune, fame!"

"Ten to one he'll marry the daughter."

"Oh dear, what a sca-an-dal!"

"And the wedding in a month. And the price of virginity is very cheap. Two and a half thousand."

"Ladies and gentlemen, ladies and gentlemen, all girls can be married off!"

What a night!

Es iz geven –

And perhaps I dreamed the whole conversation, and the forest, and the bench, and his hand on my shoulder. And it never was and it never was. And Mama wasn't standing in the door.

Those sparks in the air. Flying stars, fireflies. Quite simply – sparks from the chimney of the samovar.

"Tekla, where are Madam's eyeglasses!"

Tekla, where is your bed and your rest at night? We'll rest. We'll all sleep until morning. All of us, you and Albert and me and Albert and Albert and the pine smell and the wind blowing from the distant stars. And you and me and the king of spades.

And there will be a great spring on the moss. And I love him. And Papa won't know. And the Swede in the train. And the train will go to the forests, to the birches, to the smell of the water, to the yellowing stems and the clover. To Albert, to my bridge, to my bridge –

"I forgot to ask last night," the mother said to Nora, as they were getting dressed in their room in the morning, and she was sliding the brush over her hair. "Was the boat very crowded? A lot of people?"

"What?"

"You don't hear when people talk to you today. This is the third time I asked."

"I hear. Yes. It was very crowded. Awfully crowded. Yes."

"So how did you get Lisa on deck?"

"Yes."

"God in heaven, where's your mind hovering! Just like when you were little. I thought I asked a very simple question."

"Yes. Very simple. I didn't get on. Arin got on with her."

"Albert?"

"Yes. Albert Arin."

Nora sat on the edge of the bed. She picked up a stocking, looked at it vacantly and yawned. "I want to sleep."

"Your face is pale. Maybe you're sick?"

"No. I want to sleep."

"Didn't you sleep enough?"

"Yes, I slept enough." And she grinned happily, somewhat foolishly.

"What silliness has come over you! Did you wait long for him?"

"Not much. Until he put Lisa on board. The boat left. It was awfully crowded. I don't remember."

"Fine," said the mother. "Hurry up. We'll be late for breakfast. No, don't put on the wrinkled white one. Put on the blue one."

Nora got up. Slowly and laboriously, she wanted to shake off the night. There were no nightingales. There weren't any.

"And he didn't talk to you about Lisa?"

"About Lisa?"

"Yes, for heaven's sake, about Lisa."

"He talked a little. Why do you ask that?"

"No reason. What did he say?"

Nora was perplexed.

"I don't remember."

"It's hard to talk to you today."

"I want to sleep."

"Stop it, really!"

The mother fastened the coral pin to her jacket collar. She sighed. "I think I'm beginning to understand."

Nora glanced at her in a panic and sat down again. "What?"

The mother sat down too.

"It's hard to believe that a person sets off on a trip all of a sudden without any purpose. If, let's say, he had gone to Paris or Italy or something like that...but to come from America to this village? Who's he got here and what's he got here?"

"Us."

"That's what I said. But us? Friends, not even that. Papa was his friend, but he does know – so, you and me, he can't have come simply to see us."

"Why not?"

"What a baby you are! Because he's a mature man. Fine, a rather strange man. But that can't be."

"I don't understand."

"Of course. I don't either. But yesterday, when he offered so enthusiastically to take Lisa, I thought..."

"Enthusiastically! Take Lisa..."

"Yes. Why do you repeat every word that comes out of my mouth! You didn't have the sense not to go with them. I'm amazed, I'm astonished at you."

"But Mama," Nora stretched out the words in amazement, "you don't think Arin fell in love with Lisa all of a sudden!"

"What foolishness!" grumbled the mother. "You young girls always think that the beginning and end of everything is love."

"So what do you want?"

"Understand," the mother spoke with a hasty warmth that wasn't like her. "Albert was widowed two years ago. And now, after his daughter got married...don't you understand, now he's very lonely and doesn't have a single living soul in the whole world."

"Yes, he really is alone. Yes, I understand now, he's lonely. He's by himself and doesn't have a living soul." Nora was still talking like a sleepwalker, but suddenly she let go of the sandal she was about to put on and looked at her mother with a pair of wide-open eyes. "Mama, what, what are you saying?"

The mother shrugged. "You can't know for sure, of course. But I'm sure..." She interrupted herself for a moment.

(You can't know for sure. But I'm sure – that's their logic! – Nora was angry inside herself.)

"I'm sure he wants to get married. Why are you looking at me like that? Won't you understand such simple things?"

"And for that there's nobody in the whole wide world but Lisa!" said Nora bitterly.

"Of course," decreed the mother stubbornly, "I'm not saying that Arin hasn't met women more beautiful and interesting than Lisa in his life. But, understand, they're strangers there. And do you think that twenty-five years in a foreign country can erase from a man's heart that he's from a certain milieu? All those lovely things become acquaintanceship, a brief pleasure, even love. But when a man thinks of a woman he will have to live with day after day, it's good that that woman, well, how to put it – is a piece of his homeland."

"But Lisa isn't young anymore!" Nora unwittingly wanted to defend herself.

"And how do you see Albert, as a newborn babe? A boy your age? He needs an eighteen-year-old woman?"

"Mama," pleaded Nora tearfully. "You're talking like Shoshanna Bergman."

Yes, and yesterday he said a forty-year-old woman is quite young. She's still young. To people my age. He said yesterday! Now she didn't remember all he said last night, but only that phrase. A forty-year-old woman is still young. (And maybe all that is solid truth, maybe she's right. I'm a fool, a fool, silly, stupid...)

"And he knows that Lisa is a quiet and pleasant creature. A modest person and her demands are modest. A devoted woman, a loyal woman like her he won't find anywhere in the world. With her he can rest," the mother exaggerated her praise of her sister-in-law with increasing excitement.

She's murdering me, she's murdering my soul, thought Nora.

"Yes," sighed the mother. "It won't be easy to part from her. But if you knew how happy I'd be if she finally found happiness in life!"

Nora thrust out her lower lip. "You're talking like Shoshanna Bergman!" she said again and blushed.

"What did you say?"

Nora was silent.

"You're still too young to understand what Lisa's life is. But if we don't lie to ourselves, we must admit that we always took advantage of her. She lived only for us. That's horrible! No, understand, I believe, always, I've always believed that everyone would eventually be rewarded in this world for his good deeds."

Nora shrugged, her head bent. She felt a lump in her throat, and was afraid to say a word. And her whole world seemed to turn into heaps of rubble. Everything was ending before it began, everything! And we take advantage of her, she's right, yes, she's right.

"We have to go down for breakfast," said the mother.

And at that moment, from downstairs, under the window, Arin's voice was heard.

"Nora, Nora, Esther!"

Nora jumped up and her feet were suddenly light, and her head also cleared up all at once, as if that voice calling out had washed it like a refreshing downpour.

Arin stood under the window, his arms held out, and he held two gleaming mushrooms; on his fingers were black dirt and remnants of moss.

"Look what I found here!"

"I'm coming down," Nora called gaily. "Right away."

She quickly finished dressing, and as she ran down the stairs, her heart hummed with joy and she repeated to herself, "Nonsense, that's just nonsense. He and Lisa. It can't be, it'll never be."

And she smiled when she remembered the black dirt on his hands.

That day, the three of them agreed to get up early the next day and go picking mushrooms in the forest.

Nora lay in a hammock, leafing through some summer novel, and kept dropping the book. And when she shut her eyes, she saw rows and rows of mushrooms hidden in moss. Gleaming and sticky boletus with brown tops, and reddish truffles like fox fur. And all of a sudden, "fly-mushrooms" floated up in a row – big, blushing, seeded with white spots, like the illustration for a book of children's fairy tales. She already felt the dewy chill of the morning and the temporary loneliness in some place hidden in bushes, as in a green alcove, where the feet trample on the soft caressing moss and the ear catches in the distance the cry of "Ah-oh, ah-oh," that forest motto of mushroom pickers. And even now that damp and teasing smell seemed to rise in her nose, that fragrance of morning and rain, revealing the mushroom to those who seek it.

She lay on her back in the hammock and smiled with her eyes shut, and her nostrils trembled like the nostrils of a hunting dog from the imaginary smell of the morning in store for her tomorrow. And all of a sudden, she felt a few drops on her forehead. Her eyes that opened wide saw above her, between the branches of the pine tree, a murky gray sky. Very slowly a disturbing autumn rain began to drip.

While it was still a thin drizzle, Nora jumped out of the hammock and began untying the ropes wound around the tree trunk. Mrs. Krieger and Arin, who were just returning from a short walk among the summer resorts, approached her, and Arin helped her gather up the ropes and fold the hammock.

"Rain is good for mushrooms!" smiled the mother. "If the air clears up tomorrow morning, we'll go out and come back with a great booty. The kitchen will be very happy."

"But don't poison all the summer visitors!" warned Arin.

"Nora's an expert in mushrooms."

"As long as there isn't rain tomorrow, too…"

"Why, that's just a nothing drizzle!" said Arin.

They went up to the resort house, where the summer visitors afraid of the rain were huddling together on the verandah.

Nora put on her raincoat and went to wander a little. Arin, who remained in the room with the mother to finish a conversation they had begun, asked Nora not to go far off into the depths of the forest; he was supposed to catch up with her, to catch a walk "between the drops."

Nora walked on a very narrow path between the pine trees. The path was clear and the branches above it flickered in the tiny drops hanging on them between the long green needles. A coniferous and damp forest smell, a smell of mushrooms and sap. A tranquility of all the autumns on the solitary path.

Nora bent down and picked up a stick lying at the side of the path. It was a gnarled stick of pine branch. One of the summer visitors had carved a decoration in it of squares and the letters S.S. Somebody must have dropped it here by accident. The stick was a little wet, but the touch of the cool wood was pleasant in the hand. Nora was dragging it and inadvertently using it to turn up the yellow needles and the orange moss at her feet. Suddenly Arin was walking beside her. He put his hand on her shoulder and smiled.

"It's good here," said Nora.

Arin said, "Good."

"But I'm glad this time is passing. It's good that I'm only here on vacation. I hate these little towns, this life. If you knew how much I want to escape from here! Now I love this forest and everything in it and around it, because I know it's only a temporary stop. In two and a half months, I'll get up and go."

"Yes," said Arin, "I understand. I also wanted to escape a long time ago. I know. But I don't understand your love and yearning for the place you're going. 'Europe, Europe!' That's what you say, and 'that other life' you long for. But that Europe of yours is walking on the brink of an abyss. How will you be able to draw so much life from that death?"

He spoke at length now, without irony, without a trace of the teasing that always accompanies the conversations of grown-ups; he talked just like Nora wanted him to talk to her.

"I don't know," she pondered aloud, "and even if you're right, it will probably be hard for you to understand. I asked myself a first question, am I still 'rotting in the provinces'? You, grown-ups, tend to forget the days of your youth. You see this forest, these pine trees, the autumn and even my mother. But what's really stifling here, you don't see. You still couldn't see it. Maybe only in the evening, if you looked at the faces of those playing cards and gossiping here."

"I saw enough. But I've always known them. They haven't changed. But this smug petite bourgeoisie is the same everywhere, all over the world."

"Yes, but *those* are my relations! Flesh of my flesh!" Nora suddenly remembered the Jew in the train. "They're flesh of my flesh, and I'm responsible for them, I'm always responsible for them."

There was a short silence. Arin lifted his hand and stroked Nora's head, stroked her hair and her shoulder.

The rain was thin. The clouds moved slowly.

"And I still wanted to go to school," said Nora. "I *really* wanted to go to school. Maybe only here, in these small towns in eastern Europe, is there still that kind of youth, as one person told me, youth from the last generation. We believe, we believe there is real value in what we study, in the possibility of studying, knowing. We're exiled to a place of learning, as in the Enlightenment period, like Solomon Maimon in his day. And we don't believe in our hearts that we'll get our reward; our learning is for the sake of learning. When my friends ask me, what will you do when you finish school? I always answer, 'I'll be unemployed.'"

"Not necessarily," laughed Arin. "I think you'll be unpaid."

Nora nodded. She thought somebody had already given her that answer. It's all the same. Now, said by Arin, it was nicer.

"But what are you studying, in fact?" asked Arin after a little bit.

"Archaeology."

"That's not very practical. What do you intend to do with it, nevertheless?"

"You know," replied Nora indirectly, and her voice trembled a little. "I won't stay in Europe."

He nodded, as if remembering her letters, and he didn't have to mention the Land of Israel.

"You still hold on to that?" he asked after a brief pause, and added dubiously, "But do you know that all those you hate, this whole town and its petite bourgeoisie, all of them will go there with you, they'll follow you, if your dreams come true? Because it's for them you dreamed them and you've got to attract them to that place itself."

Nora looked at him, and her look stubbornly resisted all attack. "I know that. But there they'll be different."

Arin shrugged. "Who will promise? I, to tell the truth, don't believe it."

A wind blew. A downpour of big drops from the shaken tree blended with the thin drizzle and came down on Nora's head.

"But let's go back to the subject," said Arin. "Why archaeology, of all things?"

"Yes," said Nora slowly. "It's hard to explain that."

She was assailed by that fear of the nice words she had just said, as if she were giving away her secret and making it banal. "Didn't I say I won't stay in Europe? And there, I wanted to see things broadly and deeply. And it always seems to me that if we dig deep there, we'll get to a ground level where there are still impressions of the – God's footprints."

A moment passed after she heard the words come out of her mouth, and she feared they sounded like hollow rhetoric to the man walking at her side. She feared that that tiny glimmer of dismissal and scorn would come into his eyes. But his face was very attentive and afterward, his eyes went off and he answered with seeming irrelevance, "But freedom, Nora, freedom, if you want it, will be won in only one way. Man will be free only if he doesn't participate against his will in all the accusations of his fellow man."

"I knew you'd really understand," whispered Nora.

"Nora," said Arin, and turned his face to her. "Nora, little girl, I came here, I came here only to tell you those things…"

No, Nora thought suddenly, Arin can't say such things, no, he can't.

She stood still, wiped the drops off her forehead with a wet hand. Stood still and knew she was alone in the forest and that whole conversation was nothing but the product of her imagination. You can never bare your heart like that to live people. When you express yourself in an imaginary dialogue, they say everything you want to hear, even through argument. And you're immensely wiser than in a real exchange of words.

Here she is walking alone in the forest and making up a wise and beloved interlocutor, and telling him the essential, and he's replying. And in the end, it turns out he's not here.

And now he was probably coming out to find her near the resort house.

Nora returned to the house on that same path. She was sober now and knew that not only did that conversation not exist, it never would. For that is the punishment of imaginative people: they live in their imaginations with such intensity that they become a second reality, and since reality doesn't return twice, imagining therefore can't become material reality.

Not far from the resort house, she met Arin. He was walking toward her along the path.

"And I'm looking for you, Nora!" he called out from the distance, and approached. They turned and walked together.

"It's nice here even in the rain," said Arin, and Nora didn't reply, recalling that this was really where the imaginary dialogue began.

"What's the stick you're holding?" he asked.

"I found it," she said and handed him the stick.

Arin looked at it as he walked and, with his thumbnail, he scraped the white-greenish wood between the decorations of the orange bark.

"It looks like one of the summer visitors did that," said Nora.

"S.S.," Arin read the letters, and went on, smiling, "Sonya Slonim, Sasha Sabirski."

"Sima Solomon," Nora inadvertently entered into the game.

"Here," said Arin, returning her stick. "You'll have to decipher the origin of that object. You're the one studying archaeology. Isn't that right?"

"Yes," said Nora, and felt the imaginary conversation recurring with an almost caricatural change of character.

"Interesting field," commented Arin. "But not very practical."

"And what is practical these days?" asked Nora bitterly.

Arin sighed. "Yes, you're right. World crisis. So let's go back to the stick."

A sudden anger flooded Nora's heart in a hot stream. She didn't reply, but she waved the stick vigorously and threw it away from her among the pines.

Arin didn't sense her anger at all; he looked at her in amazement and asked, "How come? It's quite beautiful."

"No reason," she said and for some reason, she felt relieved.

"Listen, Nora," Arin suddenly began in a completely different voice. "Tomorrow morning, I'm going to the city."

Nora stood still. Her face was offended like the face of a baby who's been hit.

"And the mushrooms?" she asked after a brief silence.

"The mushrooms?" Arin didn't grasp it at first. Then he laughed. "Tomorrow morning I've got to go, Nora. Anyway, it will rain harder."

"And you'll come back at night?" she whispered.

"No. I won't come back here. I'll stay in the city."

Nora dropped her head. Arin looked at her from the side as if he were considering something.

"Come on, let's go back," he suggested.

Once again, they turned to the house. It rained a little harder. But they didn't hurry up. Her head was down.

"I'm not yet going to America, and you'll also be coming back to the city in about a week," said Arin at last. "And we'll see each other there."

Nora didn't answer.

"Are you still angry about the mushrooms?" he asked.

Nora raised her head and twisted her lips.

"Oh, that's not important," she said with the politeness of the offended.

"I want to tell you," said Arin as if he were ignoring the tone of the answer, "I was just talking with your mother. And that conversation showed me certain things. I have to be in the city as I was called to the telephone this morning about something. But it's not important. I want to see your father. I'll go to him tomorrow or the next day. My intention was…you know, I loved him very much back then. And maybe something can still be done. I've got a certain experience in such things. In these small cities of the east, things are treated so barbarically. Even in a family like yours."

He broke off, looked very carefully at Nora, who looked at him with wide-open, pleading eyes.

"Maybe I'm burdening you, Nora," he added. "But I may need your advice and explanation in this. In spite of everything, you seem to be the only person I can talk to in this case in simple and logical terms. I'm waiting for your answer, Nora."

And suddenly, there was a real connection between them. And they walked quietly next to one another. Very close, they walked together.

And only at the house did Nora recall that tomorrow she'd be left alone. And her heart once again turned over. And beside Arin, she went up the stairs of the verandah between two rows of summer visitor onlookers like a punished soldier running between two rows of bayonets.

On the bottom step of the stairs going to the kitchen sat Tekla. Curled up, she sat and wept.

Her bare feet peeped out from under the big checked apron. Her shoes were next to her, safe from the rain. The big toe of her right foot would twist from time to time and dig a hole in the wet ground.

She wept long sobs, sliced through now and then with one sharp sob and a sigh. Then she'd weep only tears again.

Nora stood still before her. At first she was about to approach and ask why she was crying, maybe try to console her. But she was stopped by embarrassment and the fear of offending a pain that wasn't hers. She stood still, and something inadvertently fascinated her in the human scene before her, in that weeping, pouring out freely as the most direct expression of pain.

So she stood and gazed lazily.

Good pets, loyal cows, if they could weep, would weep like her.

"Oh, Jesus-Maria!" Tekla blurted out. She rose up a little, picked up her shoes in one hand, straightened up, with one general broad movement, wiped her eyes and her nose with her arm, turned her back on Nora, and paddled her bare feet slowly up the steps. As she climbed, she stopped and turned to Nora. "Oh, Jesus, the young lady, why is she standing in the rain?"

And she went up and disappeared behind the kitchen door.

From there, from the slightly open window, rose the dry, vigorous voice of the proprietress. "That's the fourth time this month! You think plates grow like mushrooms in the forest!? I said I'll take it out of your salary!"

She broke a plate, thought Nora, and sighed. Such fatal weeping!

For four days now, the forest had been leaky and gray. Ever since Arin left – four days ago – the rain had stopped only for a few hours. Most of the time, Nora had to stay upstairs, in her room. When the window was open, the slap of cards on the table and fragments of angry words of the players rose from the verandah. "The queen of spades! Ten! Didn't I say!" The mother didn't talk much, and between her and Nora there was now some bad partition, as if they were lying in wait for one another. But the mother was gloomy in her silence, and Nora was obstinate.

He spoke with Mama before he left. How do I know they didn't agree about Lisa? He won't tell me anything about that. And I'm the fool!

From the corner of her eye, supposedly reading a book, she'd watch the mother and see her sitting sadly over her embroidery, her knitting, or her book. Or gazing at the window, her head leaning on her shapely white arm. But sometimes, she'd catch a silent and examining look that wanted to ask something and didn't dare. She'd return to the pages of her book and pretend to be deep in study, but didn't grasp a word of it.

Who phoned him? And why was he called to the telephone?

The days were desolate; one day followed another and was a carbon copy of the day before.

But suddenly she didn't know her own soul. What was in it, in the weeping of that farm girl? But somehow, while looking at that weeping, at the girl's bare feet, at her fair scalp, shaking on the bare arms, meaning was restored to the forest, to that rain, to herself, to the image of Albert Arin in the city.

She walked around the resort house, went up to the room. The mother was there.

She sat down and took a cigarette. She looked out the window. The trees were so green.

But how she wept! Jesus, the young lady, why is she standing in the rain? The rain beat on the window. He was already, he was already before that rain. And the forest. And we went to pick mushrooms. Papa and I. His Russian shirt was white. To search under the moss near the tree trunks. I didn't murder him on the train. And Albert. And maybe something could still be done. Maybe something was still possible. And he'll go to California. And he'll wipe out everything. And Albert and me – because in this forest, plates don't grow like mushrooms, only cards grow and gramophones.

She got up and stood at the mirror. She didn't see the face, didn't see anything except the smile.

All the time, this rain fell. Here and in the city, too. Albert walks in the street. And the whole park is yellow, and black crows among the fallen leaves. Albert climbs the green mountain. The poor back street. A red geranium in the windows. I want to go to the city, I want to go to the city. I want to see him with my own eyes – right now.

The mother entered the room. Took off the raincoat. Hung it up. Stood at the window. Said, "It's a drizzle. I went out for a little walk. I ran into Mrs. Levinstein. We went to her resort house. And there she was – what's her name? The wife of the lawyer, Glick, I think. She told me she saw you and you didn't say hello to her."

"Yes. Right. She noticed?" asked Nora with curiosity and almost happiness.

"As you'll see. I told her it was only absentmindedness."

Nora shrugged. "Too bad! Didn't I tell you two years ago, when I took care of that baby, that someday, *I* won't ask how she is. She's one of those women who told Lucy they couldn't say hello to me anymore because a babysitter is like a servant, and they wouldn't ask how servants are. And now *I* know who I have to say hello to. At any rate, not to that Glick."

The mother wasn't listening anymore. Her embroidery was spread on her lap and she was straightening a cross-stitched flower with her thumb.

"Giltman was also there," she said later. "He seemed very pre-occupied with Albert. Kept sniffing around. For some reason, they're all sure some secret is hidden here." She sighed. "I myself don't know. By the way, he said he was in the city and saw Albert driving in the car of the American consulate. I think he was just seeing things."

"I think so too," said Nora. But her face began to blush, for some reason, in her special way: from the end of the nose to the ear-lobes. But the mother's eyes were on the embroidery.

"Mama," said Nora when she felt her face was back to normal. "This rain won't stop tomorrow either. I want to go to the city."

The mother moved the embroidery off her lap. She raised pensive eyes to Nora. "Yes, as a matter of fact, we should go back."

She stood up and went to close the window; it was raining harder, and the drops were bursting into the room.

Downstairs, someone called out in a loud voice a few times in a row, "Tekla, close the windows!"

Breaking a plate was only the first of Tekla's tribulations that day.

About half an hour later, after the proprietress left the kitchen and the elderly cook, Jadwiga, a plump, clumsy woman, withdrew to the pantry to arrange the bowls of yogurt, Tekla sat idly on the long bunk made of some kind of crate that served as a bed at night and held her treasures throughout the day. Tekla sat on the bunk and gazed vacantly at the dishes, the dirty pots and the leftovers, waiting for her on the scoured wooden table.

Suddenly the door opened and a person entered the kitchen. He took a few steps toward Tekla and stood still.

Tekla looked at him fearfully, inquisitively. Then blurted out, "Oh, Jesus-Maria!"

And the guest seemed to have come from another world, from the nether world. She recognized him, but not easily. His face had changed so much! But right in front of her, literally, stood her older brother, ten years her senior.

He had left home six years before, left this country, during the time of blight, unemployment. He went to Brasilia with a group of farm workers. A company charmed them and promised them work for a fortune overseas. Since then, she hadn't known a thing about him. Letters, he didn't write. And she didn't expect any letters, she who couldn't read or write.

At first, shortly after he left, sometimes in her dreams, he appeared to her – a rich lord from a distant land, who had a gold watch. Afterward, he didn't come back even in her dreams.

"He sank in the mighty waters!" grumbled and sighed her gloomy Aunt Ona, who had raised the orphan Tekla.

And all that was left in her heart was the strange name "Brasilia." And sometimes she'd remember the brother, as she stripped off her shirt to bathe in the river: under her right breast was a red scar, a memento of a perpendicular blow of an axe the brother gave her when she was eleven years old, when she mistakenly poured out the drinking water she had brought him while he was cutting trees at the edge of the forest. And because of that scar, she was always afraid and a little terrified at the sight of every adult man who reminded her of her brother.

The brother didn't resemble the fair, dumpy, round Tekla. He was tall, had black hair, and his eyes and skin were dark. He looked like a gypsy. His face had always been bony, but now it was unrecognizably lined and gloomy. He had something yellow beneath the top layer of skin and behind the dry black flash of the eyes. And yet, a kind of reddish-yellow flush bloomed in his jutting, bony jaw. His clothes were poor, but not like the farmers. A faded pink shirt flickered under his gray jacket, and his coat was also gray. His trousers were the dusty khakis of soldiers. His long feet were stuck in worn-out, dirty soldier's boots.

Tekla stared at him a long time. He had no golden chain, no splendor of wealth, only suddenly she seemed very proud of him nevertheless.

"Sister," he only said in a hoarse voice.

She got up, went to him submissively, her head down, her lips muttering fluent words of greeting and respect, since he was ten years older than she. "My brother, it's him. When did you come from Brasilia?"

She went to him and kissed his hand, as she would kiss the hand of the priest.

He shoved her away violently (but the arm was weak), and in that shove, in spite of everything, there was a kind of affection.

When she retreated about a step, he blurted out, "People on the way told me you were here."

Then he licked his bottom lip with the tip of his dry tongue and said with an effort, "Food. Bring what you have."

Even from a distance, Tekla smelled brandy on him.

"I…right away, my brother, sit down please."

"Hurry up!" he growled at her in a choked voice and raised his hand.

Without thinking, Tekla held the rib under her right breast, defending the scar.

But he went to the bunk and plopped down.

Tekla surveyed the kitchen in a panic, pricking up her ears. The proprietress's steps weren't heard nearby. On the buffet was a loaf of bread; a glass of milk that one of the summer visitors had drunk only a little bit. On the plates were various leftovers. On tiptoe, warily, as if she were sneaking, Tekla approached the buffet, took a plate and collected the various leftovers into it. Then she took a knife out of the drawer and started slicing bread. As she did, she turned her head around and gave her brother pleading and curious glances.

Meanwhile, he took off his boots. His calves were swaddled in rags. A pungent smell of sweat filled the kitchen. His bare feet, standing on the floor, were black and amazingly thin. The toes looked as long as fingers.

Tekla put the slice of bread on the plate, stood and looked fascinated at those atrophied feet.

"I came to you to die," said the brother gloomily, his voice choked.

Tekla lowered her head. Her lips trembled, but she immediately calmed down a bit, since that was at last a kind of explanation.

She took the bread, the glass of milk, the plate of leftovers and put it in front of him. He drank the milk, his mouth twisting with disgust. Then he put the bowl of food between his knees, the bread next to him on the bunk, and carefully raised the spoon to his mouth that began chewing very slowly, like someone who finds chewing hard.

Tekla stood facing him and her heart contracted within her; she didn't know if it was because of a strange pity she felt, or perhaps from fear that the proprietress would come in, or Jadwiga, and find her misbehaving. But there was a kind of cruel decree in the thinness of his hands, his face, his black feet. And the feeling of perplexed pity grew in her. Slowly, she realized that there was nothing for her to fear anymore from the older brother, and that itself was somehow awful.

"And how was it over there, in Brasília?" she dared to ask at last.

He glanced at her furiously.

"It passed," he replied harshly after a pause, and Tekla saw how the exposed Adam's apple moved with the effort of swallowing. "Murderers! Dogs they sent there, dogs!" he grunted angrily.

"And I, brother, I thought…"

"Tell the priest!" he cut her off.

And after a brief pause, he asked, "And Aunt Ona, is she still alive, the old miser?"

"Alive."

"So. And I'll die."

Tekla sighed. "Why?"

"Why?" he imitated her with a wicked chuckle and added bitterly, "And they won't say a proper requiem mass for me. The old woman will save the few cents. And the priest – a hungry dog."

Tekla pretended not to hear the abuse of the priest, and replied only to the matter itself, and her cheeks flushed as she talked. "I've saved a little money. Mine will be enough."

"You're a fool, sister."

"Shall I give you some more bread?"

"Enough."

She was still standing before him. He looked at her as from a distance. All of a sudden, his head sank back, the plate between his knees slipped out, fell to the floor with a loud noise and didn't shatter. Strange sounds came from his throat, like a barking and a sobbing together; a harsh cough was accompanied by a groan. Tekla thought she had never heard such a racket before in her life.

"Brother," she pleaded, and held out both hands as if she wanted to stop the surge of the cough. "Please, stop, they'll hear."

But with one thing and another, the proprietress and Jadwiga were in the kitchen.

"What's this?" asked the proprietress, pointing at the brother and the rolling plate, and her skinny brown face flushed dark with rage.

The brother hunched his shoulders and stopped coughing, even made an effort to get up, but an attack of coughing stronger than the last one brought him down on the bunk. A narrow line of dark blood spilled from his mouth and went down from his chin to his shirt and dripped and scalded the bunk.

"He's my brother," muttered Tekla.

Jadwiga took a stained towel, still wet from drying the breakfast dishes, and wiped the blood off his face, off the bunk, and supported the sick man's burning head. Tekla was nailed to the spot, her hands hanging at her sides, numb, paralyzed.

The proprietress took a big step toward her; then, as if changing her mind, stood still leaning on the stove with nothing but disgust in her eyes.

After a while, the sick man's coughing stopped and the blood no longer flowed. He lay on his back on the bench, his head on Jadwiga's plump lap.

"Tuberculosis," the proprietress blurted out as if to herself. "That's all I needed. All my guests will run away."

And to Tekla, "I'll call the government hospital to put him there; you, what were you thinking of?"

"I won't go to a hospital. I came home to die," whispered the sick man in a soft voice.

"So," said Jadwiga. "There's no life in him anymore, he'll die."

"I'll take him to my aunt's house," pleaded Tekla. "There he'll die in peace."

"What savagery! What ignorance!" said the proprietress. "Maybe he can still be saved."

"There's no cure for him, Ma'am," decreed Jadwiga confidently, and the sick man nodded in agreement.

"Whatever you like," muttered the proprietress and shrugged. "But get him out of here fast, so no one will notice he was here. This is no hospital, this is a business. I wanted to help him."

"Right away, Ma'am. Oh Jesus-Maria."

The proprietress turned to leave. But in the door, she turned around and said to Tekla, "And pick up the plate. By the way, you won't work here anymore. You're fired."

After she left, Jadwiga very carefully moved the sick man's head off her lap and laid it on the bunk on a towel.

"Oh dear," she grumbled as she stood up. "Such a sick man, and drunk to boot! And you, my girl," she tapped Tekla's shoulder, who was still standing stunned at her new disaster, "don't mourn. The dead will die and the living will live. Go to your village. They'll certainly lend you a wagon. And as for this garbage" – she included the kitchen in a broad movement – "don't be sorry. You'll find something better. And him, your darling brother, he should be taken of here. For the time being, I'll lay him down in my den. I hope he doesn't die here, go fast."

The sick man listened to Jadwiga's words, indifferent and stiff, as if they weren't talking about him.

At long last, a short, depressed sobbing burst from Tekla's breast. And she fell silent. Jadwiga supported the sick man, helped him up and led him slowly to her small niche of a room.

Tekla went to the bunk, bent over it, took out a big, worn-out leather purse and a colorful kerchief. She tied the kerchief around her head and left.

She walked barefoot in the drizzle. Her village was close to the summer resorts. Only two and a half kilometers. The rain didn't bother her. Her feet tramped in the mud, paddled in the puddles. She walked and was almost calm. After she was sure the brother would die, there were no more questions.

And he did speak the truth, she thought; the aunt wouldn't hold a requiem mass. She'd save the money. I'll give her half my fortune. Because you can't do it like that. And there's no choice.

She sighed deeply. Sad to the heart. All summer she had dreamed of a new "city" dress. And now...

Her feet were immersed in puddles, her shoulders wet from

the rain. The road was familiar; the trees stood as they always had. Tekla didn't see the road.

Aunt Ona, a tall, erect, strict old peasant woman, her hair poking out from under the black kerchief, black as it was, without even a thread of silver in it, her skin dark and hard, as if forged by all the storms and tempests that had passed over the village, Aunt Ona didn't give Tekla a nice welcome.

After she heard her hesitant story, she decreed, "This place is too small to include dying people. The lady was right, take him to the hospital. I'm not a gravedigger."

"He wants to die at home," claimed Tekla.

"Fine. And why didn't he want *to live* at home? And who'll pay the burial costs?"

Without a word, Tekla took out the worn purse. She thought a little; would a third be enough?

Hesitantly she opened the purse. She counted the money slowly and seriously. She knew every scrap of paper. She put a third on the table.

Just as mutely, Aunt Ona also counted the wrinkled bills, wetting her brown fingers with saliva.

"What if that's not enough?" she tried to haggle, but it was obvious from her face that it was satisfactory. "Orphans," she said after a brief pause. "All my life I was bound to you. And all the worry was on me and on my neck. And now to die they come to me."

She whispered something and crossed herself at the icon of the saints on the wall – and the Madonna there was as dry and strict as she was.

A peasant neighbor did indeed lend them a wagon. He even agreed to go himself and bring the sick man. Tekla returned in that wagon to the forest summer resort.

Without any noise, so as not to scare the summer visitors, the sick man was put into the wagon. Tekla parted from him as she had met him – with a kiss on the hand.

His eyes were half-shut, and he didn't say a word.

The next morning, Tekla got her passport and salary (minus the price of the four plates and the days left before the end of the month), took her bundle and left for the station where the boats go down to the city. She walked – her shoes in her hands – as she walked to church on Sunday.

On the boat, she met Nora and her mother returning to the city. Nora, who remembered her fondly for her weeping on the stairs, went to her and asked where she was going.

Briefly and hesitantly, Tekla told how her brother returned, and how the proprietress had fired her.

"But you should have called a doctor! We'll send a doctor to him!" Mrs. Krieger got excited.

"No need, Ma'am. The aunt will call the priest. He'll die no matter what. There's no life left in him."

"And you?"

Mrs. Krieger had disbanded her household two months before; during the awful days before Nora came, she couldn't bear any stranger in her house, even the most passive, like those maids in eastern European cities. Now she had to look for a maid. Her vacation ended on September first.

Therefore, she began negotiating right there on the spot. Within a few minutes, Tekla was sitting next to Nora and her mother like a member of the family.

Chapter Three

Death and the Maiden

As if in spite, the sky cleared up right after Nora and her mother returned to the city. The world was steeped in that soft, clear autumnal swoon that brings out the beauty of the colors and gives them a final caress.

The day after they came, in the evening, the mother and Nora and Lisa sat at the square table and read books.

The big bay window was open. A smell of tobacco flowers, sweet and pungent, rose from below, from the garden. Insects with transparent wings danced around the glass of the lemon-colored lamp. Now and then, a vague knocking rose from outside, and Nora imagined it was ripe nuts falling from the trees. The wind came through the window and rustled the pages of music on the piano – that piano which was usually closed, and reminded Nora of the torments of childhood with the boring finger exercises – now only Lisa used it, rarely playing Tchaikovsky's Barcarole, and the Chanson Russe, and a few of Chopin's waltzes without much technical ability, but "with emotion."

From time to time, one of the women raised her eyes over the book, looked at the two others and went back to reading. Sometimes the mother would take off her glasses and wipe them and put them back on with a slightly nervous movement. That was the first year she needed reading glasses, and she still found them a nuisance. Those eyeglasses, with their dark frames, made her face look strange, serious and childish at the same time, and somehow that touched Nora's heart.

Lisa was reading an English novel, and since she had only recently learned that language and was careful about her accent, she'd move her lips very diligently as she read, like those babies who have just learned the secret of the alphabet. And sometimes she would glance at the blue Langenscheidt dictionary next to her. Her face was fuller now and not as gray as usual, and there was even some charm in it.

Nora was skimming. Too frequently, her eyes broke off from the pages of the book. She'd sit for a long time gazing and wanting to absorb that fragrant silence. But inside, she wasn't calm, and every sound rising from the yard, Lisa's moving lips, and the rustle of the music – everything awoke annoyance and discontent. We've been in the city for two days now. And Arin hasn't bothered to look in on us. A sign that he's got other interests in this city, and he's hiding them from us.

And much as she wanted to repress that thought, it kept coming up and flickering between the strange, incomprehensible lines of the book in front of her, dropping from Lisa's whispering lips, rising from the open window. And she felt a sharp insult that couldn't be overcome by logic.

In the yard, the silence stopped. The sound of measured footsteps was heard, walking as if to the slow beat of a drum. Nora knew it was the landlord on his after-dinner constitutional. Sometimes his cane beat on one of the stones next to the narrow wooden path, where he paced back and forth, back and forth, straight, tall, and sunk in his thoughts, which were probably also as slow, measured and straight as his steps. An insect was searching in one of the gardens. The sound of a girl's laughter was heard. Then there were other steps, closer, also heavy, but quick. Now they were beating on the steps to their apartment. And Nora knew it was Shoshanna Bergman coming to them.

Tekla came out of the kitchen to open the door, and Shoshanna Bergman came in. She sat at the table, as she always did, in a big armchair, not pulled up to the table, stretched her legs out, and her thighs, thinner than the thickness of her body, were open. She spread her knitting on her lap. Her lips moved and she talked all the time.

Tekla came and brought everyone tea and jam, and lingered in the door a moment, looking round-eyed at everyone sitting in the room, and her eyes beamed some inexplicable joy.

Shoshanna Bergman said, "The guest didn't come this evening either? I haven't yet had a chance to see his face."

The mother moved the jam closer to her. "Take some, please."

Shoshanna Bergman took a spoonful and put it in her tea.

"Strawberry," she stated. "And as a matter of fact, there's enough room in your apartment. Why doesn't he live here?"

The mother said, "I offered it to him when he came. But he refused. He stays in a hotel. He's more comfortable."

"Of course, of course," said Shoshanna Bergman. "It's more proper. After all, two young maidens in the house." She slowly surveyed Nora and Lisa, as if she were seeing them for the first time. Then she let her eyes linger on Esther Krieger. "And you too, now…" she sighed.

Nora changed her position. The chair squeaked nervously.

"Nora," said Shoshanna Bergman somewhat annoyed, "you know that such a squeak gives me a migraine!"

"Sorry," Nora blurted out in a voice more angry than apologetic. She felt she had been deprived of self-control.

Shoshanna Bergman didn't sense anything in those words. She went on with her conversation. "Interesting, what provincialism! The whole city hasn't stopped talking about this American of yours, what's his name, Etkin?"

"Arin," said the mother.

"Yes, Arin, that's what everybody's talking about." She looked sideways at Lisa.

"What are they saying?" asked the mother, annoyed. Lisa's face flushed.

"They say. They've got tongues in their mouth, and they grind empty words. They talk. That's how people are, everything that's none of their business is their business. You know that. Their tongue is in everything. Here, for instance, when Nora went abroad, I really couldn't cross the street; where does Mrs. Krieger get the money to send her daughter to Germany, life is so expensive there! And how is it that Mrs. Krieger's daughter went to Germany?"

"What does it matter to them!" grumbled Nora.

"Yes, I also say it doesn't matter to them," Shoshanna Bergman blurted out, swallowed a sip of tea and picked up her knitting. "I also think that's nobody's business. But – they're interested! And you think they don't ask me questions about Marek and…and…" She took out a handkerchief and wiped her tears. "My Boris. After all, I am a mother. But now, now everybody, everybody's talking only about this Arkin, who came to you all of a sudden."

And since the three women were silent as if they were offended, and apparently didn't intend to investigate what people were talking about, Shoshanna Bergman knitted in silence for a few minutes and then went on talking slowly as it were, but the more she talked, the more her desire to give news stood out.

"I met Mrs. Aaronson in the street today, and a few other people, I went to buy some yarn. And all of them, all of them ask. And not just ask. They also tell. They tell me, you understand? They say, for instance, that he's got a big fortune, and that you always supported yourselves from the money he sent from America, and now he came to check whether there's a real need for his help."

"Bastards!" said Nora, but Shoshanna Bergman didn't even turn back to her.

But this time, Lisa came to her aid. "Nora's right," she said. "That really doesn't concern us. And that whole thing…"

But Shoshanna Bergman wouldn't be cut off. "All kinds of nonsense they talk. They say, for instance, that you got divorced only–"

"How do they know I got divorced!" the mother blurted out angrily. "That was a deep secret; after all, I hardly have anything to do with people!"

"They know!" decreed Shoshanna Bergman. "At any rate, it isn't from me that they know, and not from my family. They know everything. By the way, I heard another rumor, and there may be a trace of something in that one, even though, of course, I'm not saying, God forbid, that it's true. They say that he ran away here because he went bankrupt, is in debt."

She clenched her lips and waited for the impression her words would make.

They say, they say, they say…rang in Nora's ears.

Shoshanna Bergman sighed. "I'm not saying it's the truth. But nevertheless, if the rumor is right, that he came here for other reasons" – a long and significant look at Lisa – "you really should check what's true and what isn't."

"Check!" Nora burst out. "Check! But, God almighty, what is this? What does this have to do with us?"

Shoshanna Bergman looked at her compassionately. "You're still young, Nora."

Lisa said, "Nevertheless, that doesn't have anything to do with us. And that whole story about bankruptcy…slander. And in general, they should live and let live. And we have nothing to do with other people's money."

"Well, you're an angel of God, you are!" decreed Shoshanna Bergman, dismissing her out of hand. But suddenly she felt that now it was her turn to be offended. "In general, all of you are angels! Slander! And so why are you listening? You think it's a great pleasure to walk in the streets and hear everything those people say about you? If *I* didn't know how to keep a secret…well, let's talk about something else. How do you feel in our province, Nora?"

Nora didn't reply, since the question was clearly rhetorical. So

Shoshanna Bergman repeated, "But what is he doing here, really, that man? Just having fun?"

"Two nights ago," said Lisa innocently and proudly, "we were together at the summer theater. We heard a Russian singer. He was wonderful. He was so wonderful, that singer, such a soft tenor. He sang ballads by Tchaikovsky…" And as always when she spoke of opera singers, her face expressed unbounded admiration. But this time, her excitement overflowed its banks, choked by pleasure.

"That same singer," Nora cut her off scornfully and coarsely, "is an old fool, has a voice like a slaughtered rooster, that's what he's got left."

Lisa's face grew furious. "What! How can you say such things! He's wonderful! His voice is as it was in his youth. You really didn't hear him!"

"I didn't and I won't," decreed Nora. "Not even if a thousand Arins invited me. A seventy-year-old monster stands on the stage and shrieks."

"Monster!"

"Yes, monster! Monster!"

The mother looked at Nora with reproach, amazement and sadness. "What's wrong with you, Nora? How can you talk like this?"

"How can I talk like this! How should I talk! I don't understand what you want from me!" Nora felt that every word that came out of her mouth was silly, insulting, superfluous, but she couldn't stop. "I'm talking as I always do! I don't want everybody to educate me. I'm not a baby anymore!"

"But what's gotten into you, like a lit match!" The mother turned pale.

"Nerves!" sighed Shoshanna Bergman.

"Not nerves! Not any nerves!" shouted Nora in despair, and her eyes filled with tears. "You put everything down to nerves! I just say the truth pure and simple, and you, always, always, you act like this with me! Even before I left, and now again…even then I had my fill of it…and this city, and this gossip, I can't, I can't live in this house, where all the neighbors…"

"Nora!"

"Yes, Nora! Yes, I'm Nora, so what! Why do they say we live on charity! I worked, yes. I taught stupid children. With my own money I went abroad, and they…"

"But Nora, who denies…but we…"

"But you listen to all that nonsense, and then, when I open my mouth…"

"But you were talking about the singer."

"It doesn't matter what I was talking about!"

"Hysterical!"

Nora jumped up in tears and ran to her room.

There she fell on the bed with her face buried in the pillow.

God almighty, God almighty! What am I doing, what nonsense am I doing! God in heaven, Albert –

She wept for shame that she couldn't stop her tears; she wept for an indefinable offense, for helplessness, for a rage without a reason, for a grief whose origin she didn't know. She wept like a baby, pouring out her soul, devotedly, weeping for the sake of weeping. She wept as the old woman weeps for something that can't be brought back, out of desperate bitterness, with tears that seem and are the last. Long weeping, sunk in the pillow, sunk in darkness, going out of herself and returning to pain and shame and rage.

And all of a sudden, still weeping, she felt the door opening slowly and somebody standing in the room.

She bit her lips, stopped sobbing, raised her head from the pillow, looked through the tears; in the doorway stood Tekla.

"Young miss, oh, Jesus-Maria, I didn't know…I just heard you come into the room."

"Yes," muttered Nora with an effort. "What is it?"

Tekla's face was frightened and excited, her eyes were round as though drawn by a compass.

"Young miss," she whispered, "there was a gentleman here today who asked to give you a letter. At night, when you were alone."

Nora sat up on the bed. Her tears dried all at once. Her throat was also dry with a sudden excitement. Her throat was hot, and something chilly throbbed in her chest, as if a knife point cold as ice touched her heart. Could it be? Could it be? Albert –

From under her apron, under her armpit, Tekla took out an envelope with no address. She held it out to Nora and whispered, "He didn't come into the house. He waited for me below, next to the stairs. When I went down with the bucket, he asked, 'Do you work here?' He looked at me so hard, oh, Jesus-Maria, I was scared! I told him, 'Yes. I'm the maid for the ladies.' Then he said, 'Give this to the young miss, to Miss Nora,' he said, 'when nobody is with her,' he said, 'at night.' A gentleman he was, old, with a beard…"

"Oh," Nora groaned, and once again tears rose in her eyes. "Good, good, thank you, go."

Tekla tiptoed out. She shut the door carefully. And opening the envelope Nora wasn't surprised at the sight of that writing she had known all her life:

My daughter,

You're one of them, too, one of those mortal enemies. You, the only one I believed in! Bloodsuckers and mortal enemies turned you against me too. But they'll get theirs. I'll foil the plot. I'm alone in the battle. You left me too. But you'll come back to me, when you know the secret. Look and see, the end isn't far off. One day soon I will open their eyes. All of them are mad and crazy, listen to the advice of the old father, beware of them.

And then, all of a sudden, in an extremely even and clear handwriting:

Regards to Mama. Albert told me you managed to rest in the dacha. How are you now? Take good care of yourself, especially your nerves. See you soon.

Papa

Nora put the open letter on the table. She grimaced. She lay down again. Her eyes filled with tears again. And the tears flowed from the corners of her eyes and poured into her ears and made her hair wet.

Now she didn't feel she was weeping. She lay there, shed tears and listened; beyond the corridor, in the dining room, Shoshanna Bergman's short thin laugh rolled away and Lisa's laugh replied to it; then chairs were moved, knitting needles rang, steps shuffled. Then muffled words of women parting came from the corridor, and Shoshanna Bergman's heavy steps squeaked on the stairs.

And a tap on Nora's door.

And even though Nora didn't respond to the knock, the door opened and her mother entered the room. She looked at her with a questioning silence, stood embarrassed a little while. She came and sat down on the edge of the bed.

In her voice was a very distant echo of dull resentment and concern. "So, what's wrong with you?"

Without a word, Nora gave the mother the letter. Suddenly she felt she was weeping only because of that letter. It didn't occur to her that the letter came after the weeping. She didn't want to lie, but somehow, she was mixed up about what came before and what came after.

The mother grasped the issue as an explanation for the weeping. Scanning the lines of the letter, her face grew more serious, and tiny lines formed around her mouth in an expression of submission, and her eyes were the eyes of a person who accepts the judgment.

She finished reading and put the letter into the envelope.

"Who brought it?"

"Tekla."

Carefully, with loving solace, the mother stroked Nora's head. "My silly little girl. Well, we have to get used to it at last. Didn't you tell me that it was an illness like any other, like any other illness?"

The tears kept pouring from Nora's eyes. The mother sat and went on stroking her hair. "Stop, stop, calm down. You knew. Soon you'll leave here. You'll go back to your concerns, your studies."

"Mama, and you, you'll stay here."

"Our lives," she said dismissively. "Don't think about that anymore. Get undressed and go to sleep. Don't think anymore."

She stood up and tiptoed out of the room, afraid to wake Nora.

He who walks and casts his seeds, weeps. And heavy is the yoke.

God almighty, the yoke of our youth is too heavy to bear. Give me strength to bear my youth, to accept my youth with love. To bear the great awe, walking and weeping, walking and bearing. Walking and stumbling. And getting up – seven times.

The new post office, like all the new government buildings in that small state, was a little more splendid than it had to be. And even though it didn't go beyond bourgeois taste, something in it bordered on the absurd, because of the search for a "special style" that had the pretense of coordinating the demands of modern man in a technical age with big vaulted Venetian windows and pink marble columns like both Renaissance and ancient buildings. The milk chocolate brown of the outside walls calmed the eye of the spectator, but inside the building expensive marble piled up, too much marble.

The girl selling stamps behind the small window curled her straw-colored hair very carefully. Her lips were rouged, and her checked muslin blouse was a little too starched. But her eyes, watery blue eyes, and her broad nose with its few freckles peeping with simple honesty from under the coat of powder, and especially her wide, healthy, reddish plump hands, almost as much as her manicured fingernails – all that showed she had recently been a milkmaid in her remote village. And if you removed her makeup, she'd be a twin sister to Tekla. Most of the clerks in that small state had the same expression as the rustic Tekla.

And maybe that was why she carried out her task with a perfect "clerkish" awareness that doesn't give up anything; precise and important in her own eyes, without partiality and without friendliness. And Nora, whose only interest in that girl was to buy a stamp from her, felt as if she were standing at a very high counter, and was suddenly small and helpless compared to her.

Every contact with government clerks, even if they're selling stamps in the post office, had always given Nora a strange dread. So, this time too, she hurried as fast as she could to get away from the window where the clerk was sitting. She grabbed her change nervously and almost fled for her life to the mailbox, licking the stamp on the way (a childish habit she couldn't break) and sticking it on the envelope.

The mailbox was also solemn: big and splendid as an alms box in some church. Nora dropped the letter into the gaping maw of that box, and felt relieved.

The letter she sent was thoroughly insignificant – a friendly note to that redhead Antonia, who had been on the outing with her on the gray morning she told Arin about. But the very act of sending a letter had always strangely weighed heavily on Nora; after the letter was swallowed up in the mailbox, something of it seemed lost. She felt an irreparable loss, an act that was done and could never be taken back, almost a physical feeling of separation and loss, as if she were suddenly a little lighter, and not that liberating lightness that makes you willing to leap, take off, fly, but a lightness of lost weight, physical insecurity.

She stood a little while at the mailbox, wondering, Can I get the letter back? Then, with a tiny shrug of renunciation, she went out and very slowly descended the broad, easy stone steps of the post office.

On the main street, lighted by the autumn sun, traffic was slow and quiet, the weekday morning traffic. It was all polite. Nursemaids pushed baby buggies over the trampled sand of the avenue of lindens turning green-gold with the fallen leaves. Ladies and servants came and went leisurely in the big shops. A few men, most of them with briefcases indicating that they belonged to various "departments," crossed the street now and then and disappeared into one of the side streets with their government institutions. The buses were half empty and moved lazily and heavily.

Swept up by the slow pace of the hour, Nora slowly walked to the curb and was about to cross the avenue when a voice called her name.

She recognized that voice, and her breast was flooded with a wave of joyous and happy fear. And as she turned her blushing face around, the voice called her name again.

Arin was standing a little distance away and waving for her to wait a moment for him.

Nora saw that he wasn't alone. A tall young woman stood facing him, leaning on a long gray car. Nora couldn't see anything but a red coat and a red hat and some sparkling and radiant freshness in her fair face beneath the beautiful flame of the hat. The woman parted from Arin with a handshake, sat down in the car and drove off.

It all took only about half a minute, and Arin was walking toward Nora. But in that half minute, the happy fear that had stirred in her at the sound of his voice was snuffed out completely and was replaced by a sharp stab of offense. And she recalled that it had been four days since she had come to the city and he hadn't deigned to come by and ask how she was.

As he came toward her, he called out, "When did you come, Nora?" and his face lit up with a thin smile, mainly in the corners of his lips, and his eyes gleamed with a strangely sweet glow, which Nora hadn't seen in his face before.

At first, she smiled back at him and held her hand out while she was still far away, but she realized at once that that smile wasn't meant for her, that what lighted up Arin's face was simply the fresh reflection of that woman in the red coat. And when Nora shook his hand, there was that firm and evil glassiness in her eyes that aged her face and made it ugly.

Arin repeated his question.

"Four days ago," Nora replied dryly and resentfully.

But he didn't notice and said with a paternal scolding, "How come so fast? It's good in the forest now."

"It was raining," said Nora.

"Oh, yes," he said. "But now it's so nice."

His speech was a bit hasty, unlike his usual way, but very slowly his eyes came back and looked *at her* and smiled *at her*. And in the face of that look, Nora's dry anger was removed.

"And how is Mama?" he asked.

Now she said in a new voice, with a kind of naïve confession, "We really were expecting you all those days. We wanted to see you."

"So did I, every day, I was about to come by to see you. Lisa did tell me that you had come back. But...I was busy."

They crossed the avenue together and walked to the park across the street. As they walked along the avenue, Arin smiled at Nora. "You suit this autumn today. Slightly pale, and the brown color becomes you." He put his hand on her arm to protect her from a boy riding a bike who burst out at the side of the avenue.

She was silent and smiled. She felt his touch as a caress of her arm even after he took his hand away, and she was glad he had noticed the way her face looked.

Like most young women, even if more sober, Nora had a special relation to her clothes, but not to their objective beauty. She had "lucky" clothes and clothes for "black days." And every dress and coat had its own special quality. That soft brown coat, the soft little hat, had a history of successful days abroad, and now she remembered something, and her confidence, easily shaken, returned to her.

"Aren't you in a hurry?" asked Arin.

"No, I've got time."

"So maybe we can sit here, on the bench," he pointed with his chin to the park beyond the sidewalk. "I'd like to tell you something, but not while walking."

They went into the park.

"In an autumn garden, like a pair of lovers..." A verse from a poem that had never been written flickered into Nora's head.

They sat on a tree-lined side path, rounding across from the right wing of the opera house, which was very ugly on that side with its bare concrete – its beautiful façade facing the main boulevard. Next to the vaulted roof of the theater was the high, exposed crest of a poplar, and on its peak a big tattered crows' nest. There were a lot of crows in the park. They flew shrieking over the trees, over the heads of the nursemaids and the German "governesses," who came here with the children. But their shrieking was one of the characteristics of the place, and out of habit, it didn't grate on the ear.

Behind the bench where they were sitting was a lush, wide-branched chestnut tree. One of its heavy fruits fell and burst at Nora's feet. The thick, thorny green shell opened and showed the soft white belly, and the shining brown ball of the chestnut escaped and rolled away from her a little. Nora picked it up; with pensive fingers she stroked the cool, slightly damp pip and ran her thumb over the rough orange concavity on one side, and her middle finger over the shiny smoothness. Then she put it on her palm and held it out to Arin.

"When I was little," she said, "I'd gather chestnuts. Somebody told me you could make purple ink with them. We, my friend Milly and I, tried but never succeeded." She laughed dimly, somewhat timidly, and Arin laughed along with her.

"But I didn't stay angry at the failure," she went on. "I love the chestnut. See how smooth it is."

Arin took it from her and stroked it with a smile.

"Yes," he said. "A sight for the eyes and a touch for the hands. These are things the eye sees every single day. Don't they always confirm for us, always anew, that in spite of everything, life is very precious, worthwhile for us to live?"

"I don't know," said Nora slowly. "I don't know. Maybe not what we see but what we could see. It's hard for me to explain that. I think things we see are like a hint of other things that could be seen." She blushed and broke off.

Arin slowly shook his head. "I'm not sure I understand."

"It's very simple," said Nora. "Or maybe I think so, since I've always felt that. Here, for example, if I walk on a beautiful street, and there's a high garden wall there, I always think that behind that wall is the most beautiful thing. I always think that if I could peep

in, I'd see something wonderful there. More wonderful than anything I'd seen so far."

"Yes," said Arin in his low, slow speech, whose hastiness had
now vanished. "I do know that. And I even remember a summer day
many years ago. I was walking alongside a red brick wall. There was a
heat wave. The wall was high and long, maybe a kilometer long, and
behind it treetops. And all the time I thought that behind that wall,
there *had to be* something marvelously beautiful. Something magic
as a legend. At last I climbed up on a pile of stones and peeped in."

He fell silent.

"And what was there?" asked Nora.

Arin twisted his lips in an unhappy smile. "A cemetery."

Nora gave him a sad look and fell silent. The toe of her shoe
had inadvertently drawn a big letter on the sand of the path. Suddenly she sensed that that letter was A, and she quickly rubbed it out.

"But that story of mine isn't a moral lesson, Nora," he said after
a short silence. "Not behind every wall is there a cemetery. I'm sure
you'll peep in and see a beautiful garden. And I'm sure this life deserves
to be lived, warts and all, in spite of all the cemeteries. I believe," he
said warmly, "I believe that no ugliness and no suffering cancels the
beauty and the joy. And in this life, Nora, there is beauty and joy.
I'm not sixteen years old, Nora, and I say all these things to you as I
would say them to myself. There's nothing a person can't overcome,
and with this fact we always triumph. Life is very precious, Nora."

A little amazed at this speech, which brought back his hastiness, Nora stretched her neck to him like a curious baby about to
peep through a high fence. After a brief silence, she said, "There's no
evidence for those things. That is, I want to know the essential thing:
do you really believe that?"

He thought and seemed to be examining her face and his
own words at the same time. And then he said simply, "Yes." And
he repeated, "The only evidence of these things is belief in them."

A dark chubby toddler came to the bench and wanted to get

her ball that had rolled behind it. Arin leaned back and, reaching his long arm down, he picked up the ball and gave it to the child.

"But today I wanted to tell you," he began in a different voice, an apologetic voice, after the child had gone, "that during these days I went to your father's house, that is, the place where he's living."

"He wrote me." Nora bent her head and her face became gloomy.

"He did?" Arin took out his cigarette case and offered it to Nora. "Will you smoke?"

"No, thanks. Not now."

"As you like." He lit his cigarette and inhaled. "Yes, we talked about you," he commented. "But I want to tell you, please forgive me for bothering you, but it seems to me I have to tell one of you. And you, if I'm not mistaken, are the only one who can understand something. That is," he grew confused, "with Lisa, there's no point in talking. She herself goes to visit him. But that's not proper. That is, she does everything she's supposed to, as far as I could see. And really well. But she does everything as if it was *her* catastrophe, and she and not he has to bear it. And so she's sometimes too careful, and that drives him crazy. There are movements, there are looks he's most sensitive to. She was there the day before yesterday in the morning, before I visited, and I found him in a condition that was immeasurably worse than the day before she came. I don't know, of course, if that was the reason."

"Oh," Nora blurted out, her mouth twisting and shaking at the left corner. But Arin didn't look at her, probably intentionally. And that made it easier for her. She was silent and listened.

"Yes, I couldn't tell your mother that either. Pure and simple, I don't dare interfere in her business. But you...I told you back in the forest that I wanted to see and know if anything could be changed."

"Yes?" Nora replied with a nervous question.

"And I thought," Arin went on without paying attention to her question, and didn't look at her. "Understand, and don't get mad; he was my best friend and I've got a certain right – I thought it had to do with money, and I...it's all the same. In short, I'm definitely not a professional, but those words: schizophrenia, hebephrenia, paranoia, definitely don't get to the heart of the matter. I've got a certain experience. I didn't want to talk about it. I hate doctors of nerves of all kinds with a mortal hatred. But I'm sure, Nora, I'm very sorry, I'm sure that nothing is to be changed here. One thing and one thing only is logical; let him live like that, but don't torture yourselves. That's all. That, at any rate, is how it seems to me. And you, Nora, if you meet him, be a good girl and try to be calm really, as calm as possible. And mainly, it shouldn't be artificial. You understand? And for now, it's better if you don't visit him. Right?"

"And he?"

"He? I visited him almost every single day. And he's reasonable and sane for the most part. But almost every time, something bursts out. For a little while. All those delusions. That is, our delusions, the healthy ones as it were, about that mental state. Healthy people always tend to believe that the world of the mentally ill is awful, but interesting from some perspective."

Nora shook her head a few times. "I know."

Arin smiled sadly. "I feared that nevertheless you didn't know. Forgive me for saying that. But I…I knew him before. He was one of the few people I knew who wasn't limited, his world was truly broad, despite the environment in which he lived, he was not narrow-minded. Not at all. And now he's got some world into which he sometimes wants to invite others. And in that world, built as it were on the basis of two or three ideas and visions, only one single thing exists: he himself. He, the persecuted, he the tortured, he the saint, he the king-messiah, he the god. That's why I said nothing can be done. That world, despite all its torments, a person won't give up. I know. Yes, I know. We too, when we're sane, Nora, wouldn't give up that center in the big world inside every single one of us."

Another chestnut fell from the tree and burst. This time, only half the shell came off, and the brown pit peeped gaily from the white pith. Arin touched it with the tip of his shoe, looked at Nora's face at long last and smiled. "Look, no, you yourself won't be able to see at all. But I suddenly see three eyes like one another as three drops of water. Two in your face, and one here, on the ground."

But Nora didn't let him change the subject. At first *she* wanted an excuse to get off the topic. She really didn't want to hear it, wanted to run away. But his last words touched something in her differently, and she cut him off almost resentfully. "And how is it there, in that house?"

"Very nice," replied Arin, and rolled the chestnut away from him with his foot. "Lisa didn't tell you?"

"No," said Nora bitterly and her nervous hand opened and closed the button of her left glove. "I saw her whispering with Mama. They don't tell me anything. They're sparing my nerves."

"Ease up, Nora, you're exaggerating. I'm sure she at least described the house to you."

"She said something. But I wanted to know how you see it."

"A nice house. A spacious wooden house. With a rather big garden around it. A vegetable garden on one side. And his window faces the fruit trees. A light room, whitewashed. And most of the furniture is made of birch. Rustic, but nice. I didn't see such things in my youth. All that's in his room. In the landlord's rooms, everything is in the familiar style from before the last war: sideboard, samovar, thick colorful porcelain dishes, icons. They're Russian Orthodox." He pronounced the word "orthodox" with an English accent, and Nora didn't immediately understand what it meant. "Old people who have no children. He's some kind of low-level clerk, but the main thing in his life is working in the garden and the house. Taciturn people. Both of them are very serious. But they're of a certain type, you know, that only coincidentally, because it didn't occur to them, aren't disciples of some religious sect. And it's good that they're like that. They very gladly bear some yoke. Last night I was there. We all sat at the table. Around the samovar, of course. And your father read them holy scriptures in Russian translation. They sat and listened with awe and reverence. Serious. They were silent."

Nora listened a little while as if she were listening to a fairy tale. Her mouth was slightly open. But then her lips clenched again in silent bitter grief.

Now Arin didn't take his eyes off her and slowly nodded. "Believe me, child, I'm not softening or beautifying anything. That's how he is and you have to accept things as they are and keep quiet."

"Keep quiet?" Nora repeated. "But, but I, between one thing and another, I'm too quiet. I took off the yoke. I put it on others. I'll go away in two months. And afterward, even afterward, I won't stay here."

"That's good."

"Yes, good! And it's all on them. Mama and Lisa. And I saved myself," she mortified herself with her words. "I know they see me as a person who loves nobody but herself. And they're right. But when I think that Mama may be left alone some day, that Lisa can finally decide she's had enough. And rightly, rightly. After all, she's no more obligated than I am, after all, I," she was agitated, "I should bear everything, not her. But in fact, she's had enough." She fell silent with pain and said with an obvious effort, "She's still a relatively young woman, as you said, and her own life…"

"Lisa?" Arin blurted out with sad amazement. "Where will she go? Haven't you noticed that Lisa is the only one of you who has found her mission in life? And that mission is to be a victim. And the only thing she'll gladly forgive you is your love for yourself because love of others belongs only to her."

"Yes," said Nora, and felt very relieved. "Sometimes I think so too. But it's evil to think like that. And some change seems to have taken place in her recently…in the last few days."

Arin shrugged. "I don't know. I didn't know her before. That is, I didn't see her before."

And suddenly everything about Lisa became marvelously clear.

"And forgive me," said Arin, "if I've hurt you. I thought I had to tell it."

"Yes, yes," Nora answered quickly. "I thank you very much. And I…"

"Why don't you finish?"

"I think you – behaved as a friend, that you're a true friend!"

"Is there any doubt?" he laughed.

Nora blushed slightly and bowed her head. "No. But you…we haven't been together for even a week. And anyway. We don't know anything." Once again her words were confused because she didn't dare tell him she didn't yet know for what and for whom he suddenly came to this city.

Arin didn't answer, her words were whispered and he may not have heard them at all, or perhaps he ignored them deliberately.

There was a silence. Arin looked at the little children playing in the sand. Nora looked up at him from below, from the side, with her head down. His face was tired now, but numb. Once again she remembered the encounter. She remembered that beautiful woman in the red coat. The memory was like a thorn. He asks me. He tells. He talks about my issues. And so do I. I'll take courage. Me too.

She raised her head, gazed at him with hostility. "And that lady in the red coat?"

Arin looked at her with an amazed question. "What lady?"

"The one you parted from when we met today? The beautiful woman," Nora's voice dropped.

"Oh, Helen," said Arin, as if the woman's first name explained everything. For a brief moment, the trace of that fresh smile, like a glowing prism of her, reappeared on his lips. But since Nora didn't take her hostile eyes off his face, the smile died out and was replaced by a slightly tense weariness. He felt obliged to explain. "She went to the university with my daughter Paula, and about a year ago she married your attaché in our country." He chewed a little and added for some reason, "Her mother was a Jew, I think."

And he fell silent.

Nora suddenly felt guilty. His daughter's friend. His daughter is six years older than me. Married. Six years older than me.

"The sky is very overcast," she said.

The glow of the boulevard grew dim and gray. The nursemaids looked at the sky with worried eyes.

Nora got up.

"Maybe you'll come with me and eat with us."

Arin also got up and apologized. "Forgive me, I can't; maybe I'll come by in the early evening."

"I won't be home in the early evening," Nora replied dryly. "I have to pay a sick call. My aunt is sick, Aunt Zlata. They want me to go there. In fact, I should have visited her before this. I promised them."

"So, see you this evening?" said Arin.

"This evening."

And when they parted at the gate of the park, he shook her hand warmly and stood for a while, watching her cross the avenue.

That smell on the stairs! That mixture of smells of dying fish, rot, dust, and rags that hadn't been aired in months; that smell of Jewish corridors, of pale Jewish children, who didn't know soap and water; that stench of unwashed dishes and leftovers of Sabbath dinners, and the choking air of sealed apartments whose windows were shut both summer and winter.

In the dark of the staircase, Nora stood still, struck by those smells. At that stench, its force and violence, everything was null and void. Her liberation, her year of escape, her life in a foreign country, with its own fragrance, as it were, her forest a few days ago, Albert Arin – everything, everything suddenly seemed gone in this oppressive air, in the choking of this staircase.

A nauseating, hateful, and shameful mixture. That searing shame of impotence and helplessness, the shame of the person involved against his will, besieged her, as she felt back then, facing the Jew on the train. And there was no refuge. Once again she felt the silly, absurd responsibility, the responsibility for the phenomena of that life, for all its bad smells, for that stink that rose to her and revolted her and entered into her from the open door of that strange apartment, an apartment on the first floor of her aunt's building.

Her steps were heavy and her eyes were fixed on that open door and the figure of that masculine woman and the figure of her tall, coarse son, standing in the corridor of that apartment.

The masculine woman stood in the doorway and fixed heavy dark eyes on Nora. There was a strange beauty in those eyes, in the coarse red face. An upsetting, misleading beauty that was somehow depressing and shameful. The dead uncle used to call that neighbor by some strange Sholem Aleichem name. "Chemeritsa" – Nora remembered and lowered her head at the heavy look. And behind her, the woman's voice rang out as she explained to her stupid son the purpose of Nora's visit in that house, "To visit a sick woman she's going, the sick woman on the second floor!"

A visit to the sick. Family love. Love of a woman her mother's brother married for some reason so-and-so many years ago. Bad memories of a suffocating girlhood, of a loathsome life she had wanted to escape but which pursued her were embodied within this house, within these stairs, within that aunt who lay sick, there in her room on the second floor.

Those Friday evenings, and that obligatory visit to the aunt's house, that dumpy, broad, flat woman, taking the pots out of the oven. Gefilte fish you had to praise to the sky, and that prison of depressing and stifling family warmth. Only the uncle's little bit of humor would make up for something. But the uncle isn't here anymore.

"But you can't go in like that!" Nora thought, and wanted to bring up from the distance, from the depths of childhood, some Sabbath morning, and the house of that aunt when she still lived across the river – the broad, clear river with green banks, a slope of bare stones…she was good to me, thought Nora, but those words in the thought were weak and strange. She was good to me, she repeated the thought to be sure, and forced herself to touch the bell.

An aging spinster, wrapped in a gray wool kerchief, opened the door to her. A silly amazement, obsequiousness and hostility were frozen in her long heavy-chinned face. Her broad sweaty hand was entwined in Nora's fingers. Nora wanted to remember her name and couldn't. One of those miserable creatures who surrounded Aunt Zlata after she was widowed.

In the dimness of the narrow corridor, between the coat closet and the stand loaded with jackets, Nora shook the raindrops off her coat. The smell of medicines came from the clothes, the closet, the long face of the old maid leaning on the doorpost with her hands clasped on her chest, who didn't take her eyes off Nora as she took off her coat.

No one was in the big dining room. But nonetheless there was something of a sense of crowdedness, as always, as on those Friday evenings in her childhood. An angry-faced oak table under the dark needlepoint runner. A concave, worn, greenish sofa. A few books on the cheap shelf in the corner, the uncle's books. And opaque windows that turned black in the evening, and behind them lurked the street. The street and its smells.

Long-Face seemed to slide behind the heavy screen that separated the dining room from the small bedroom. She crossed it. Her whispering voice, and another exhausted voice. And she reappeared and took off. Nora went into the sickroom.

The aunt, placed among a lot of puffed-up pillows, hoisted herself a little on her elbows. A kind of smile twisted her thin thirsty lips. Her voice was frail. Lost among the big pillows.

"Nora?" she said. "Sit down, sit down. When did you come?"

And not getting an answer, she shut her eyes and sank back into the pillows.

Nora remained alone. With the little windowless room. With the rustle of the heavy screen behind her back. With the mute illness of the aunt. Two beds. The one on the left belonged to the uncle, who, two years ago, used to wake up at night and choke in his serious heart disease. And he would choke and hold his right hand on his left arm and try to smile and tell a joke, and his reddish face would suddenly fall back and hit the hard headboard of the wooden bed, despite the many pillows at his head. Now that long-faced old maid probably slept on that bed. Two beds. And between them tiny, tall, narrow night tables. They hid the chamberpots. The smell of footbaths. And on their gray artificial marble tops – bottles of medicine and a glass with remnants of cooling tea. On the bed on the right was the sick woman. Her round head, flat as a pancake, was attached to awkward shoulders without passing through a neck. That rheumatic poisoning, which the doctors still hadn't determined, poured a heavy black onto her wrinkled skin. Her thin hair, black and gray, her shut eyes. And in the round closed area of her face, her whole small world was inlaid, a world of pots and pans in the kitchen, a world of a ledger and percentage book, a world of naked sensibility and suspicion, lying in wait for everyone who came to her, a world of canine devotion to the memory of her husband who wouldn't be reached, and the world of trust and belief in her own righteousness, in her own morality, in the honest path of her life, creeping in those narrow alleys for more than fifty years now. Tiny drops of sweat glistened on her forehead.

She'll die, thought Nora with a stupid cruelty. She'll die, she'll die.

"How are you, Aunt?" she forced her lips.

"Getting better, thank God," answered the aunt without opening her eyes.

She always suffers in silence. Bearing her torments in silence, her mother's words rose in Nora's memory. But this suffering in silence Nora couldn't count as the aunt's good quality. Only toward the dead uncle was her silence truly heroism and love of her fellow man. She restrained her character to keep from tormenting him. She didn't reveal anything to us because she was suspicious, because she feared that we wouldn't treat the suffering properly, that we'd steal something from her little world, that we'd want her death. There was some anger at us in that silence which announced to everyone that we weren't as good as she. We had harsh stone hearts. That silence, that enclosed us in a cage of our evil and was suffocating, suffocating…

She'll die, Nora thought again. Such a death! Such a dull and miserable death.

Like most people her age, who refuse to agree that this life goes on without purpose or shape, Nora also kept in her heart that vague faith in the purity of a person's leaving life. A faith in a final elevation, which may but doesn't have to lead the person to a better world than this; but death itself, at that last moment of the person's existence on the earth, must, must be something superb, sublime, superhuman, beaming and imparting its radiance to others. "A cemetery," she recalled Arin's words. Maybe the illusion of that death had something greater than others, precisely because she knew intimately the other boundary of the forces of mind and consciousness of the person – the madness. Since she knew its physiological ugliness, the oppression and suffering it imposes on everything around, the turgid abyss of suffering with no consolation, not even the most banal. Maybe because of that, maybe in opposition to that, out of self-defense, the most precious thing to her was the poetic image of death. But now – before her eyes this cellar death, low death, abstract, miserable, small as a bug, with an ugliness that has nothing demonic. "To die like that! To die like that!" – she thought with a flaring animosity, as if out of malice, this sick woman displayed her desperate dying. And she felt she was addicted to that death, given to it without any defense. That, against her will, she had a part in that death, as she had also had a part in that life.

The sick woman opened her eyes. Her look was weary, indifferent, and yet very tense.

"What did you do in Berlin?" she asked suddenly.

Nora began telling. She told her superficial things, she almost didn't know what she was saying. Here, in this room, between these beds, in this opaque dimness, all the colorful things, things she had seen only a little while ago as liberation, as refuge, as *life* – had no more flash, no more soul, were null and void.

To get out of here, to get out, God! To go, to go – the desperate, heavy longing of one who can't escape hummed in her. And she talked.

The aunt wasn't listening. Somewhere in the story, in the middle of some cut-off episode, the searing poison began bubbling up in her little eyes. Nora felt it, and something told her the sick woman was reading her mind, guessing her hostility, her pitilessness, her desire to run away and leave the sick woman to death. The poison in the aunt's eyes pierced and oozed into Nora's flesh, made her tongue heavy; her story got complicated, she seemed to have been talking for a whole hour, while in fact only about ten minutes had passed.

Once again the sick woman raised herself a little on her big pillows, her sharp pale tongue licking her thirsty lips.

"How's Papa?" she suddenly blurted out.

Nora didn't answer immediately. She knows! she thought. And somehow she knew that that was only a rhetorical question, but she didn't know what was hiding behind it.

"Better, thank you."

The sick woman shook her head.

"No, no. You can talk frankly to me, I know as well as you do that he's incurable. Better! What's better in this matter! You don't have to tell me things like that. But you know, you had better take good care of your own health."

"But I…that is…I feel fine, really," said Nora helplessly, and immediately regretted her words.

"So!" said the sick woman mockingly, and her voice became clearer, and something like inspiration was in it. "Fine! According to you, you feel fine. Mama told me that, in Berlin, you met that cousin from Warsaw. Your mother told me he's got a nervous disease – that, how do you call that? That is, we simple people, we'd say he went crazy. He's very sick, eh?"

"Yes," said Nora in a choked voice. "But he, maybe he'll get better," she concluded with a desperate self-defense.

"You think so?" mocked the sick woman. "A girl your age, my darling, isn't a baby anymore. You should know and recognize the truth. That man is from your father's family and your father and also…"

What will she say now? What will she reveal now, God, why did I come here! But aloud she said only, as if she was trying to put up a last bulwark, "But you know, Papa…that happened in the war, it's only shock!"

The sick woman clenched her lips. "Shock! We all went through the war, didn't we! Weren't we all in hard situations? And your uncle and I, weren't we in Ukraine during the pogroms? Didn't we sit in a cellar for two weeks? But if you don't have madness in your blood, you won't have any shock! You know how your uncle Solomon ended in Russia?"

Here it comes, now it comes! Nora felt a nightmarish dread. "He died of tuberculosis," she said. "During the war in the Carpathian Mountains, he caught cold and…they told me…" She didn't have the strength to finish the sentence.

"They told you!" the sick woman sat up among her pillows. Something wild twisted her flat face. A force suddenly rose in it, a kind of nameless power. And a strange power; at that moment, the face was bigger, more human in its evil flame.

"They told you, they *didn't* tell. So, I'll tell you: your father's family hid the truth because it wasn't nice for them. Your uncle died of his madness, in a lunatic asylum your father's brother died. That was his 'tuberculosis'!"

And then, dropping back into the pillows, weary and old, she lay among them like a cat, her eyes extinguished, and her lips still muttering, "It's in your blood. In the blood of the whole family. All the Kriegers. I'm telling you this for your own good. A grown-up girl. Just for your own good."

Nora didn't see anything else. Dry tears filled her throat and wouldn't rise to her eyes. Her head was very heavy, and tatters of her thoughts darkened her consciousness. Filth, filth, she thought, filth and bondage. And there's no way out, no way out. And I don't want to go crazy. That's the verdict. I don't want to, I don't want to, impossible for me…

In the fog of awareness there suddenly rose the face, white as sour milk, the face of that German doctor from the Charité, who asked about her heredity for some minor test, and her voice sounded professional, dry. "But why can't you treat that as a disease, like a cold, for example?"

Why don't you know? Why? Like a cold, like a cold, like a cold – the words rumbled in Nora's brain.

"Just for your own good," the sick woman repeated, only with mumbling lips.

Something slipped out of Nora's hand and she didn't bend over to see what it was. A broken glass seemed to ring. And maybe that was a coin falling out of her wallet. She got up and without a word went into the dark narrow corridor. It was cold in the corridor. Somewhere in the coat was a right sleeve, a left. The long-faced spinster came out to lock the door behind her.

I won't go crazy! Nora wanted to tell her, but she knew she wouldn't believe her anyway.

In the staircase was that same choking smell, and the Chemeritsa's door was ajar and her stupid son was standing in the corridor of their apartment, illuminated by a very dim electric light, and he was praying in a loud and silly voice.

She didn't know how she got home; she walked, walked a long time, longer than she had to. In the street were lighted buses and a lot of people and glittering display windows, and umbrellas and electric streetlamps swaying in the wet wind, and a thin drizzle that had been falling since twilight.

And her feet in the light summer sandals splashed spitefully in all the puddles. And her shoulders, maliciously, bumped into all the passersby and their umbrellas.

And only in the staircase of her house, when she almost opened the door, did she suddenly feel waves of chill and heat passing alternately through her body, and thought with dread, What will I tell, what will I say when they ask me?

But in the corridor, when she took off her hat, she heard strange voices from the room, and Tekla came out of the kitchen beaming with silent excitement, which she had shown as soon as she came to work in the Krieger house, and she said, "Young lady, guests!"

Nora sighed with relief. Guests, that's very good. Won't have to tell everything.

Once again, strange waves of shaking chill and blazing heat passed through her body and she dropped down exhausted on a chair under the coat rack and started taking off her wet shoes and socks.

"Fine, Tekla," she smiled weakly and apologetically to the waiting servant, "please bring me other shoes and socks, ask Mama."

For a moment, her head spun and sank in the gloom.

Her mother came with the shoes and socks in her hand. "So you were there? What's there?"

"As bad as can be, as bad as can be," Nora blurted out and felt that her eyes suddenly emitted some wild and jolly flash that didn't match her answer.

Her mother didn't notice her look and sighed, "The poor woman! And you're late. We've already eaten," she said and gave Nora the shoes. "You got caught in the rain. You'll catch a cold. I left supper for you in the dining room."

At the mention of food, Nora felt nauseous; her mouth was bitter and her tongue was heavy.

"I already ate there," she lied inadvertently, happy the mother didn't question her any further; she slipped on her shoes and socks and stood up.

"Guests," said the mother, and led the way.

The guests were gathered in the mother's room, which also served as a living room. Its walls were somewhat sloping, since the apartment had in fact been an attic; the low ceiling cut the walls like the roof of a lopped-off pyramid. A green carpet covered the floor; comfortable, green silk armchairs and a small crooked sofa surrounded a round table. On the wallpaper were pictures of orange leaves long as seaweed, and heavy greenish drapes decorated the windows. "Aquarium," Giltman had called that room. And indeed, the picture "Maiden from Sienna," which had been in fashion in those days, and which Nora had sent to her mother from Berlin, that smiling mask, hanging on the wall, also enhanced the impression that everything here was underwater.

In the room, Nora found Giltman, Arin and three girls she knew who had come to visit her.

"The aquarium is already full of goldfish!" Giltman called out when she came in.

And even though Nora had heard that joke of his more than once, she was glad because it saved her the trouble of greetings and the words of the first encounter.

The two girls sitting on Giltman's right and left were Nora's classmates from the Gymnasium – Hannah Milner and Nehama Bloch. Hannah, short, with a broad jaw, straight hair, dark and energetic, had a strange admiration for Nora, which seemed to contradict the sober practicality of the commonsensical girl. Nora was somehow the only romance in her life, a kind of symbol of another life, more poetic and not down to earth. Nora didn't know why she saw her that way, and was always a little ashamed when Hannah expressed something like that in her dry, monotone style, a style that couldn't be indirect. She sensed there was some fabrication here that wasn't her fault, but she was fond of Hannah's stubborn look, her overblown movements, her mind, which was sharp but very limited, all her confident ways, which had had that greediness in absentmindedness which indicated, without too much explanation, that she was the daughter of her parents: dealers in raw materials in the market in that city, rich people who hoarded every penny and lived a life of poverty and filth in an alley near that market.

Nehama Bloch was a very ugly girl. Her chinless face was sprinkled with freckles, her eyes watery gray, her dark brown hair was stiff and curly with that unique "Semitic curl" no comb could control. Unlike Hannah, she was a completely blurred creature, that kind of human vegetation that comes up in the desolate abysses of life, untouched by any wind, their soil not refreshed by any healthy vigor.

In point of fact, there had never been anything between her and Nora, but now and then she would come to her house, and Nora never knew why. But this time, Nehama sat straight, almost arrogantly. It turned out she had gotten engaged a week before. Her fiancé was a pharmacist who was supposed to open a pharmacy with his future wife's dowry. The wedding was set for late September, and Nehama was very important in her own eyes, and her face said that she expected congratulations from her envious entourage.

The third one, sitting at some distance from that group, in an armchair next to Arin's chair, was Lucy Kurtz, Nora's friend from the university in that city, where Nora had studied three semesters before she went abroad. Lucy was tall and slim with long legs. Her fair heavy hair was in an unfashionable bun on her long skull. Her eyes were brown and her face was so white and delicate that something in it suggested a thin frost, although a frost that didn't come from her. In the expression on her face, the weak smile of her big soft mouth, the way she sat, which was almost lying, there was something of a constant weariness, a kind of tolerant and pleasant, premature renunciation. Even her closed blue dress wrapped her body with that weariness of renunciation which gave her a side effect of charm in refined, almost elegant, negligence. Now she was smoking slowly, and between one drag and another, she'd move her long-fingered, short-nailed oval hand far away from her. And her elbow, where the sleeve of her dress ended, was leaning on the armchair, and the middle finger tapping the cigarette looked like the neck of a swan.

Lucy was a native of Petersburg, apparently from a good family, but she never said what her parents had been before the war. Nora knew only that her father had died many years ago, and her mother, who lived in some remote town, made a meager living teaching German and English. Lucy herself, who studied here in the university, worked more energetically than her weakness would indicate, and before Nora left, she handed all her students over to Lucy.

And now that Nora saw Lucy in her "aquarium," she felt a kind of shame that, all the time she had been in this city and the forest, she had been concerned only with her own feelings and hadn't even given one little thought to her friends. Maybe it was this shame that didn't let her approach her now and express her joy at seeing her. She shook hands limply, as with the rest of her guests, and sat down not next to her, but next to Hannah.

Sitting, she was uncomfortable. Now and then she felt a strange buzzing in her ears and a chill in her chest. But all that was good and dissolved her and washed away the thoughts of her visit to the aunt, and in a strange way took her mind off Arin, too.

"And we," said Hannah, "were talking about you, of course, when you weren't here. Everybody is amazed that you chose such a profession! Even though I said that nothing fit you better than a profession that doesn't fit anything in the world."

"A woman's logic!" laughed Giltman. "Fits! A profession isn't a dress."

"And it has no real chances," Hannah went on. "And Mr. Arin says that all the professions together have no practical value in our day because the world is facing an economic and intellectual crisis and everything may be null and void."

"We," said Lucy, pausing briefly as she always did after the first word, "always lived in a crisis. Nothing can scare us."

Arin smiled at her. "From a certain perspective, that's not too bad. Maybe in times like these, a young person can afford a period of study, and study that is definitely interesting to him, since the practical value is the same everywhere."

"And yet," said Hannah with the aggressiveness of an incipient argument, "there will always be sick people and there will always be a need for doctors! And I don't regret that I chose medicine. Not from a practical perspective either."

"And there will always be quarrels in the world and brawls and arguments about money and marriage, thank God, thank God, lawyers aren't superfluous in any society," said Giltman.

"You've probably been told more than once that there will soon be more doctors and lawyers than their clients," stated Arin. "But that's not the only issue, unfortunately."

"So, what to do?" Hannah demanded practical advice.

"Not to expect anything," Nora blurted out.

"You should always expect something," said Arin gravely.

"I don't understand the argument of the young ladies at all!" Giltman cut him off. "After all, you've got the simplest way out."

"What's that?"

"To get married. Nehama is smarter than all of you."

Nehama blushed.

"When?" asked Lucy politely, as always.

"In a month!" declared Nehama and laughed both proudly and embarrassed. "Nora! Do you know, our girlfriends said you got engaged abroad to an Indian! Friends from school said so."

Nora shrugged. "I don't understand. They always spread such silly rumors about me, our girlfriends!"

"But you were always like that!" said Nehama, and was almost offended.

"What does that mean?" asked Arin. "Indians always wanted her hand?"

"No, that's great!" Nora suddenly woke up from her freeze and laughed maliciously. "The girls from our school always thought of me for some reason…did I know? As some sort of strange creature. Yes, yes, I still remember, when I was in the ninth grade, I once stood in the hall next to the coat rack. You remember, the coat rack was there. And Nehama stood off to the side a little, and somebody else. I had a terrible cold that day and I'd wipe my nose on a handkerchief. And all of a sudden, I hear that other girl saying to Nehama, 'You see, I always said Nora isn't an aristocrat. Aristocrats wipe their nose like this!' She took out a handkerchief and sniffed it very delicately, as if she were sniffing a prize rose, slowly, with one nostril after another."

Everybody laughed. Only Nehama lowered her head and muttered, "You always tell things like that!"

And Mrs. Krieger, who was offering fruit to the guests, scolded, "But Nora!"

"Nevertheless," said Hannah, "school days were nice. Maybe the happiest days of our lives…"

Suddenly Nora felt very sad. Happy school days, 'childhood, the golden age!' as Tolstoy said – those happy days – and the bad, evil memory thrust before her eyes that awful picture she always wanted to forget, forever, all her life.

The yard of the Gymnasium is full of children. Recess. Summer. A few weeks after the beginning of the school year. The boys playing soccer. The girls drawing hopscotch games or strolling in couples over the yard and pushed by the players running around. As they do, they are all chewing bread and butter, bread and goose fat, rolls. Nora has forgotten her lunch at home. And there, at the gate of the yard – the father. He came to bring her food. She runs to him and takes the package from his hand. "I'm not hungry, Papa," she says, but he's not listening, his eyes are straying over the yard, over the children running around, distant, hard eyes. Fear goes through Nora's body. She knows what eyes like that mean. "Goodbye, Papa." She tries to get away from him. But he follows her into the yard. "Papa," she says, "don't come in. They're laughing at me that you bring me food."

But he's not listening. "The children," he blurts out, "the children, their heart is still pure. Their heart is still pure."

"Papa," Nora pleads, "don't come with me, they're laughing."

"The children," says the father, "they'll understand. Nora, I'll tell them, I'll tell them the truth." He raises his cane, a big flame kindled in his eyes.

For a split second, she also sees the flame in his eyes as a flame of holiness; for a split second, she believes in him, believes in him, believes that a miracle will happen and he'll be a leader, a prophet, a Messiah. But then, she knows what it all means. And when he gets to the mound of sand inside the yard, and starts climbing up on it with his cane raised, she grabs his sleeve and wants to pull him down, to stop him, and pleads, "Papa, Papa, there's no need!"

For a moment he lowers his cane and pushes her away. "Out, damned one!"

"Papa!" she calls in despair.

But he's now standing up above and opens his mouth and shouts, "Children, little pure-hearted sons of Israel!"

In a minute, they stood gathered around him. At first they stood attentive and amazed, and she murmurs from below, "Papa, there's no need!" And tears flowed from her eyes. And he spoke. Suddenly the first sounds of laughter were heard, shouts of "Lunatic!" And somebody in the back shouted happily, "That's Nora Krieger's father! He's crazy! He's crazy!" She turned around and clenched her fists and was about to attack the one who shouted those words, but all she saw was rows and rows of teeth bared in laughter. All of them were laughing. And her fists fell helplessly, and she was pushed and ran among that cruel dense crowd, crying and hearing the father's voice behind her back and feeling his raised cane and hearing, "Crazy. The father of Krieger in the third grade–" And two teachers and the principal were already running to the crowd of rambunctious children, and one of the little ones cast a clod of earth at her. The principal came and grabbed her by the arms, held her shaking shoulders in his strong hands, pressing like a steel vise, and she was almost carried to the nurse's room next to the teachers' lounge. She was put into the hands of somebody and there she was placed on the sofa and given a few drops of Baldrian. She lay withdrawn in her tears, her hands clasped in front of her, she lay for an hour or two, or even longer, and didn't know how that spectacle in the yard ended.

When she came home, she didn't find the father there. Only later did she find out that her mother had been called in and, with the help of the principal who managed to persuade the father to come into his office, she sat him in a car and took him straight to the hospital.

Nora did not return to school until a week later. The children didn't talk about that incident, but their looks haunted her, either pitying or with the arrogance of "knowing." The happy days of childhood –

Don't think –

Nora wrenched herself away from the torments of memory. It was the living room, and these were Nehama Bloch, and Hannah Milner, who were then in the yard.

Hannah was telling something, and after a tense effort, Nora grasped the words. "And so what? Everything didn't turn out as we thought. When I was little, I always dreamed that when I grew up, I'd have a long dress and long hair. Now I'm grown up, my dress is short and my hair is short." And she shook her shorn head with the straight hair.

Listen, see – Nora was tempting herself. And she looked into Arin's face and suddenly knew that last night before she fell asleep she had wanted to remember that face and couldn't. You never could remember a person's face, see a person's expression when he wasn't there, a face that is more to you than the face of a passerby, more than the face of one of many friends. Now, now I see what a special line, rising from the mouth to the forehead. She wanted to etch the line in her memory, she wanted to recall its rhythm as an aid, so it would be like those hollow and empty words you etch in your memory in a certain rhythm, with a special intention to remember their melody.

"Nora's face is so tired," said Lucy. "Maybe we'd better go now." And she stood up.

Nora also stood up and wanted to make her go back to her seat. Suddenly she felt very weak.

"Mama, a little water!"

Mrs. Krieger hurried to the kitchen. Nora stood surrounded by all her guests and muttered, "It's nothing, it's nothing, it'll pass."

But some hard lump was rising from her insides up and up. And suddenly the faces and the furniture were swimming before her eyes.

Arin supported her, hugged her and led her from the room. She leaned on him, completely in his arms. She clamped her mouth shut and thought, Don't let it happen. Restraint. Don't let him see me ugly. Restrain for one more second.

In the door, the mother met her holding a glass of water. And she turned around and accompanied Arin, who was leading her to the bathroom. There he put her into the mother's hands.

Later, when she stood at the sink and vomited into it, she was very relieved.

He didn't see! was her first thought, and then another one, almost happy. So I'm sick, it's all physical, only physical, thank God!

She sat on some stool, leaning on the wall, and thirstily drank the tepid water her mother gave her. Then she heard the voices of the guests saying goodbye in the hall and another voice calling her name.

Apparently it was Lisa who returned, the last consciousness flickered, and she had no more strength to think any other thought.

Doctor Nikitin, the Russian physician, who cured Nora's flu when she was a little girl, came the next day to examine her.

"Thirty-nine point eight. It's almost forty!" he said with a sigh, shaking the thermometer to get the mercury down. "Not nice, young lady, not nice at all."

Nora lay and looked at him dry-eyed, her head aching terribly, and she constantly licked her lips with a hard tongue, and let him poke and press her exposed body, and listened to him murmuring to himself the various diagnoses that came into his mind.

"Stomach flu, it could be, it really could be, hmmm...or maybe typhoid...but it could also be..." He blurted out some Latin name Nora had never heard. "Let's see, let's see..."

Mrs. Krieger was busy, going in and out of the room.

After the examination, the doctor sat in a chair at the bed and smacked Nora's hand lightly. "Not nice, young lady, not good. We old people are getting older and you young people have to live and be healthy. You're at the university now?"

"Yes."

He stood up a moment, stroked his beard, went to the desk, and picked up some book.

"What's this?" he asked absentmindedly.

Nora glanced wearily at the book and saw it was one of the

volumes of Ehrman she had taken out of the state library in Berlin. "Hieroglyphics."

Doctor Nikitin put the book back on the desk as if it had burned him, and he stood and looked at Nora with eyes that were both scared and discerning.

Nora caught his look and suddenly burst out laughing. Waves of laughter rose to her head and made the pain in her temples worse, even though she couldn't stop; the old doctor's panic was so ridiculous. At long last she stifled the laughter and said softly, "But I'm fully conscious, doctor!"

And when she saw him shaking his head both offended and suspicious, she explained, "It really is hieroglyphics. I'm studying Egyptology."

"Oh…" sighed the doctor, relieved, sat down and muttered again, "Yes, yes. We're getting old."

And Nora felt she had to console him and comfort him somehow.

"When I was little, doctor, you'd always tell me a tale about the goldfish."

He smiled and took her hand, and slowly started stroking it.

"Yes. To tempt you to swallow bitter medicine. You were a little capricious, young lady Nora, weren't you? And how is it now?"

And after a silence, he started the old story. "Once upon a time there was an old man and an old woman. The old man and the old lady lived on the shore of the blue sea…"

Nora shut her eyes. The doctor got up, a bit scared. "Headache, eh?"

And he addressed Mrs. Krieger, who came into the room just then with an ice bag. "Yes, yes. Put ice on her forehead."

And he stood before her and comforted her. "It will be fine, my lady, it will be fine. I'll look in on her again this afternoon."

Doctor Nikitin didn't grasp the nature of Nora's illness. He'd come twice a day and express various suppositions, as was his wont, hesitantly and carefully, and add every time with an affectionate admonition, "Not nice, young lady, not nice!"

But on the fourth day, her temperature fell, the headache passed, and what was left in Nora's body was only a pleasant weakness and some warm appeased laziness.

That weakness kept her in bed for ten more days, and those days were very quiet and nice, the happiest days of that autumn.

The mornings were wonderful. The mother went back to work, and Lisa was also steeped in her office from the morning. Nothing was heard in the apartment but the plodding of Tekla's bare feet, and sometimes the sound of her monotonous singing, which brought to Nora's room fragments of rustic words about the white lily and the mint in the garden.

Sometimes rain beat on the window of her bright room, but most days were clear, and in the morning, broad, trembling sunbeams rested on the rug beside her bed.

Twice during that time, Lucy Kurtz came by to find out how she was, short of time, between one class and another, but not in a hurry. Her weariness and beautiful negligence added to the accompanying charm in those hours of appeasement. And her few soft words didn't disturb Nora's rest.

Every single morning, Arin came and sat at Nora's bed for a long time and talked with her a great deal. And every single day, as soon as she opened her eyes in the morning, Nora would wait for him to come, and would listen carefully, but not in dread, for the footsteps climbing the stairs, and she could always tell his footsteps from those of others.

After he'd leave, she'd ask herself whether she loved him, and most times the answer was negative. It was nothing but friendly admiration. It was nothing but the charm of meeting. But in the hours when she'd lie there from morning on and wait constantly, without any other thought in her mind, she knew from her happy expectation that she did love him, only him, even though that love was absurd, even though he was almost the same age as her father, even though she didn't want to love him.

In the evening, before she fell asleep, she'd want to picture his face and would see his blue tie, his gray overcoat, his shoulders, his hands, his hair and the silver strands in it, but she couldn't see his face. Only sometimes, in a dream, it would come to her for a moment, as if it were teasing her and would suddenly change very much and could no longer be grasped.

Once, at dawn, she dreamed she was standing in the Bergman house at the long looking glass at twilight and combing her hair. And suddenly she sees in the mirror that he's approaching her from behind and standing behind her back, smiling. She immediately turned her face to him, to see him, to see him and not his reflection, and he was her father. When she woke up that morning her eyes were wet.

Arin would talk with her now not as he had talked with her in the forest. He talked at greater length, with greater freedom, and his sentences weren't cut off. And there wasn't in his speech that slight mockery, that's always squeezed into the words of the elderly when they talk with the very young. He'd tell about himself, his wanderings and his life, would sometimes make a mistake with abstract things, landscapes he had seen, and books he had read. Maybe the repose of Nora's little room gave him the grace of good conversation or maybe he loved as he talked to see her eyes before him listening, picking up, absorbing his words. And Nora was a little proud that he always chose those morning hours when she was alone in the house and that he only came to her and for her.

Once, when he was sitting like that at her bed and smoking a cigarette with a relaxed calm, she said to him, "I'll remember these days. I'll remember everything. The room and the purple chrysanthemums on the table. Lucy brought them to me yesterday. And you in that chair. And how the lines of sun cut the smoke coming out of your mouth. Years from now I'll remember every detail, even if I'm very old. I almost always know what will stay in my memory. Even the sun on your nose I'll remember."

He shifted a little, absentmindedly wiped his nose, as if wiping the sun off it, and Nora saw the glowing spot play on his long, nicotine-stained fingers. Then he stood up, tapped the ash off his cigarette into the white glass ashtray on the table and said, "But memories are the main thing, Nora."

He sat down in the chair again. "Memories make us what we are. Precisely because we remember the small things, the unimportant things, as it were, but they're so much ours. When I recall my youth, for some reason, I remember more than anything our bedroom, in my parents' house. On winter evenings. There were four long, narrow beds there. My younger sister slept in one, and my brothers slept in the other two. And my bed was made, but I hadn't yet laid down in it. I used to read standing up back then. For some reason, the lamp in our house was on a high cabinet, apparently so its light wouldn't be too bright and disturb our sleep. It stayed on all night long because my little sister was afraid of the dark and used to wake up at night sometimes. And I would stand between the heater and the cabinet and a very dim light would fall on the pages of the book. I remember reading the poems of Mordechai Zvi Maneh, and my head was ablaze with excitement, and in the heater some little door was always shaking and its iron was clanking, and one shutter, which was always broken, would rattle and bang from outside. As if those things had gotten broken and weren't fixed on purpose, so we'd always remember them, so they'd always be part of our lives, our being."

He stood up, put the cigarette out in the ashtray, then stood at the bookshelf and ran a fingernail over the volumes, as children or virtuosos strum piano keys, then he pulled out a copy of Verlaine's poems in a gray binding with a red leather back, opened it, read the title page, closed it and put it back on the shelf. Nora watched his movements as if she were watching a tense drama.

He came back to the bed and, still standing, said very slowly, "I read the poems of Mordechai Zvi Maneh," and he stubbornly began retrieving from his memory:

> All around reigns calm and quiet,
> On a cliff so horribly alone,
> A strong wind will come awaken
> The poet sitting on a stone.

"What didn't we read into those rhymes back then! Understand: not from them, but *into* them," he emphasized. "It's hard for me to imagine now, but I do remember that that's how it was."

He sat down.

"Did you write poems when you were young?" he asked, and from that "when you were young," Nora sensed that he didn't really see her at that moment.

"No," she said, "I've never written poems in my life."

"I did," he said.

"I know. Spanish. *Siempre vago.*"

"Spanish," Arin laughed. "And other languages too. The common denominator of them all was that they were all bad."

He was silent a moment; a hesitant smile hung on the ends of his lips.

"But the memories," he said, "they're what give us our private, individual character, they're what make us what we are. The facts of our lives, marvelous as they are at times in a person's life, are nevertheless common property. We share them with others. And only what is kept in memory, unimportant things, as it were, they're what constitute our real being. They're that culture a person gives to wine, let's say. Filling all the barrels equally, and the barrels are no different from one another, and now comes the boss of the winery and puts into one barrel that teeny-tiny thing, the culture of vermouth, let's say. And that barrel isn't just wine anymore, that whole barrel is vermouth. It has its own special nature, a special essence."

"And bad memories," asked Nora, "constitute a bad nature?"

"There are no bad memories at all," said Arin. "There is only a bad attitude toward memories."

"No," said Nora, and her face became harsh. "There are bad memories. Definitely bad. In the most objective way. I know."

Arin looked at her intently and said, "Yes, you're right. There are very bad memories."

Nora blushed. She wasn't pleased with her victory in the argument, and so easily. In fact she would very much have wanted him to argue the opposite.

But he said, "But it's not a matter of good and bad. It's not a moral matter at all," and he looked at her again and added, "But once, in the forest, remember, you promised me something! And nevertheless you go on thinking constantly of that matter."

"No," Nora apologized without asking what he meant. "I'm thinking of something else altogether."

He didn't ask what, fearing that in such cases he was liable to touch a hidden and painful wound. But she did go on. "You said as for the smallest and most unimportant things, and I thought about an unimportant incident. But I can never forget it. It was summer, the last days of June. It was a Sunday. Very hot and stifling. All my friends went out of town. I had an end-of-the-month 'drought.' That's it, quite simply; I didn't have a cent in my pocket and I stayed in town. It was a heat wave. A stifling blaze. And I thought I was so lonely and sad in the big empty city. As if all my friends had died, and I was the only one left. Or maybe more precisely, as if they were all living somewhere else and I was dead and walking in the street, and that's how I would have to walk forever, alone in that awful blazing heat. I don't know, but I felt something like that back then. And after I had lunch in some cheap and ugly restaurant, I went back home and thought all those thoughts. And suddenly, around some corner, some fat bourgeois man came toward me, you know, one of those with a beer belly and a smug red face. He looks arrogantly in my face, under my hat brim and decrees aloud with quiet confidence, '*Selbstmord*' ['Suicide']."

She fell silent and her face grew angry, as if that bourgeois man was still in front of her.

Arin nodded. "I imagine your expression then!" and he smiled. But a minute later, his eyes grew dark. "All this is very cruel and very German. I wouldn't want to live in that country."

Nora leaned on her elbow and raised her head. "It doesn't have anything to do with Germany!"

Arin didn't respond to that remark; she shrugged and said, "The main thing is that it was true. I truly was close to suicide. What that bourgeois man said was a kind of confirmation, as if he was the agent of certain forces leading me in that direction."

"And you remained alive," said Arin.

Nora bit her lip. And her face, which had been pale as she told her story, blushed again, as usual, from the end of her nose to her earlobes. "I always remain alive, always!"

Arin laughed aloud. "That's good, Nora! That's very good. Life is precious. Life is worth more than all our suffering. Just life."

For a brief moment, he was assailed by a strange nervousness and started walking around in the little room, pacing. Then he stood still, both long hands leaning on the desk, and looked beyond it, out the window, to the yard.

"But remember this day, Nora. Remember it well. And mainly, what I told you just now. I said life is precious. In spite of everything. Because there is no disaster and no disease of body or mind that can lower its value. None. Those things you heard from me, Nora. I'm the one who told them to you."

She, from her bed, saw nothing but his ear and a thin crescent of his cheek, and didn't know if he was laughing or speaking seriously.

That day, after he left, she wanted to sum up what she thought about her life, and couldn't.

She put her hands under her head, lay on her back, without a thought. In the dining room, the clock struck two long full rings.

Now, she saw Arin's absent face clearly before her eyes, and the sun on his nose. And once again she knew she'd remember that forever. And she was weak and happy in her weakness.

Another time, on one of those quiet days of recuperation, Arin said to her, "I got a letter from my daughter today."

Nora, who was reclining among big pillows supporting half her body, leaned her head on a tiny pillow and rummaged around in her thoughts: what should you say to him?

I always forget he has a daughter. He doesn't talk about her at all. What should I ask him? Do I have to ask him how she is, or what she writes to him?

But before she opened her mouth, Arin said, "She doesn't know how to write letters. It's their style, that generation. Everything's as from a primitive textbook. But that's not the point. Everything comes at me suddenly as from another world, a lost world."

Since Nora was still silent, he added, "Her husband also writes a few words. A standard handwriting! Both of them."

"What does her husband do?"

"He works in Hollywood."

And when he saw a flash of curious interest in Nora's eyes, he chuckled, "Don't look at me like a little girl who's just heard someone mention Jackie Coogan. He's not a movie star. He's an accountant."

"I'd like to see your daughter's face," said Nora.

"I may have a photo," and he started rummaging in his jacket pocket. "She's very American, my Paula. A sentimental and energetic woman." He found a leather wallet, pulled out an amateur photo and gave it to Nora. "Haven't I shown you that yet? Oh, yes, your mother saw it."

A young woman smiled from the photo, with even teeth, her forehead and eyes shaped just like Arin's. Nora wanted to tell him that, but just then he began, "She looks just like my wife," and Nora seemed to catch a hint of hostility in those words. She was silent. But the longer she looked at the photo, the more she was struck by the similarity between father and daughter.

"We used to be great friends," said Arin, "in those days, when I'd hold her hand and take her to school. She had two braids, and the children would always come to her and touch her braids, and she was very proud of that." He smiled as at a distance, shook his head. "Did you also have braids when you were a little girl? I think that determines a lot in the life of a little girl."

"No," said Nora. "My hair was always cut. Many other things determined my life."

Arin went to the window, looked outside. "In your yard there's a dovecote. Who do the doves belong to?"

"The children. I think the doorman's son and the son of the math teacher in the Russian Gymnasium are partners. At any rate, that's how it was before I left."

"Yes," said Arin, and he came to her bed and held out a hand for the photo. "And now she's a grown woman. Married. And everything…well, let's leave that. She's not at all like you, Nora," and his eyes looked at her very fondly.

As he was about to put the photo in the wallet, another photo slipped from between his fingers and fell right onto Nora's hand. Nora grabbed it and involuntarily looked at it. She recognized the daughter in it, too, but next to her was another figure, which immediately fascinated her: a young woman leaning on a fence and holding a tennis racket. She beamed a grin over the picture. In a split second, Nora knew when she had seen that beaming smile.

Arin turned his face away. Nora saw that he wasn't pleased. She felt like she was reading someone else's letter. But when he looked at her again and his face was lost, she was suddenly assailed by hatred of him and the strange woman in the picture.

"I saw her here," she stated.

He replied as then. "That's Helen," and he was silent. Then he reached out his hand and took the photo from Nora. And when he put it back in the leather wallet, his face was very calm. "She's a friend of Paula's," he said, and added as back then, "I think her mother was Jewish."

"She's very beautiful," Nora blurted out hostilely.

"Yes," he said simply. "She's very beautiful."

Then he smiled and sat down, crossed his legs and drummed with a finger of his right hand on his raised knee. "Didn't I tell you," his voice was now slow and drawn out as on the day they met. "She's married to your attaché in our country."

"Yes, you told me." Nora wanted to penetrate the closed expression on his face, but the face was completely opaque, indifferent, and strange.

"Yes, that's Helen…and Paula. But that has nothing to do with you," he laughed and his face grew soft. "Strangers."

"Sometimes," said Nora, also very softly, "I think people are always interesting. Especially…"

"Especially what?"

"Especially," she hesitated a little, and yet she concluded, "if they interest our friends."

"That's not a criterion. By the way, at your age, can you really be interested in people who don't really touch your life?"

Nora wanted to make a very fast spiritual accounting and admitted, "No." And after a short break, "But sometimes, even while riding in the underground, I'd choose a face and want to decipher who the person was, what he did, what he thought and felt, and the face would haunt me for days, and I couldn't get rid of it. Sometimes, when I was alone, strange faces would surround me and I knew they were also fates, and I knew I'd never see them again. And yet they were with me, bothered me. I had to make an effort to forget them, to get away from them."

"That's something else," Arin stated. He stood up, took a few steps in the room. Nora sensed that he felt some sudden emotion; he wanted to shake off the dust of old thoughts.

As he walked, he said, "That's how we live, for the most part, *next to* people, and not *with them*."

He stood leaning on the bookshelf and smiled at Nora, or perhaps at nothing, beyond her.

"At your age, everything is still understood and everything will be redeemed. But us?" He raised one hand a little and opened his clenched fist questioningly and sat down again.

"Here's a story, Nora," he said in an indistinct voice. "And one man, who has spent many years with a woman who was devoted to him with all her might, he realized one day that he didn't see her. Quite simply, didn't see her. It was like this: that day, he came across an old album, and in the album was a picture from the early days of their love. In that picture she was photographed in her splendor, as they did in those days, you know, those photographs that seem like not just the clothes, but also the face in them is stiff with starch. By the way, I love them to this day, those photographic wonders. And there she is standing in that picture and her black braid is hanging on her shoulder, a thick plait, braided from an abundance of soft, very black hair, and the man was a little sentimental and remembered with a throbbing heart how, in those days, he loved that woman's soft beautiful hair. And just then, she herself comes into the room and asks him something inconsequential about the shop assistant, who was sent to the bank to cash a check. And he looked at her, and when he opened his mouth to answer her, he suddenly saw that her hair was fair. Reddish-blonde hair crowned her head, and in the picture it was black, he remembered it as black. And it was as if someone had hit him in the eye. And, without knowing what he said, he blurted out, 'When did you dye your hair?' She looked at him coldly and answered in a voice of practical amazement and mockery that was like her usual conversation – she was a woman who knew how to control her emotions! She replied, 'Five years ago. And what made you ask me all of a sudden!' And she shrugged and demanded a real answer to her question and left the room. And he sat, after she left, looking at the old picture and asked himself, How many years had it been since he had seen her? And he didn't notice at all that the color of her hair had changed. And he asked himself, Does she know he doesn't see her? But afterward, that day, as he passed by her room, he heard her crying. She was a bold and stiff woman and didn't tend to cry. He didn't go into her room. What could he have said to her? And that person, Nora, wasn't naturally bad-natured, a person who ignored others. And here–"

Arin took out his cigarette case, opened it, let his fingers rest on one of the cigarettes, but didn't take it out. He sat bent over, rapt, bowed.

Nora knew she had been shown an episode from the married life of the man sitting in front of her, and it was the "third person," and the literariness of his words revealed that. She didn't think of his wife. She thought of him, and she was infinitely sorry for him. If she could have held out her hand and touched so lightly the hand holding the silver case, or said something – but he shook himself out of his paralysis and smiled at her. "Are you allowed to smoke yet?" he asked. And changed his mind. "No, no. Better not." He took a cigarette for himself and lit it. As he smoked, he went on talking. "Those are everyday stories, Nora. Either that way or some other way, they're repeated about the closest people. Look, in general, how many people live next to us without a word, like dogs, like cats that are in the house, and we don't guess that they also have a complicated, twisted emotional life, and the importance of those lives isn't less than ours? And since they can't talk, or won't talk, it's convenient for us not to see them, not to try to figure out even a fraction of their soul, pass by them without noticing, like an object. We tend to let our look linger on 'interesting' people, as we call them. But what is the real issue? We see a book, sometimes we look at a beautiful vase, not to mention a flower on our table, but the person walking next to us, when do we deign to look at him? In your house, in the kitchen, some barefoot girl is walking around. What's her name?"

"Tekla."

"Yes, that Tekla, did you see her, even once, as a human, a human discovery? Did you ever suspect that she also has her own emotional life, that isn't simple at all?"

Nora remembered Tekla's crying in the forest, and therefore she could answer yes.

Arin was amazed to silence, since he had clearly assumed from the start that Nora's answer would be different. Therefore, Nora thought she had to explain. "I once saw her weeping. In the forest."

He laughed and touched Nora's hand and stroked it placatingly.

The two of them were silent a moment and listened to the thin, monotonous singing coming up from the kitchen accompanied by the banging of the pot on the stove. Arin tilted his head to the door, as if hinting at who was behind it, and said surprisingly the very same words Nora had thought in the forest that day. "She has the eyes of a good pet. Look at her and see."

And the day Nora first left her sickbed, she had an opportunity to peep through the screen of Tekla's life.

At about ten in the morning, she got out of bed and was shuffling from room to room. The apartment looked new to her. In the green "aquarium" there was a great serenity on the deep silk of the furniture. In the dining room, in the window bay, sunbeams played on the dark leaves of the ficus plant standing there in a wide pot; the beams shone on the stiff flash of the leaf like the smooth surface of a mirror. A big, black-blue autumn fly was buzzing and banging into the glass of the window and trying to get through that transparent wall, as if demanding his right to take his last breath in the fresh air of summer's end. And aside from that buzzing there was total silence throughout the apartment.

And as always in isolated moments of silence, now too, Nora was tense with some vague expectation of something about to happen.

She peeped out the window and saw the letter carrier in his dark blue uniform walking on the narrow wooden sidewalk the old landlord used as a "promenade." A minute later, she heard heavy steps coming up the stairs of their apartment. The steps pounded and stopped. Nora imagined that the letter carrier stopped in the middle of climbing that little windowsill that served as a kind of mailbox for the Krieger family.

She forgot the doctor's warning not to go outside, jumped up and ran to the corridor to take the letter. And as she opened the door, on the stairs in front of her next to that little window, stood Tekla and the letter carrier hugging and kissing. At the squeak of the door opening, Tekla turned her head around and separated from her partner. Nora closed the door quickly and retreated, escaping to the inside room as if *she* had been caught in an act of love.

When she sat down again, withdrawn, in an armchair next to that window bay in the dining room, she was scared and a little upset with that strange amazement that accompanies unexpected discoveries. It wasn't Tekla who occupied her thoughts, but her partner, the letter carrier. It was so strange to see that figure she had known for years outside the automatic framework of his activity. If she had seen a telegraph pole start dancing, she wouldn't have been any more surprised than now, when she saw the letter carrier hugging Tekla. "Letter carrier" was a function and not a living creature with the reactions and feelings of a feeling and reacting creature; he was always one figure that didn't change. Once a year, two years, three years, he would change his face, his height or the color of his mustache, but he himself was always stuck in a dark blue uniform, bringing letters and putting them in the fixed place on the sill of that little window, and if they happened to meet in the courtyard, in all his metamorphoses, he would answer the question – "Is there a letter for me?" – with that same automatic joke, "They're still writing, Ma'am, they're still writing!"

And all of a sudden, the letter carrier sets Nora's imagination in motion in a completely different way. In a human and living way. She remembered Arin's words about those living people all around, living beside us like those pets, and we don't see them at all. Suddenly, she started thinking about the letter carrier – what was he before that? What did he look like if he didn't wear that blue uniform? And he's probably from a village, like Tekla, and in his childhood he ran around barefoot in a meadow and herded geese. Or maybe he was from the suburbs and lived in one of those little wooden houses on the edge of the city, whose little windows were divided into four absolutely equal squares with a flame-red geranium always peeping out of them? And how does such a person feel his body in the evening, before he goes to sleep, when he returns home and takes off the uniform and remains there with himself and his private, absolutely private, unofficial face? And in Tekla's eyes he also has a private face…and what's the meaning of that toil, day after day distributing letters to human beings, wearing yourself out walking to those same houses, the same neighborhood, climbing the stairs? All of a sudden, she remembered with miraculous clarity as if from an old photo on her retina the face of the old letter carrier who would bring Arin's letters, and whom she'd await impatiently because of those letters. An old man he was, and his mustache was gray, and he must have had a wife and children, and maybe even grandchildren, and Nora felt almost physically the pain in that old man's legs as he climbed the stairs of strangers' houses.

What did it mean to be a letter carrier? And in the most illogical way of thinking, Nora began pondering various professions and different ways of life bound up with them. So many forms of life, so many possibilities of living, existing in the world!

And she felt that passion of youth that comes with convalescence. The desire to live, to live really, all that life, to feel the touch of life, its bold spirit, its sharp air, to feel from all sides, to live in all metamorphoses.

First she saw herself in a dream of her future – being in the mountains on the edge of the desert. Temporary tents, and ground that conceals inside itself the history of man and God. That stingy ground that for thousands of years keeps a secret of human treasures. Manual labor and fruits of the mind. To stand, to hold in your hand an ancient clay vessel, half broken and beautifully shaped, or to sit bent over in one of the great libraries and decipher an inscription written on a parchment in a very ancient language – or to walk on that very ground and bend a bare knee, to that hot dry land and plant a tree…or maybe to live a completely different life, to go with a scientific expedition to the heart of Africa, among black-skinned people, to get to wild places, to walk for days with caravans, to feel great thirst and hunger, and to come, after weariness and trembling and hunger, to a place that no one knows of, and there to discover new ways of life, new plants, songs and dances the world doesn't know anything about – or maybe, to live a life that doesn't exist any longer, and to be born a hundred years earlier in the house of aristocrats in one of the estates hidden in a big park, to wear a sheer white lamé dress that reaches the heels of the little shoes and to walk on a boulevard of poplars and to touch smooth stones with the tip of a nice, airy parasol, and at twilight to feel your heart beat at the sound of carriage wheels coming from the next estate – who's coming? And at night when everyone's asleep, to take out of the secret drawer a love letter with a dried flower in it, and read it, read it countless times and shed tears – or to live the life of action and revolt, to sacrifice life for a great revolution, to sanctify with blood itself the happiness of future generations, to hide, to work underground, to be imprisoned and to keep stubbornly silent during interrogation and torture – or to be sick for years, many, many days, and lie in a rest home on a broad verandah in a chaise longue, to lie for whole days in the mountains facing a green valley, a grove, and see the tall treetops move slowly in the wind – how many lives, how many kinds of life there are in this world! And there's not even one, not even one kind, with all the suffering and pain involved with it, that isn't worth living. But better than anything if it were possible to try and live them all, all of them at once.

Tekla interrupted her thoughts. She came into the room, stood in the doorway, covered half her face with her hand, a rustic gesture of shame as old as the village itself, and muttered, "I, young lady, I really…it's he who was cheeky…and I…"

"Those are your private affairs, Tekla," said Nora considerately and seriously, wanting to hide her embarrassment behind an emphatic maturity.

Tekla apparently didn't grasp the meaning of the words, but their tone calmed her.

"The young lady won't tell the mistress. Or Miss Lisa!" She looked pleadingly at Nora.

"Of course, of course!" said Nora, even though she did intend to tell her mother as a most ridiculous tale, since she knew there was nothing at all in it to hurt Tekla, since Mrs. Krieger loved to marry off her maids and was praised for that by the girls who wanted to do housework.

"Is he...a bachelor?" Nora dared to ask.

"Of course, what is the young lady thinking!" answered Tekla proudly, and a flash of bliss lit up in her eyes. But she lowered her eyelids, came to Nora, and handing her a crushed gray envelope, said, "A letter he brought me, young lady," and she was silent for a brief, helpless silence. "And I can't read."

"Give it here," said Nora. "I'll read it to you. Sit down."

Tekla sat at the table, not far from Nora's chair, leaned her elbows and rested her face on her fists, like a child preparing to hear a tale.

Nora glanced at the letter. Twisted and forced letters, words blurred heartbreakingly, told Tekla of the death of her brother, who departed the world about five days before and was buried in his village. And Nora didn't yet begin to read aloud; she glanced with innocent curiosity into Tekla's eyes and asked, "Why didn't the letter carrier read this to you?"

"It's none of his business, young lady. The letter is from home," Tekla decreed.

Nora sighed. "Bad news in the letter."

Tekla's face didn't budge.

"They write you that your brother is very sick."

"I know."

"And he..." Nora searched for words that wouldn't be cruel. "He...that is, he is no more." And since she didn't think Tekla understood her, she was forced to explain. "He's dead."

"I know," said Tekla. "He told me he'd die. He was sick."

Nora looked at the girl, at the quiet in her face, and that quiet almost seemed stupid to her. Silent, wondering and hostile.

"And did they hold a requiem mass for him?" asked Tekla, after a brief pause. "I gave my money to Aunt Ona. Please read the letter, young lady."

Nora read the stingily brief lines to Tekla, with an appendix by some neighbor who knew how to write, a very laconic story about the death of her brother and an accounting for the money that was paid to the priest. And regards and a bow to the receiver.

"Thank you, young lady," said Tekla. She took the letter, stood up. Bowed unusually and went off to the kitchen. Her face didn't move, as at first.

Strange creatures, thought Nora. What a way to treat death!

A few days later, she found Tekla sitting on a low stool in the kitchen and crying.

"What's wrong with you?" she asked her.

Tekla lifted her red face, wet with tears, to her. "My brother died, young lady."

Nora stood before her, helpless and stunned.

"I had only one, young lady," added Tekla like a weeping mourner. "One and only one I had, left alone of my whole family, a lonely orphan!"

Her eyes dried. She wiped her face with her sleeve.

"They tortured him to death in a foreign land," she shook her head and trilled. "In a foreign land, in Bras-ilia."

When Nora told Arin about that, he laughed a lot at her amazement at the letter carrier's love, but didn't show any interest in Tekla's experiences or feelings. And when Nora wanted to develop a kind of theory about how simple people treat love and death, his face grew desolate before her eyes, and she felt at last that he wasn't really listening. That indifferent silence, his absentmindedness, and the boredom in his face offended her and embarrassed her. She quickly finished what she had to say and crushed her story so as not to be cut off in the middle of the paragraph, and felt like a student reciting a hackneyed lesson to a strict teacher, and she failed.

After she uttered the concluding paragraph in a falling voice, Arin sat before her and gazed and drummed his thumb on the table. Nora waited a little while, maybe he'd say something – but he didn't.

"Didn't you yourself want to prove to me that people live along-side us like those pets," she blurted out at last, half scolding and half apologizing. "And we don't see them."

He glanced up questioningly.

"You said," Nora added, "that the simplest people live a com-plicated emotional life, and we ignore them. You said we don't want to look at them properly."

He woke up a bit, shrugged and declared, "I said? I don't remember."

His mouth twisted bitterly. "Looking at our fellow man! A wasted effort. What can we know about our fellow man, their emo-tional life, when we don't know a thing about our own emotional life."

The words "emotional life" were stressed mockingly, even though he himself used them in that conversation which, for some reason, he now disavowed or maybe forgot. The tone of that expres-sion now came from above, like those words he had said to Nora when they met. "Are you still wasting away in the provinces, young lady?" But the little bit of friendship in that mockery was lacking. Tormented by his contradictions and his mockery, she looked at him and didn't know what to say or do.

He was nervous that day, leaning in the chair, rejecting the ash-tray in front of him, as if it weren't an object but some concept stuck between his thoughts and disturbing his speech. "Understand our fellow man?" he repeated after a rather long silence. "We don't even come to terms with our own soul. You can never understand a per-son partially, and we can't understand him as a whole. To understand how those human beings love and die, we've got to grasp a thousand other things. We've got, for example, to understand how and why that Tekla of yours, who loves you so much, and that precious let-ter carrier of hers, who smiles at you with innocent affection, would be ready and willing, during some pogrom, to murder you and your family with that same simplicity and that same sense of righteous-ness they live and die by, and without the shame that attacks them when you find the two of them hugging and kissing on the stairs."

"I don't believe they could do that," Nora denied sharply.

He didn't look at her face, shifted the ashtray to another side.

"Please, I'm not saying that they, those two, would do such a thing. But many like them are capable of it. Many, good, innocent, pure-hearted, simple people with emotions. And we can understand that in them only if we understand ourselves well."

He stood up and looked at Nora, as if he suddenly realized it was she he had been talking to all the time. And as if he now wanted to say something aimed straight at her, he sat down again and opened his mouth, but his look was caught suddenly by the picture of the "unknown woman," and she obviously disturbed him and he could no longer remember what he had been talking about before.

"What's that?" he asked, jutting his chin toward that picture.

"The Unknown Woman of the Seine," Nora replied unpleasantly, since she wanted to continue the previous conversation.

"That doesn't tell me anything," said Arin.

"The mask of a girl who was pulled out of the Seine. Apparently she drowned herself."

"I wouldn't hang a picture of a suicide in my room."

Afterward he fell into a heavy silence until Lisa came and sat next to him and started a hushed and excited conversation with him about something that had happened twenty-five years earlier and the two of them remembered it. And Nora felt completely left out of their being and their life.

Ever since Nora's recovery, Arin had changed completely and was no longer soft and friendly as during those ten good days. He was usually upset, or distracted. No longer did he visit every day, and he almost always came at dusk when the mother and Lisa were at home. And frequently, in conversation with him now, Nora encountered his adult mockery or his open indifference to what came out of her mouth. All that pained her, and sometimes when she was talking to him, she was like a blind man walking around in the room, constantly bumping into the sharp edges of the furniture. And when she was alone, she sometimes looked like a complete fool in her own eyes. "Why do I talk to him? What can somebody like me give him?" But she sensed that he didn't feel well, that something was oppressing him now and that she couldn't guess his pain or help him even a little. An offense, feelings of inferiority, impotent rage, and wounded pride tormented her at night after his visits. And yet, she waited impatiently for him every single day, standing in the window bay in the dining room and looking at the wooden path in the long courtyard, stretching from the gate to the threshold of their apartment. And standing like that, she would suddenly imagine things that deep in her heart she knew were only a delusion. She would suddenly think, inadvertently, that he was sad because of her, and that he came only at those times when the mother and Lisa were at home, because he was afraid of himself and of the closeness between them. And that maybe, someday, he wouldn't control himself and would say to her, "I'm many years older than you, Nora." And she would lower her eyes and answer, "I don't know arithmetic." Her heart pounded and she'd begin feeling a sense threatening her body under her dress, and her breasts were heavy. She would immediately scold herself, and the image of the woman with the beaming laugh, that Helen in her flame-red clothes, would stand before her eyes. And Nora would bite her lip and repeat in despair, "Fool, you're such a complete fool!" And after a while, she'd find herself sitting across from Arin, a well-bred student, and wanting in vain to break his desolation with choked fragments of conversation, and she knew he didn't see her.

Lisa stood up and left the room, returned a minute later holding a bulging album. She opened its thick pages and showed Arin old photos, and the two of them laughed softly at that shared past, which Nora wasn't part of.

Then came Mrs. Krieger and Shoshanna Bergman along with her son Marek, and Tekla and cups of tea and cakes and red-cheeked apples in a big bowl and soft juicy pears.

"Eat, eat, Marek!" Shoshanna Bergman would plead with her son and would select the nicest and biggest and softest pear and hand it to him, and he'd eat heartily. And Shoshanna Bergman would whisper something to the mother, and Marek would ask Arin questions about America, and Nora sat and listened to his brief answers and looked obliquely at her mother and Shoshanna Bergman and asked herself for the thousandth time what connected those two women who were so different? And she'd miss the answer to one of Marek's teasing questions, which always hid an ambivalence that didn't stem from intelligence.

Arin looked at his watch and stood up as if he were about to leave, but suddenly he changed his mind and sat down. Lisa, who had also stood up when he did, looked at her watch and didn't sit down again. She had some evening work outside her office at some private firm, and it was time for her to go there. She sent Arin a questioning glance, as if inviting him to accompany her, but at that moment, he was deep in conversation with Marek, who was explaining some interesting combination of cards he had seen at his club the night before. Lisa shrugged her thin shoulders very slightly, almost unnoticed, and left the room with a careful nod, like someone who doesn't want to disturb the group, but her mouth clenched as she did it, with offense.

About five minutes later, Arin stopped Marek's flow of words and said to Mrs. Krieger, "Did Lisa leave yet, Esther?"

"Yes, just now."

"And I was going to go with her!" he exclaimed in a self-contemptuous voice. "Well," he looked at his watch. "I have to go anyway." And he left.

Nora went out to the corridor with him.

On the stairs, he suddenly stood still, and shaking Nora's hand, he said, "Good days. Know, Nora, if the weather doesn't change, maybe we'll go to the forest someday. For a few hours. To stroll."

Nora looked at him with wide-open, excited eyes.

"Do you want to?"

He left and she went back to the room, wanting to dull the beam in her eyes a bit. Shoshanna Bergman was spreading her knitting on her lap and interrogating the mother. "When is he going back to America?"

"I don't know."

"Strange, very strange. Alone?"

"I don't understand your question."

Shoshanna Bergman glanced up significantly at Nora, smiling cunningly. "And where is Lisa?"

The mother sighed.

"You saw. She went to work."

To the forest, Nora repeated to herself, to the forest.

Mighty forests and gardens with fallen leaves. The autumn world will turn gold in the jewels of its pears. Last birds will call out in their flight south. The shadow of their spread wings is cast over the harvested fields. The big river beyond the forest will hum and weep and sing. Barefoot children with suntanned legs will come out of the grove, and in a basket – mushrooms, smelling of the mossy depths of the forests. The last birds on their voyage south will defy the moving wings of the windmill. Autumn clouds will pass. And we will go and sink into the deep moss, and will glide over the pine needles. The deep autumn at our feet, and a flock of red leaves falls on our shoulders. Our beautiful epilogue, our delicate epilogue, our pure-eyed epilogue, our cold-eyed epilogue.

But the trip to the forest didn't take place. The day after Yom Kippur, Aunt Zlata was taken to the Jewish hospital, and the doctors all decreed that her days were numbered.

And since Nora hadn't told her mother or Lisa what had happened to her on that visit to the sick woman, she had to go to the hospital to see how the dying aunt was.

It was ten in the morning, and the pungent odor of medicine made the visitors dizzy. In the corridor, next to the room where the aunt had been put, stood a group of people, most of whom Nora knew only distantly. And a few of them were completely new faces. Members of the aunt's family, some of them from nearby small towns.

One of them, a dumpy Jew with a pointed beard, whom Nora had often seen and didn't remember his name, was spinning around like a screw, went into the dense group of relatives and came out of it. And his tongue kept mashing short verses, whispering, along with significant looks as sharp as needles.

Nora stood next to that group, scared of the monstrous twilight and the twisted faces of the people staring at her with curious eyes.

"A bad sign, a bad sign," said a woman. "That they immediately give her a special room all to herself."

Somebody who apparently didn't catch her drift said, "Well, it must be influence!"

Nora took one step closer to that group, and that bearded man immediately swooped down on her and ordered, "You can't go in now. The doctor's there."

"In any case–" some hesitant voice started from inside the group, and was cut off.

Just then the door opened, and a nurse beckoned to Nora. "Please."

Nora bent over and went through the high, vaulted door, as if she were going into a small cave.

The room was dim, like the corridor; the ceiling over the bed was vaulted, like the door, and the bed itself was very narrow. On it, as on the purification plank, lay the aunt covered with a white sheet. Her body was flat and almost didn't stick up under the bedclothes.

Nora slowly approached the bed and it seemed to her that death itself was accompanying her and pushing her to the sickbed. Standing next to that bed, she recognized the face before her. The face had become very small and had turned yellow, and its circles no longer closed as on that day, in the aunt's house. Its expression had become sharp and even her chin was obvious now and poking out over the scrawny neck. And by some miracle, that face, which didn't look like the everyday face of Aunt Zlata, was now closer and clearer than that face itself throughout her life.

And Nora no longer remembered what had happened in their last meeting. That flat body on the bed, like a purifying plank, and the damp hair above the smooth, yellow forehead, suddenly made her feel great pity. The sick woman's eyes were sunken and the skin of her cheeks was like wrinkled leaves. But those sunken eyes were wide open and alive and they saw and recognized.

The narrow slit of her mouth moved and it might even have wanted to smile. Nora bent over to the sick woman's face and, overcoming the strange and heavy smell rising from the bed, she listened.

"Nora," whispered the aunt.

"It will be fine, Aunt," Nora's lips muttered something without knowing what.

Now it was clear that the dying woman really was smiling. Her weak voice overcame some obstacle, and her words were quite clear.

"Nothing will be," she said. She was silent a moment, a wave of pain passed over her face, and she talked again. "Your uncle loved you very much, Nora," and she sighed. "This is no place for you to spend your vacation."

Her head didn't move; only her eyes passed over the hospital room and its vaulted ceiling as if explaining what place she meant.

Stunned and gripped by regret, Nora sat on a stool next to the bed and couldn't speak a word. The sick woman once again clenched her lips, shut her eyes a moment, and when she opened them a minute later, they were dull and extinguished. And the whisper coming from her now was a kind of echo, like an automatic continuation of what she had said before, as if Nora had already left the room and the sick woman still went on talking to her shadow. "Your uncle's dead. And so am I…and you go, go into the fresh air." Her stare briefly shuddered with fear, looked for a place to hold on to, but slipped over Nora's face, not seeing her, and was fixed on the ceiling.

Nora stood up and as she turned to go, she pushed someone who stood behind her. It was that long-faced old maid who lived in the aunt's house. Her rusty eyes were fixed on Nora's face as on a sucking question.

What does she want to know? A thought of impatience passed through Nora's heart.

In the corridor the bearded Jew approached her and said, "Well?"

Nora shrugged and waved him off. And suddenly she felt that her cheeks were wet.

She turned her back on the whole group of relatives and left, and at the door of the hospital she bumped into her mother and Lisa.

The next morning, before dawn, Aunt Zlata died.

It was a chilly and clear day, and all the way to the cemetery, the wailing of the long-faced old maid split the pure, clear air hanging over the city.

A small group of people followed the coffin, the first ones bent over and distressed, the last ones plodding in slow motion. The Jew with the sharp beard and some fat woman Nora had never seen before supported the wailing old maid. Now and then, the fat woman would join her wailing and lament in a weepy voice, "And she lived a perfectly righteous life, a righteous woman among the Jews, a mother to all the poor and destitute. What a heart she had, a heart of gold, a heart of pure gold…"

They were followed by the mother and Lisa in a gloomy silence, and now and then the mother wiped her tears. Nora knew that even now she was inadvertently mourning her brother, who had died some time ago, the jolly, good-hearted uncle, who was Aunt Zlata's husband.

Behind Nora walked Shoshanna Bergman and one woman, a dentist, whom her whole family had known forever.

"She was so modest, so modest! And bore all her torments in silence," Shoshanna Bergman said at the beginning of the walk.

And shortly after, Nora heard, "That's what I think. At the bank. Quite a sum. And most important: jewels. He used to spoil her like an only daughter. Children they didn't have. He'd buy her very expensive jewels. And she never wore them in her life, afraid of the evil eye." A brief laugh. "Yes, she believed in such things, but she had diamonds and pearls. At any rate, I think the Kriegers won't get anything. You see how they swooped down on her from all the small towns. And that wailing old maid, did you hear? That's not without motive either."

"But if her husband was Esther's brother, then by law…"

"Law shmaw! Don't you know Esther? In such matters, she's like a child–"

"And I thought…"

"Listen, listen to that one wailing!"

And after a brief pause, "And how's Boris?"

"How can he be in jail? Oh, those troubles! But now I'm hoping they'll trade him for some priests imprisoned in Russia. My heart is breaking, he'll go there and I won't see him at all. But it's better like that. And my Marek, you know…"

And at the gate of the cemetery, the dentist said in a thoroughly desperate voice, "Did you notice how yellow Nora's teeth have become? A real shame! A young girl who doesn't take care of her teeth. I already told Esther to send her to me. Nora!" She tapped her shoulder from behind. "Please turn your head."

Nora turned her head, but at that moment, the funeral entered the graveyard and the old maid behind the coffin burst into a wild shout that rose above her previous wailing. Everyone ran to her; she stood and beat her chest and wailed. Somebody growled at her and she fell silent immediately. And the funeral proceeded among the mounds of the graves, accompanied by the banging of the charity box and shouts of "charity will save you from death."

Will save you from death. That's the life wisdom of generations. And in the depths of his heart every person certainly believes he'll be saved. He alone, and nobody else. I, I alone. I will die.

But in my heart there is no pity. None, none.

How beautiful is the elm tree leaning on the fence in the red of autumn leaves. How beautiful is that high – oak – tree.

And that's death, too. That's death. Autumn.

If not for –

I would be walking beside you now. Beside you, arm in arm. And in the valley the grass turns yellow.

Here, that's how it is always, always, always and forever. Death before her, and she's thinking only of herself.

Her face was small and the sheet was straight on the flat body. Like a purification plank. And your uncle loved you very much. But in your blood there is madness. In the blood. Blood.

My blood is on my own head.

And my head won't grasp death. And my heart – a stone. Heavy. Cold. Cold, and without pity. Without compassion.

And yet, my God, protect this city. Protect its little Jews. All of them, all of them. Even if they weren't righteous, they're innocent. More innocent than I am. All of them.

My left shoe is tight. Just yesterday I planned to go to the shoemaker. How nice are your steps in your shoes – your steps in the graveyard.

Death, death, death is walking before you.

And Nora's teeth are turning yellow. And my Boris and my Marek. A shame, a young girl.

Young people will also die.

Didn't you see them: famished, swollen, yellow, empty-eyed, they'd walk in the expanses of Russia and cry out for bread. And I'm little, so little.

Lisa's crying too. They've got tears, all of them. I don't. And I'm not thinking of her at all. I'm not thinking of a person's death.

What, did I say something? He wasn't listening. And what do we know about other people, we don't even know anything about ourselves. "Emotional life is complicated," he said. And the mockery, the murderous mockery.

And she isn't anymore. So modest, bearing her torments in silence. A righteous woman among the Jews. And her hatred, her hatred for all of us. Your uncle loved you very much. And I won't go crazy. Now, after her death, no one will know what happened in her house that day. And I'll forget, I have to forget.

And her face was small and her look was fixed on the ceiling.

And the Kriegers won't get anything.

That Jew with the beard, what's his name, finally? What's his name? Mironovsky? Marinovsky? No. On the tip of my tongue.

I'm not thinking of her. And it doesn't matter, death doesn't matter to me. And I wept yesterday.

Trees rose among the graves. Dead trees between the graves of humans. Graves of children they are, and charity won't save from death. Won't save, won't save, from love, from death, from madness, from life, from this awful life, from the inability to live it forever, forever – nice are your steps in your shoes, my love, my tormented love, their death and mine.

We'll get up tomorrow and she won't get up again. She won't bang the pots at the little stove. And between one thing and another, there will be day, a great white day, countless days, days will come, days will be counted, our days, my days, life, life, life to the end, life with life and death, and walking among graves behind the wall, behind the high wall and the beauty of its gardens –

And there will be the world –

As the body was lowered into the grave, Mrs. Krieger leaned on Nora's arm, buried her face in her shoulder and wept. Nora stood stiff, turned to stone, and felt her mother's forehead beat on her shoulder, the thin shoulder. And the cold annoyance of wickedness rose in her, and her dry eyes were wide open and unwittingly photographing everything before her.

Chapter Four

October

Rain fell. The drops stuck little nails in the puddles. Daylight was gray. The gleaming pavement turned black and then silver.

Nora and Lucy Kurtz left the humanities building and when they saw that the rain didn't let up, they stopped in the door. Since they were outside, Nora opened her umbrella, not noticing that above her head was an awning to keep off the rain. They stood on the little porch, a kind of semicircle, above the stairs leading down to the street, and continued their conversation.

"I have no future, no future at all," said Lucy. "Don't you see that yourself? I'm not deceiving myself. When I finish studying here, if I'm lucky, I'll be a teacher in some small town, and if not, I'll support myself here with private lessons, as now."

"But there might be some change," Nora commented without much confidence.

"I don't think so," said Lucy. "No chance. I was at home during the holidays and my mother gave her opinion on my mood. She said, 'At your age, I was full of life, full of faith and hope. Nothing stood in my way.'"

"They always forget afterward that youth isn't sweet at all!" said Nora.

"No. Not that. They grew up in a different time. The world was open to them. A completely different world. And different conditions."

The door of the university creaked; the history professor came out, and when he passed by the girls, he tipped his wide-brimmed hat, revealed his long hair that almost came down to his shoulders. He went down the stairs and went off into the rain.

"He's the only one," said Lucy, "who makes you forget the intellectual poverty here. You remember his lectures on the history of England?"

"Yes, they were great." And Nora was glad she could comfort Lucy. "My history teachers aren't in the same league."

"But in general, if you only knew what I'd give to get out of here!" Lucy refused to be comforted. "A few days ago, I was dragged to Ella Katz's wedding. I didn't want to go, but I didn't have the strength to refuse. A whole lot of people. All the same. They drank till they were drunk. At last, your Giltman came to me, drunk as Lot, shook one of my hands, then the other, and poured out his heart. 'You know what our tragedy is? We're all sure even now that we'll have no choice but to marry some fat rich girl, to sell ourselves!' Their tragedy! He couldn't find a better word than that."

"His parents are very poor," said Nora sadly.

"It's all the same. Almost all of them are like that. Even those whose parents are rich. If at least they kept quiet! But," her face suddenly lit up, "do you know Eliyahu Rom?"

"Yes. From childhood. He was a friend of Boris Bergman."

"Boris? The one in prison? Yes. He told me. You know, that group, they're the only ones with any vision. And they've got a future, or faith in the future at least. If I were a little more interested in politics, I would follow them."

"After all, they're not the only ones," Nora shrugged. "Even though they are friendly guys and are believers–"

"And they do have a world view! Even though I can't bear to listen to every sentence that starts with 'Lenin said…'"

"Yes, but what I meant was: if you went my way, that's also faith in the future. To build a new country, it's no small thing!"

Lucy sighed.

"I don't know. I told you I don't understand anything about politics, but your people, all that petite bourgeoisie…"

"There are others, completely different ones, but you don't have–"

At that moment, a jolly voice cut in. "Humanists are afraid to melt in the rain!"

And another replied, "Lest they drown in a puddle!"

Nora and Lucy picked up their heads and saw Hannah Milner with a group of medical students crossing the street to them.

"Like doves under a canopy!" called Hannah, pointing to Nora's open umbrella. "Come down! The rain has stopped!"

Nora folded her umbrella and went down to the group of students, most of whom she knew.

"Where are you all coming from?"

"An exam."

"From flunking an exam!"

"We flunked anatomy!"

"All of you?"

"All of us, the eight of us standing before you and another fourteen who didn't join us. Altogether, twenty-two people."

"The fourth time we flunked. Never mind, Jirbitsky examines seven times at least."

"But when did all of you manage to flunk? It's only twelve o'clock!"

"With lightning speed. Within an hour and a half, he slaughtered twenty-two people. One by one!"

"This day will be signed and sealed in the history of the state. The second of October, in the year one thousand nine hundred thirty-one A.D., twenty-two young men and women were shot with the rifle of anatomy in an hour and a half!" declaimed a tall redheaded fellow.

"And what are you going to do now?" asked Lucy.

"Now we are going to submit a group request to be examined in another week. And he'll examine us and fail us for the fifth time."

"Yes, but now, that is, this moment, we're going to not think about it and go celebrate the event in the Milk Center."

"With yogurt and potatoes!"

"Join us, humanities people!"

"I'm leaving, I have a class," said Lucy.

"To hell with the class!"

"No, really, I can't." She turned to leave.

"And you, Nora?"

"I'll join you."

They left.

"Listen, Nora, even abroad, where you are, do they fail anatomy eight times?"

"I don't know. I think that there, they generally take exams twice during all the years of study. Ask Haim Liebman, he studies medicine in Jena."

"But that Jirbitsky, that Jirbitsky!"

"Pure and simple: a sadistic bastard."

The group turned to the main street. The rain really had stopped. Between the clouds, a strip of blue sky peeped out.

"Look! Look!" shouted Mira Goldstein, a small, nimble student with a small turned-up nose and somewhat slanted Asiatic gray eyes. "The sky is blue above, the weather will be nice. If the strip of blue manages to cut trousers from it, it means the weather will be nice."

"What do you care! Anyway, you'll have to sit on your I-beg-your-pardon and memorize anatomy."

"And I like to study when it's raining."

"Nora, you haven't yet been in the Milk Center? Can it be? Now the whole city goes there for breakfast. It's a noble custom."

"Our nobles hoard yogurt with potatoes, à la pastoral!"

"That suits them. Those are their memories of the village from yesterday. The parents' house of the heads of our state."

"Hush, there's no freedom of speech here. They'll arrest you!"

"No, listen, seriously! Last night I met Meir Shapiro."

"Which Shapiro? From biology? The one who speaks Hebrew 'in principle'?"

"Yes. And you know how he talks: accusative case here, accusative case there, and the wrong conjugation. In short, 'The professor failed me the exam.' And so, last night, all of a sudden, he says to me, 'You know, I ate lunch today at the Milk Center, and it was really good. Very good. All the students eat there, all the professors eat there, everybody eats there, even the ministers!'"

Laughter.

"Now everybody who fails anatomy will eat there, as well as Nora Krieger."

"Come on in, I'm ordering yogurt with roasted minister!"

"Minister of Education, don't forget!"

The dairy was tastefully arranged with comfortable white furniture, big windows and the finest dairy products; it attracted a big crowd in the morning. Nursemaids would give their charges cocoa and pasteurized milk, and feed them sour cream and cheese; ladies and gentlemen sat at the tables and ate yogurt and steamed potatoes on plates. The dairy was a government institution and served as a kind of advertisement for the production of the dairy-rich land.

When the group of students entered, the big room wasn't full as usual since the rain had kept the clients of the Milk Center at home.

At one of the tables sat Giltman and Dina Globus. Giltman waved and called out with mischievous pathos, "Greetings. How many times now?"

"Four! And how do you know already?"

"Some of your failures passed by here and gave us the news."

The gang took seats at a big table. Mira Goldstein said, "When do your classes start, Nora?"

"Next month. In November."

"What luck! And we're already toiling."

Nora felt good in that happy and joking group. There was something simple, social and affectionate in that "acting up" with yogurt and potatoes. And not for one moment could the students get rid of the impression of the exam, and kept returning to the subject and rehashing it and twisting everything like a caricature.

"What did he tell you, Mira? What did he tell you?"

"Didn't you hear? He asked me something about the muscles of the heart."

"Yes, yes."

"And I got confused, that is, not completely confused, but I didn't answer right away. So he suddenly roared, 'And what does the young lady think, the heart suits only her romances!'"

"Yes, yes, he said 'romances'! I also heard 'romances.'"

"He was drunk, that Jirbitsky. Drunk as Lot! But I went to him, I sniffed brandy."

"He always comes drunk to exams."

"And to lectures."

"But today he outdid himself."

"In point of fact, it's all very sad," sighed Hannah Milner. "And who knows how it will end."

"We'll be examined five more times, at least."

"That's his way, dammit!"

"And why did she cry, that gorgeous girl?"

"Who? Corinetta?"

"Yes. Why did she cry?"

"You don't know? That's all they've been talking about. Almost impossible to tell. Nora doesn't study medicine, and that whole matter can be told only in the medical school."

"Never mind, let Nora cover her ears for a moment!"

"But how come you didn't hear it? He asked her some question about…"

"Oh, I understand, he always asks beautiful girls questions like that."

"Didn't I say so? A sadistic bastard."

"And that's why she cried?"

"No. Apparently, she couldn't answer, or hesitated. At any rate, he said to her, 'The lady doesn't know such a simple thing? She has to study some more. Come to my house and I'll show you!'"

"Villainy!"

"But maybe he means…"

"He knows very well what he means, that's his famous vulgarity."

"But yet? Could it be? He said specifically, 'I'll show you!'"

"Yes. That's abuse. We should complain to the Rector."

"That's sending the mouse to bell the cat."

"What Rector! The Rector won't help. He's an even bigger anti-Semite."

"But, Mira, in this case it's not anti-Semitism, that Corinetta Helena isn't even a Jew."

"Oh, yes…but anyway…"

"Very simple. When the professor is as drunk as Lot, he behaves like a sailor."

"Ow, I burned my tongue on a potato!"

"You deserve it!"

Nora was sitting with her back to the door and didn't see who came into the dairy. Suddenly, she saw Giltman winking at her and making strange signals, as if inviting her to turn around.

She looked where Giltman was aiming his eyes and saw Arin helping a tall woman take off her raincoat. And even though she saw only the woman's back, she immediately recognized Helen. Nora turned her head back, shrank in her chair and she thought she turned pale.

At that moment, Hannah Milner said, "Why are you blushing so much, Nora? When you sit with a group of students who have failed anatomy, you have to get used to jokes that are a little racy." Apparently she was referring to something that had been said and that Nora hadn't heard.

"No, no, please, talk as you like," Nora blurted out without paying attention.

She sat huddled up, afraid to move and reveal her offended spirit. She wanted to listen to the words of the jolly group; and what they said, which had amused her just a few moments ago, now sounded trite, stupid and tasteless.

They found a fine time to be glad! she thought angrily. That's also a joyous event! How to get out of here? And what does all that have to do with me?

But a minute later, all that did have to do with her. "Look!" that tall redhead pointed beyond Nora's back. "She's not ugly at all!"

"A proper *shiksa!*"

"Really, pretty..."

"If that one were to fall into Jirbitsky's hands, he'd make up some sticky questions!"

"Yes, a girl like that would fail twenty times so he'd have a chance to see her more often."

"But truly beautiful."

"Who are you talking about? The blonde? Yes, an athletic girl!"

"They're speaking in English."

"But I know him. My word, I do know him."

"Looks like a Jew."

"Absolutely, absolutely. Nora, look, it's that American I met at your house when you were sick."

Nora glanced furiously at Hannah Milner and said without turning her head, "Yes."

"My lady, you have eyes – in the back of your head!"

"Hush. It's vulgar!"

"You know her too?"

Nora said with emphatic coldness, as if defending Arin's honor, "She's a friend of his daughter."

"A friend of his daughter!" shouted someone. "Really, she hasn't got bad taste, his daughter!"

The tall redhead raised a spoonful of yogurt to his mouth as if he were raising a glass of wine, and said, "Here's to the friends of our daughters!"

"Here's to the daughters and the friends!" answered the others in chorus.

There was laughter, and Nora wanted to join in to hide her tormented embarrassment.

At that moment, Arin stood up to select a dish at the counter, passed by the table of the laughing students and saw Nora. He waved to her and called out, "See you tomorrow! I'll stop by in the morning."

Nora nodded and smiled back at him.

"An old Jew," determined somebody next to her.

Nora heard the words and got angry. She wanted to give a brazen answer, but suddenly she was gripped by a great fear. Old Jew! she repeated to herself, and understood that he could probably be seen like that as well.

When Arin returned to his place, he didn't look at Nora, and when she stood up to leave the dairy with the whole group, she didn't dare look at the table where he was sitting with the beautiful woman. And only in the street, through the window, did she see a small hat and fair hair beneath it.

That afternoon, the mother had a teachers' meeting at her school and Nora was left at home face-to-face with Lisa.

Only now was it clear to her that all the time, she had unwittingly avoided staying alone with Lisa for long periods. She didn't really know what had created the division between them now. But she thought that Lisa didn't want to be close to her either and didn't want to talk with her alone. As if a breakdown had occurred in their relations – apparently that evening when Nora spoke coarsely about the Russian opera singer Lisa had praised.

Now, when Lisa sat before her, as usual, on one leg, the other hanging above the floor, leafing through a novel by Arnold Bennett, and glancing at the English dictionary in front of her, Nora suddenly remembered how she had met her at the railroad station, remembered her lost and expectant stance, her running and shouting, "Porter, taxi, taxi!" And she knew that she, Nora, was very guilty toward her.

The guilt dragged up memories, and the memories dragged up new guilt, and there was a desire to approach, admit her sins, ask forgiveness, and she didn't know for what or how.

She inadvertently dropped the sock she was mending on a wooden darning egg onto her lap. There was a big hole in the sock, and the yellowish-pink lacquer covering the egg peeped through it, and Nora suddenly remembered the oblong yellow-pink Crimean apple Lisa had brought her one fine day in the middle of winter. That was about a year and a half after they had returned from Russia, and Lisa came to them from another city to live with them and help her sick brother and his family. There was a housing shortage in those days and all four of them lived in one big and very cold room, with screens and cabinets dividing one bed from another, and they wanted to turn it into an "apartment." The mother wasn't yet working in the school and would sell hand-embroidered tablecloths; the money was small and the customers were few. And Lisa, a typist in an office, would give Russian and German lessons after work, and was the main provider of the house. Everything was tight and Nora knew very well the limits of her wishes and requests. And one winter day, after a bad attack that came on Papa, when Nora was curled up in a corner behind the cabinet weeping silently in great despair, and wanted to be very small so they wouldn't notice her, and her crying and her fear – Lisa came behind the cabinet and without a word gave her a big Crimean apple, wrapped in soft pink paper, like those apples in the windows of the big delicatessens which Nora would look at admiringly from afar as almost legendary things, beyond her own world. She knew very well on that day what that apple had cost Lisa –

Nora tore her eyes away from the hole in the sock and looked at the aunt sitting in front of her, and saw that she wasn't reading anymore. Her long, ageless face was still bent over the book, but her eyes didn't move and her hand didn't turn the pages. A moment later, she raised her head, repressed a sigh and said to Nora, "Do you have a cigarette?"

Nora got up, the sock dropped out of her lap, fell on the floor, and the egg clanked dully.

"In my room," she said. "I'll bring it right away."

When she came back from her room with a pack of cigarettes, Lisa was standing at the open piano, one hand strumming the keys. She stood like that a moment, then the little finger shook, and one note, very weak, wavering, and miserable, was heard and fell silent. Lisa's face was twisted as if from a burn; she lowered her hand, closed the piano, and took a cigarette out of Nora's pack.

"I want to smoke too," said Nora when the two of them sat down again at the table, and she lit her cigarette with Lisa's.

Lisa tapped the ash and said, "I saw Albert today. In the street."

"So did I," said Nora, but for some reason she decided not to tell the details of the meeting at the dairy.

"He was coming toward me," added Lisa. "And he didn't see me. There was a woman with him. Did you see him too?"

"Yes."

Lisa sucked on the cigarette noisily and exhaled the smoke, thrusting out her lips.

"He didn't tell us that he had friends here outside our family. Although it is conceivable, of course. We can't assume he's been sitting here alone in his hotel all the time." She sighed, shrugged, tapped the cigarette in the ashtray. "Wonder who she is," she said as if to herself.

"Helen!" Nora blurted out suddenly, just as Arin had blurted out that name when Nora met them the first time, as if all the explanation and all the justification were in that name.

Lisa looked at her in astonishment. "What? You know her?"

"No. But I saw her before and asked him. He told me her name is Helen and she's a friend of his daughter. In America, she married the military attaché of our embassy."

Lisa looked at her with tense curiosity.

Now Nora shrugged and summed up, "More than that I don't know either."

At any rate, she was slightly proud that Arin had told her more than he had told her mother and Lisa.

Lisa said, "I think she's very beautiful."

"Yes, very beautiful," Nora agreed and added, maintaining her control over information others don't know. "I also saw a picture of her once in his hand…along with his daughter, Paula."

Lisa shook her head a few times in innocent sadness. "So maybe *that's* why he came here!"

Nora bent down to pick up the sock to hide her excited face. Maybe because of that, maybe, maybe. And suddenly, her heart beat maliciously; what did she think? That he came because of her? That it was her he wanted here? That the prince came to fit the glass slipper on Cinderella's foot?

But when she picked up the sock and put it next to her on the sofa, she had to look into Lisa's face, and then she understood that her face didn't express a hope disappointed now, but expressed, as then, as always, all the hopes disappointed long, long ago. And once again there was something moving in her thin, docile shoulders, and her pale lips and her slightly swollen eyelids over the profane sadness in her eyes.

"Anyway," said Lisa, "I'm glad he came. If you only knew how many memories connect us! And in general, when was the time right to meet a person? You're still young and your life is different, you see so many people, and hear interesting things, and we here…I'm not complaining, God forbid. But the office, and the Bergmans and the few people we come in contact with – and suddenly here comes a person–"

Her face was covered with a slight flush, and her voice rang and jerked, and once again it sounded very much like the voice of a young girl, and her smile was apologetic and thin, as if she were afraid to grin, lest it be too frivolous.

"You know, Nora, not always was I against your going abroad," she confessed suddenly, out of the blue. "I wanted to tell you that right after you came, but I couldn't. I think our situation, you know… when rich maidens travel, or at least those who are well-off, and that's no effort, you understand…but in our situation, I thought that those were luxuries."

"I know you think that, you don't have to say it specifically," said Nora, and couldn't hide the cold hostility that crept into her voice.

But Lisa didn't notice. "I think," she added, "that every person should do what he has to. Yes, what he has to, to adapt to his conditions, to bear the yoke and submit to it. To submit because that's what's demanded of him. But maybe you're right, today I think you were absolutely right." Her face was obstinate, as if she were about to rebel and throw off the yoke of submission. "Maybe every person has to think of himself first and foremost, his life, his happiness, and if not, how will he end up?"

Nora felt that this time, Lisa didn't intend to hurt her. She knew that at this moment, she wasn't accusing her of exaggerated selfishness, even though her words, always revolving around that circle of expressions itself, weren't excessively complimentary, but on the contrary, at that moment she was almost Nora's ally. Her ally in her war for her own life. And nevertheless, the words "to think of himself first and foremost" seared her ears and she was ready to stand up and throw this in her face. "We'll never come to an understanding, Lisa!"

But before she could draw the conclusion that summed up all evil, the door to the corridor creaked and the mother's voice was heard talking to Tekla.

Nora and Lisa stood up and went into the corridor. The mother stood in the door, gave Tekla some packages she had brought from the city, and shook the raindrops off the brim of her blue hat.

"It's raining out," she smiled at her daughter and sister-in-law. "Really autumn. Cold and wet."

The next morning, Nora strolled with Arin on the riverbank. A very light rain would fall and stop, fall and stop, not like the mild, constant autumn damp.

Arin walked beside Nora, bareheaded, wearing a white raincoat, and attracted the looks of the few passersby. But he didn't pay attention to them.

The gray river under the gray sky hummed stormily. Its narrow banks seemed too narrow to hold it. Two big rafts cruised at its center, moved quickly with the stream and left behind them a clear silver wake in the murky water. The smell of the water, the smell of fish, the smell of wood and tar rose from the river. Now and then a strong short gust would burst out from somewhere and spray sharp drops in the face of the pedestrians. And when it quieted, the air was silent and heavy as lead; under it the humming movement of the water increased.

Not far from the bridge, some barges were tied to the shore, bobbing on the little waves and pulling on their chains, like recalcitrant horses who want to set out. The creaking of ropes and the clanking of rusting chains was a kind of syncopated accompaniment to the long dejected melody of the river.

Nora and Arin climbed onto the bridge and walked slowly, looking at the flowing expanse beneath them. Suddenly, when they came to the middle of the bridge, Nora grabbed Arin's hand nervously, almost convulsively, and stood still.

"What's wrong?" Arin asked her in astonishment and dread, looking into her bulging eyes.

"Nothing. One minute. Wait."

She shut her eyes a moment as if to get rid of dreadful sights. Then she smiled weakly. "It's strange and ridiculous," she said at last. "I remembered a dream I had last night. Just last night."

"And it scared you so much?"

"Yes. I dreamed the two of us, you and I, were walking on this bridge, and we came to the middle, and suddenly you left me and walked on. I'm about to follow you, and I see that one board from the floor of the bridge is torn up. And under it – water. Black, and so deep. And I'm standing at the abyss and I can't pass over it. I'm here

164

and you're there," she pointed to the two parts of the bridge. "And here, in front of me, is that hole, and underneath – black water flowing fast, dizzyingly fast. Just last night I dreamed that. Understand?"

Arin listened very closely. "Yes. It's quite awful. I know." After a brief silence, he said, "But it's not so awful, it's only a dream. When you're awake, it's possible, pure and simple, to pass over that pulled-up plank and get over the bridge, isn't it?"

They stood leaning on the railing.

Nora let go of his arm that was holding her, and he took her hand in both of his.

"Why did you come out without gloves? Your hand is so cold!" He rubbed her hand and then stuck it in the big pocket of his coat. "There. That's better."

They walked, and Nora felt the caress of his big hand in his pocket. She was afraid to speak, afraid to breathe, walking beside him feeling a shudder of bliss, her eyes glued to his quiet face.

Now it comes! Now it comes by surprise. Comes, comes, and you can pass over. And I'll pass over it because it's possible, it's possible.

But his face moved, and it was as if he shook off her admiring look. He let go of her hand, and she had to take it out of his pocket.

She lowered her head, and to herself she cursed and abused herself with bitter mockery, "Fool, stupid, what a ninny!"

Meanwhile, they crossed the bridge and were standing at the wooden steps that climb the mountain.

"Shall we go up?"

Nora forced herself to speak calmly. "No. It's not worth it. It's clay, and in the rain it gets soft, and there's a danger of slipping."

"Too bad," said Arin. "And the stairs are shaky?"

"Shaky."

"So. There aren't many changes here. I remember climbing up this mountain one day when I was young. In the spring. After a rain. I lived in this town about two months altogether."

And after a pensive silence, "Even in our hometown, mine and your parents', this same river flows. Shall we go back?"

"Let's."

On their way back, it started drizzling again. It was piercing, and the river bristled beneath it. Nora said, "Even waking, it's not always possible to pass over it."

Arin squinted. "You went back to your dream?"

"And I'm sure that even when awake, there are situations when it's better for a person to jump into that hole, into the water. And that's it."

"There are no situations like that if the person doesn't create them willingly."

"It's easy to talk. With talking and nice words we haven't yet taught anybody to live."

"If only you saw, Nora, what human beings can do with their lives after they've managed to pass over!"

"I haven't seen any."

"You have. With your own eyes."

Nora persisted in her refusal.

"Who?"

"Your mother," said Arin.

She hesitated a moment before she replied, and at last she said, "But my father!"

Arin measured her with a long look. "You see him only from the perspective of your own life, Nora. But he, even like that, is living his life."

Nora's eyes filled with tears. "I don't know, I don't know anything about his life. But sometimes I think it's a duty to show them, the mentally ill, the possibilities of jumping into the water. Yes. That would be good for them and everybody else. Everyone would be rid of torments."

Arin was silent. And she felt that this time, his silence wasn't forgiving, she felt that he too judged her as guilty; his face turned very pale, his face chilly. He hates me now. And Nora suddenly knew with awful clarity that she had done something irretrievable and she didn't know why.

She whispered, "Maybe I blurted out something stupid…"

He answered her harshly. "Yes. You said stupid things."

They entered the alley that connects the riverbank with one of the town squares. They stood at the advertisement of the opera. Arin read the name of the visiting singer appearing in *The Barber of Seville*. Then he nodded and said to Nora, "Good God, child, how young you are!"

At home, Nora found a letter from her friend Antonia. The letter came from the Tyrol mountains, where the redheaded girl's parents had a house. An autumn wind of mountains blew from her straight lines, and there was a call for a meeting in them.

Nora walked around all that day missing her life abroad, and at night, in bed, she reread the letter. To drop everything here, forget, go.

She couldn't sleep that night; last night's dream haunted her and she imagined that the moment she shut her eyes, she'd see the rickety bridge and the abyss beneath it. And on waking – it could be passed over. Don't fall asleep, don't fall asleep. And I want to sleep so much. And I can't.

She turned on the light, picked up a book on her bedside table. *A Selection of Hebrew Poetry.* Nora opened the book with no specific intention, and her eyes fell on the bifurcated lines of Rabbi Moses ben Jacob ben Ezra. Somewhere, in the middle of the poem, were lines that, for some reason, she didn't connect with what went before:

It is the light that goes on glowing through my youth,
And glows yet brighter as I grow old.
It must be of the substance of God's light,
For otherwise it would be fading
As my years and strength decline.

Detached and cut off from the logical connection of the religious poem, those lines referred inadvertently to what she was thinking, was afraid of, dreaded, and expected.

It is the light. And thanks to it we live our lives. It is the light – and it is. And what is it? It is the light.

She closed the book, turned off the light, and lay there repeating the words until they completely lost their spoken meaning and became music that has no connotation.

And suddenly, as if from those words, or perhaps in some connection hidden even from her, she remembered one man, not young, rather tall with a wide brow, one of her acquaintances in Berlin, Elhanan Kron, who would stand leaning on the window at the "Seminary of Semitic Languages," leafing through some book with square letters, and she heard his voice: "To choose a language as you choose a ring. That right to choose a language like a wedding ring and make a blessing over it, 'I thee wed.'"

It is the light. And perhaps this is the light –

Sights of the last year revolved around her. To get back to them, to forget everything, to get back.

But suddenly her whole body was shaken by one sight before her which wasn't so awful, as it were.

Until that moment, she was sliding over her memories, memories of the year of her salvation, as a passenger in a night train passing lights and stars and crescent moons, and here, all at once and urgently, the train stops at a station lighted with a bright yellow light. And there are no more charms of night or charms of movement to cover the reality. And there are only details of things, and they're all filthy. That's how the train of Nora's memories now stopped.

She saw her room, her "furnished room," in Berlin. She saw the soft, worn easy chair next to the lamp standing on a high pedestal. She saw the picture of "Old Fritz" behind her, the window open onto the dead yard, where one melancholy tree lived out a life sentence.

She saw the pale face, as if it were smeared with a film of grease, the face of Rüdiger, her friend, and Antonia's boyfriend. His sharp nose, his fair face, and those "three hairs" always standing stubbornly on his scalp, impervious to the comb. Grandson and great-grandson of a distinguished family, great-grandson of the enlightened prime minister of the enlightened king, from an estate on the Prussian border, the place where the German Junkers were conceived, born and raised. He sat sunk in the armchair of a furnished room where a Jewish girl from Lithuania lived. He was one of those who rebelled against tradition and was proud of his land. His family demanded he do what they wanted: either agriculture or the army. That was the custom of those men from generations back, and he rebelled and went his own way. He chose music, and his teacher and mentor was a Jew who wrote operettas. And his sister – "older than me in retrospect, but younger than me when we're in company" – did the same. What was her name, that sister? Brunhilde? Krimhilde? Something from their ancient songs…Valkyrie? Valtraut? Yes, Valtraut! She also left her parents' home and went to a workers' colony, to the "Levina" factories, to give their children piano lessons.

"…and just imagine, we come home, from far away, as the car approaches our estate, I see the flag with the swastika waving on our roof!"

"Good thing I didn't go with you," said Nora.

"Y…yes. You understand my situation. With me, in the car, Loni sits, and Loni is…"

"A Jew, just like me. And what did she say?"

"What could she say? She didn't say anything."

"I think that in such cases, silence is fine," commented Antonia.

"Because there's no choice!" said Nora angrily.

"The essence of failure is contained in silence," Rüdiger blurted out. "I ask my sister Valtraut, 'Valtraut, who do you vote for?' And she answers, 'For them, of course.' Just imagine! 'Why?' 'Because they make the most noise!' The Nazis. So, what do you say?"

"And you?"

"I'm an artist. I'm pretty sure no art can exist in such a regime. If they win, I'll pick up and escape across the Polish border. Very simple."

If they win, thought Nora now. If they win.

And suddenly she knew. He was also lying to himself. He wouldn't pick up and run away. He would be with them. Would be one of them. He'd go, he'd stand, he'd walk, he'd salute, he'd wear a brown shirt, he'd march in their ranks and sing the Horst Wessel Song.

She saw him so clearly in the dark of night that she almost felt a physical pain in her eyes.

That too was the rickety bridge, that too. And I have to pass over it, over that abyss too.

And this is the light.

And this is the great darkness becoming stuck to and caught up in that light. How long is the night.

He'll go put on a brown shirt, he'll go, and thousands and tens of thousands like him will march to the light of the torches. And we are crushed under their feet. Our good friends. Our good friends until when? And Antonia?

What was he to Antonia? I think that on that night, when the two of them stayed in his room – but I didn't see.

Everything, everything swoops down on me and bothers me all at once.

As in childhood, as in childhood, as in nights of childhood.

"Nora's so infantile!"

"Don't mention delicate matters between the sexes in front of her."

"Here! This is the absurd Russian education that blocks their development for another few years, and then they burst out like a volcano."

"My baby!"

Who spoke?

There are many who spoke.

It's not she, not this one.

Where did I run away to? To whom and from whom?

Here, in this city, beyond the river bristling with rain, here in miserable huts and hungry eyes in windows.

Your poor, Israel, your poor.

The little ones, huddled, wretched, who say "Hear O Israel" every single day.

And their toil, and their toil, you, young lady, have no part of it. Ungrateful, boastful. Bragging!

Who taught you to read with square letters if not that town and its Jews?

Who taught you to open a book at night and ask for a solution in the poems of Rabbi Moses ben Jacob ben Ezra, if not that town and its Jews?

Who taught you to dream the dream of your future, with a tremble, to pronounce the name of a little land on the shores of the Mediterranean, if not this town and its Jews?

And for whom, and because of whom did you want to live, if not for them, for the people of this town, its Jews.

Beyond the river bristling with rain are their wretched huts, porters, shoemakers, beggars. All more worthy than I.

Beyond that bridge –

Why does my flesh burn? Why do I mix up all the realms?

And this is the light – and if they do win in the end? That fear. He took my hand, yes, yes, that's why my flesh burns, and not from the fear of the Nazis. He took my hand and put it in his pocket.

The night is so long. I'll sleep, I'll sleep. They say you have to count, if only to a thousand.

One…he told me that awake…two…that you can…three… there was…no, never mind, count – one, two, three, four…he went… five…s-ix – s-seven, eight…and the bridge over the stormy river… from the start – one, two, three – and maybe –

Two days later, Arin came and brought tickets for the whole family to *The Barber of Seville*, for the guest appearance of the famous singer. The tickets were very expensive. Arin tended to be a spendthrift; he rented a box and wanted to turn the trip to the theater into a festive family event. Nora feared that the whole thing had a whiff of parting. Anyway, the gift surprised the three women, and Mrs. Krieger protested affectionately, "But Albert, why a box? I haven't sat in such a place since nineteen-fourteen!"

"What do you care, Esther!" he dismissed her jokingly. "For once you'll sit at the opera like Duchess de Longia!"

"Forget your duchess!" sighed the mother.

There were two more seats in the box and Arin very graciously offered them to Shoshanna Bergman and her son Marek, since they happened to be in the Krieger house when he brought his tickets. Nora wasn't very happy about that, but Mrs. Krieger looked gratefully at Arin; she always felt in debt to her friend Shoshanna Bergman for those days after the war when Shoshanna took her into her house. She thought she could never repay her.

"Why, that's wonderful," she said. "We'll all go together."

"Why, that's wonderful," Arin answered. "I've found a man, to help me against four women."

Shoshanna Bergman, who lovingly accepted the chance gift, nevertheless couldn't refrain from commenting sarcastically, "You don't really think you'd be dominated by four women!" She couldn't forgive him the fact that she was unable to discover his secrets.

In the evening before the performance, there was a lot of preparation in the Krieger house. Arin was to come at eight and take them to the theater in a carriage or a car. And at seven-thirty, every corner of the house smelled of eau de cologne, and the three women were running around the rooms excitedly completing the details of their outfits. Even Mrs. Krieger, wearing a black velvet dress with a thin pearl necklace, the only piece of jewelry she had left, except for her ring, from the good old days – adjusted the waves of her hair whenever she passed the mirror, coming to help her daughter and her sister-in-law pin, button, smooth and adjust their dresses. She took great care of Lisa's closed brown silk dress, very attentively pinned the yellowish flower to her shoulder, her only ornament. She had tested its place – higher, lower – on the shoulder and near the collar, and tested whether it really suited the distance from the button and the sleeve seam, but as she did, her eyes went off now and then and excitedly and fearfully examined her daughter, who thrust her long thin arms into the short sleeves of the white evening gown.

"Nora, go ask Tekla to button you up in back!"

"You're beautiful, Mama!" exclaimed Nora, and turned around on her high heels and ran to Tekla.

Mrs. Krieger blushed like a little girl and concentrated more on her sister-in-law's dress.

"Here, that's fine! Listen to me, Lisa, put on a little lipstick. You don't know how that refreshes your face! Really, just this time!"

"No matter what," replied Lisa submissively, after looking at herself and her sister-in-law in the mirror, "it won't help me much." And she laughed with twisted lips. "The president won't fall in love with me."

Nevertheless, she stood at the mirror and smeared her lips with a red pencil, but she wiped off the color, shrugged and moved aside.

Mrs. Krieger went to the mirror and picked up her box of powder.

"Mama! Mama!" Nora burst into the room, shouting bitterly. "Those damn buttons! One is missing, Tekla told me it's missing."

"I told you to check the dress before you put it on," scolded the mother, but she immediately picked up a needle and thread and now, since she had done her duty with her sister-in-law, she began working almost devoutly on her daughter's dress.

"Turn around a little, that's right. That's right. I'm finished here. And now – why haven't you done your hair? Gather up the curls. Yes. You went to the student ball in that dress? Just something on your neck. The little chain. Yes. That's enough. White is always pretty. Look in the mirror," she concluded, and couldn't hide her maternal pride.

Nora stood at the mirror, her face inflamed with joy, her lips smiling, the sparkle in her eyes, her long bare neck, turned dark a little by her white dress, now it all looked very lovely to her.

I'm really not so ugly! she thought briefly and happily. Somewhere behind that thought hummed in her great joy: this evening is decisive, this evening has to decide! And she didn't know what would be decided, but the pleasure swelled up in her and was reflected in all her movements and gave her charm.

I'm not at all like Lisa. I'd advise you to smile. Her teeth are yellow, that woman said. A lie. My teeth are beautiful, straight. They're white and shining. And so are the lips.

"Well, enough twirling in the mirror," said Lisa, who peered into the room again. "We still have to put on coats and galoshes; Albert will soon be here, and he wants us to be ready."

Nora glanced at her reflection in the looking glass one last time, as if she were parting from some character who was suddenly dear to her. Her breast moved, throbbed with some happy and incomprehensible fear. If Lisa hadn't been looking at her critically, she would have waved at her, at the girl in the mirror. Then she turned around and left.

"Mama, you're absolutely the most beautiful woman!" she whispered again in her mother's ear, and caressed her as she walked to the corridor.

"Stop, Nora, you messed up my hair!" growled the mother affectionately. "Here are your galoshes!"

"At long last," Lisa blurted out with a chill that didn't come from the depths of her heart and an apology not directed at anyone. "We're not going out to a ball, we're going to hear an opera."

At the cloakroom, Arin helped Nora off with her coat and surveyed her with a smiling eye. "Beautiful!" he said, and his face beamed satisfaction.

Nora saw herself in the big looking glass on the wall and once again she was flooded with pleasure at the sight of her supple, thin figure, the sight of her excited cheeks.

"Look at Mama!" she whispered to Arin, so Lisa wouldn't hear.

"Didn't I tell you, Esther," Arin said to Mrs. Krieger. "Your natural place is in a box at the opera."

Mrs. Krieger blushed again, like when she heard her daughter's praise.

Everything was beautiful. Even the fat Shoshanna Bergman looked good in her lead-colored opera gown.

Ladies and gentlemen were taking off their coats at the cloakroom. The big looking glass reflected festive images. Splendid gowns of high-class women overshadowed Nora's modest evening dress, but she felt fresh, light and young in her white silk.

Arin was also feeling the giddy mood. His movements were a bit lighter than necessary; he spoke in a whisper and laughed out loud, and was somewhat strange in his hasty excitement.

"How many years since I've been to the opera!" he said. "The whole thing reminds me of my youth."

They climbed the wide white stairs with the red banister and sat in the box. Nora, Lisa and the mother in the first row; Marek, Shoshanna Bergman and Arin behind them.

The brightly lit opera house was filling up and humming with restrained voices and Nora thought everyone was as happy as she. That hall, with its three stories, its boxes and its red plush seats, was the pride and joy of the small state.

"Nora, give me the opera glasses!" Lisa asked and started looking at everything around.

In the orchestra, downstairs, in the first rows, sat rich citizens, most of them Jews, and officers whose polished uniforms and shoulders gleamed with the copper stars on them. In the nearby boxes, the ones facing the stage, sat senior officials and ministers. In the center box were the wife and daughter of the president, and behind them sat the Minister of the Interior and next to him a small, very old woman, wearing a rustic dress with a white kerchief on her head.

"Look at that," Marek poked Arin sitting next to him. "That's our minister, and that old gentile woman next to him is his mother! You can see that, just yesterday, they were pig herders. They really need operas!"

Arin looked very carefully at the old woman sitting withdrawn and tiny in the box as if she wanted to fade into it and disappear, and nevertheless there was also an expression of pride on her face whenever she raised her eyes to her pug-nosed, heavyset son sitting very confidently and comfortably, and his face, also a peasant face, expressed the serenity of someone who had reached a place of honor.

She seemed to be strict about the honor of the two of them and the honor of the kingdom.

"Yesterday she was milking cows, and today she's sitting here and representing the state!" chuckled Marek.

Arin nodded. "No, that's very touching. To bring an old mother like that to the theater without any shame, that's almost greatness."

"Pig herders when they're at home among themselves," decreed Marek disdainfully.

Nora knew that tone, that way of expression: the good citizens of that city were ready and willing to forgive the leadership of the state all their political mistakes, all the fascist deviations, and the Jews – even the persecution of the Jews, if it didn't directly damage them and their relatives. But that they were peasants, villagers who weren't ashamed of being villagers – that, those "aristocrats" didn't forgive.

"Pig herders, pig herders, pig herders!" the lips bubbled with contempt.

But at that moment, Nora's attention wasn't free for much contemplation. The sight of the gleaming, festive theater won her heart. Never had she seen that auditorium like that, since her seat had always been in the "pigeon roost," in the "standing room only" section, way, way up, where her student friends were probably huddled now too. Up there she was hidden from the world and the world was revealed before her. And today she suddenly felt on display to the eyes of that whole audience. But since that audience was on display to her eyes, she felt fine.

"Who's in that box?" asked Arin behind her back.

"The Foreign Minister and his wife. She was an opera singer. And the one who's offering her the box of candy is the French ambassador, if I'm not mistaken. That's the diplomatic box. We also have diplomats, and they're called that because they're given a diploma in the pig sty!" Marek whinnied like a horse, happy with his successful joke.

Lisa suddenly turned her head and blurted out angrily, "What's that? You think you deserve the position of minister?"

Shoshanna Bergman gave Lisa a crushing look and said, "And you, you think there aren't Jewish men who could do the work better than all those together? All the teachers in school used to say about my Boris that he had the brains of a minister!"

Marek then replied, "And have you forgotten that in nineteen nineteen, and twenty, at the beginning of their political independence, our Jewish brothers were sitting very high up and teaching them how to do that work, and after they learned how to hold the reins, they threw them out? The slave did what he was supposed to, the slave can go now. And now, here they are sitting here like high-ranking lords, with an ancient tradition in politics, house of lords!"

"Well, as for tradition," laughed Arin, "and especially the behavior of the diplomatic corps, it seems to me that we Jews can't be guides."

Lisa took the opera glass again and was looking at the first rows of the hall.

"Who's that standing there, Lisa?" asked Shoshanna Bergman. "I'm nearsighted. Isn't that Mrs. M?" The name of one of the "faces" of the city was blurted out indifferently.

"Yes," said Lisa. "She's looking here."

Shoshanna Bergman nodded a polite greeting to the high-class lady. But the latter was looking at Mrs. Krieger, who was sitting silently with her beautiful arm leaning on the red velvet of the box and didn't see Shoshanna Bergman's greeting.

Very slowly, many of the looks from the first rows of the parterre began turning to the group in the box. Some sent greetings, some looked with open and arrogant curiosity. One woman, with a silver fox fur stole, whispered something in the ear of her neighbor wearing a purple gown, and pointed at the box. The other woman stood up and put a lorgnette to her eye.

Nora saw her mother's face turn pale and the smile was wiped off of it. She turned her head back to Arin and said, "Didn't I tell you…" and didn't finish.

Nora knew that the group looking at them were distinguished rich people of the city; most of whom had known her mother before the war, when Esther Krieger was the wife of the architect Krieger and one of them. Now that she had become a handicrafts teacher in the school for poor girls, she was beyond the pale of that group; they no longer recognized her. Nevertheless, they couldn't restrain their curiosity at seeing her appear like that at the opera. Nora knew that tomorrow her mother would be the talk of the town, and they'd find ways to send all the sarcasm and gossip to their isolated house.

Shoshanna Bergman also grasped what was going on here. She leaned over to her friend's ear and whispered, "What do you care? I would feel, I'm here, whether you like it or not!"

The light went out, and everyone was relieved. The conductor stood at his podium; Rossini's notes descended like dew on all those heads in the darkness of the hall.

Lisa bent forward, put her chest on the upholstered ledge of the box and pressed against it almost painfully. Her neck was thrust forward, her chin jutted out, elongated, her mouth moved slowly in complete oblivion; sometimes it seemed that if she tried just a little harder, she'd manage to separate her head from her neck and send it flying into the orchestra. She was the most musical one in the family, was drawn to music and hypnotized by it, like those snakes that obey the flute. She loved it, all of it, without any distinction, from the trite and sentimental ballads coming from the mouths of the girls of her generation, to the symphony orchestra. Nora watched her out of the corner of her eye and imagined her ears growing and sticking out under her grayish hair in the dark. But her mouth, always dry, was now lustful, active, alive.

Mrs. Krieger, on the other hand, was almost indifferent to the notes. She felt only a slight pleasure and the caressing, very complex excitement, which included the notes and the theater, and the people around her, and sitting there festively, mixed with memories of days gone by; all of them together gave her attentive face a charm of both contentment and calm.

During the last year, Nora had decided she didn't like opera very much and that it was only a ridiculous art whose time had passed; that, in general, all that "sentimental junk" didn't deserve to be heard and should be shelved, and everything should start all over; only Prokofiev, whom her friend Rüdiger loved to play, could inspire a new romanticism in melodies with the spirit of the age. That was how the members of her society in Berlin talked, divided in their opinions between Mahler, Prokofiev, Stravinsky, Hindemith, and Arnold Schoenberg, and she too, who didn't really have a musical education, followed them, believed them, even learned to feel things as they did.

But at the moment, hearing the jolly overture, suddenly all the fine judgments were forgotten, all the theories and comments were forgotten, and her ear happily picked up those honeyed old-fashioned notes. Awake and dreaming at the same time, she saw everything more sharply in the dark of the theater, and with the strange processes of apperception, she was very attentive, and nevertheless had time to think irrelevant thoughts. She sat and heard and felt that Arin was sitting behind her, that he was here, that he was here with her, very close, that he was breathing behind her.

Now and then, when the orchestra thundered forte, her heart would again be filled with that happy fear in daring toward something, toward something that would happen and would decide. And suddenly she saw herself from a distance, remembered how she had gone to the opera for the first time when she was eleven years old. It was New Year's Eve, and her father and mother surprised her and took her to the theater. It was like permission to leave childhood. The opera was performed in the old theater, the one her father had built back then, that wretched building used mainly for dancing and where they used to hold the Gymnasium's Hanukkah balls, that very building Nora saw the night she returned home. They sat in the balcony and below, very far away, on the stage, was the magical musical world. That lighted square, like a frame of a mottled picture of wonders, sent its melodies and images to Nora. Lords and ladies from the distant past were moving and hovering and singing their complaints about the pleasures of the torments of their love. They were performing *La Traviata*, and Nora didn't hear that the small, ad hoc orchestra played Verdi off-key, melodies she had known from Lisa's singing when she combed her hair or washed, and she didn't see how shabby and tasteless the cardboard set was that shook with every step of the great Alfredo, who was too tall for that stage, and how hoarse, how ugly and provincial was Violetta in her very pink, shiny, stiff satin dress which failed in its attempt to hint at Parisian fashion and the character of a great courtesan of the last century. What was the value of all those things? All the ridiculously small things? And that was *opera*, real opera, a show for grown-ups, opera with an orchestra and chorus and singers, and she, Nora, an eleven-year-old girl, was allowed to watch that great wonder, that magic; and maybe she was allowed to be part of a great love at long last, the love sung by Violetta as she lay dying, and perhaps she was also allowed to die a death of love with her, a kiss of death –

And now, too, in spite of everything – in spite of all that had happened since then – things were slightly similar. The curtain went up. A slight rustle passed through the theater. A tension of impatience at the appearance of the famous singer. The overture ended, and Duke Almaviva wandered around under the windows of Rosina. The happy Figaro appeared and offered him his service. Who would look at Figaro? Who would listen to the trills of the duke's voice? She, only Rosina, drew that big audience to the theater this evening, and in contrast with her, even Rossini himself was null and void.

Here she is on the beautiful balcony. Here, her voice pours out with mischievous sweetness. She sang Italian: *"Una voce poco fa / Qui nel cor mi risuonò."*

Even though the singer was very famous, there was in her and her excellent voice something of the real charm that attracts the heart. She was still quite young, and her walking on stage and her movements didn't yet have the theatrical rustiness of jadedness and confidence of success or that unwise arrogance that makes most opera and ballet stars forget the necessary charm of good taste. Like most of her colleagues in the art of singing, she was plump, but not yet clumsy, and her round face didn't reveal a double chin, even to the opera glass. Her full shoulders moved pleasantly above her very low-cut gown, and it was nice to see her exposed breast even under the layer of powder rising and falling with her voice rising high and sliding down to the low notes. She didn't "play around" much, she did only what she had to; the movements she couldn't avoid because of her role. The rest was completed by her voice and her natural grace. Therefore, there was a smile on every face right after she appeared, and Nora, who took the opera glass for a little while from Lisa and mistakenly glanced into the depths of the orchestra, saw that a smile of real esteem and real relief hovered even on the faces of the two illuminated violinists.

Nora also smiled and felt part of Figaro's deceptions and conspiracy with the duke and Rosina, felt loved, happy and graceful as her, and for some moments, she felt that she too, if only she'd open her mouth, that crystal clear, ringing voice would come out of it.

Suddenly she felt a hand touching her arm lightly and cautiously. Then the warm hand caressed the arm and stroked it. Nora didn't dare turn around, didn't dare breathe; numb, and devoted to that hand she sat blissfully frightened. And why did she have to turn around? She knew, just from the touch, from those long fingers clinging to her bare arm, with her whole being she knew what person was holding her. The characters on the stage began to blur before her eyes and she no longer grasped who was walking around there and singing, didn't know what the chorus wanted, what the orchestra was playing. Her head was spinning, the happy fear overcame her, and she was completely in that touch, and in the tune rising in the distance from that lighted square where something was going on and there was no need to understand what was going on.

How much time passed? It's your hand, your hand, your hand, Albert, Albert, Albert. You and I and the music, Albert, Albert, Albert. Lost in that dark, only with the touch of union. I knew, I knew this evening, this evening was for me.

The last notes cheered in triumph, joy, frivolity. And before the curtain came down and the lights came up, applause burst out. Nora didn't move and the hand on her arm didn't leave, and it didn't move either. And the lights came up. Short of breath, eyes frightened with joy, Nora glanced behind her. Arin's seat was empty; he was standing at the edge of the box leaning on the wall and applauding. On his chair sat Marek holding Nora's arm. Nora didn't understand immediately. And when she did, a searing shame flooded her and everything shriveled in her and revolted. With a sharp, coarse movement, as if she were shaking off some disgusting insect, she pulled her arm out of Marek's hand.

"Why did you grab me!"

He apparently grasped the disgust in her voice and laughed maliciously, "Are you made of china, Norake?"

"I'm not Queen Pik that you can grab my hand!" Nora hissed in a venomous whisper.

"Fool. I thought you'd grown up," Marek shrugged.

The mother and Lisa and Shoshanna Bergman were already talking around them. "Isn't she wonderful! Isn't she wonderful! Such a coloratura! And what ease, with no effort of breathing!"

The curtain rose again, and the singer returned and curtsied. Nora looked at Arin, who kept applauding, like a robot, with slow, monotonous movements unlike the rhythm of the other applause, and his eyes kept looking at one point. Nora wanted to look in that direction, too, and she saw the diplomatic corps, but part of it was hidden from her by the wide cloak of the president's wife, who held out her hand for a kiss to some general sparkling with stars on his uniform. From where she sat, Nora couldn't see what Arin saw.

She glanced at him again. As he moved his head decisively, he stopped clapping (so did the others) and put both hands in his pockets. He shifted his eyes from that point he had been looking at and said to Nora and Lisa, "Shall we go out for a smoke?"

His face was pale and his smile was forced and tortured.

Nora stood up. Lisa and all the others wanted to stay in their seats. Helping Nora pass among the chairs, Arin took her arm, high up, near the sleeve.

Marek shot her a poisonous and mocking look and growled, "Oh, that's it!"

"Idiot!" Nora whispered to him as she passed.

And her heart beat: what a fool, *that* was the hand! How come you couldn't tell?

At any rate, her good mood, the pleasure of her expectations, didn't come back to her.

Arin walked beside her in silence. In silence, he took out his case and offered her a cigarette.

They stood still and smoked, leaning on the wall not far from the broad stairs where the audience streamed to the foyer.

That foyer was very big; blue velvet easy chairs lined its walls, and in the center was a mosaic floor in a wide circle. On those edges the audience walked around in circles, like horses in a circus ring or like a toy train on its tracks. Those who came out of the circle came out of it centrifugally; for some reason, no one dared break the line and approach the center of the mosaic.

Arin, who looked for a long time at the revolving audience, commented about it to Nora. But she knew that from her previous visits to that theater. There wasn't a person who didn't notice it.

The spinning circle spat out a young couple near them: Lucy Kurtz and Eliyahu Rom. They came to them.

"Nora, you're here too! That's great! Nora, you're so lovely in your evening gown."

Nora looked at Lucy's modest, blue dress, and suddenly felt very guilty.

"We're sitting way up, in the 'dovecote,' but you hear everything and even see a little. And where are you?"

Nora glanced up at Arin, as if asking his protection. He said, "Nora betrayed her class today. 'Uncle Sam' came and brought her down from the heights of her seat to the bourgeois box."

"Oh, that's why you're wearing an evening gown. But that's very beautiful, Nora, really."

Nora wasn't as sure of that now as when she had left home, or when she stood at the mirror in the cloakroom. Eliyahu Rom, Lucy's escort, stood gloomily and glared at them.

There was a short silence; Arin turned aside a little and his eyes searched the audience walking around.

"And you certainly don't remember me," said Eliyahu Rom, nodding his stiff hair that bristled above his broad forehead, whose bones stubbornly protruded.

"I remember well," said Nora happily when he removed his examining look from her (like many shy people, he averted his eyes from the person who addressed him, and only after an internal struggle and after a decision did he look again at his interlocutor as he talked). "We played croquet together once."

"Yes," Eliyahu grinned, and decided to look again into her wide-open eyes, straight into her eyes. "With Boris."

"And you hit my leg with your mallet, because as I walked I moved your ball, which was right at the wicket."

"And you wailed like a dozen cats!"

The three of them burst out laughing, and for some reason, Lucy laughed harder than all of them and said, "I imagine the two of you together, I imagine it!" And she rested a caressing look on Eliyahu's face, which was higher than hers.

"And here you are, a young lady!" said Eliyahu.

"I'm not such a young lady," Nora replied, and glanced appraisingly at the train of her long dress and raised her head to look for Arin to come to her aid this time, too. But Arin was no longer at her side; maybe he had gone off and gotten lost in the crowd, and maybe he had returned to the box.

"He went there!" said Lucy, as if she were answering a question that was asked, and nodding toward the crowd, which looked like a kind of dam in the aisle between the foyer and the bar.

"We'll go too," said Eliyahu. "Our seats are upstairs...by the time we get there..."

And shaking Nora's hand, he said, "Boris talked about you when we met. During a visit."

"His mother's here now," said Nora, but the two had already moved away.

Nora hesitated whether to go look for Arin in the crowd or to go back to the box. Suddenly she felt deserted and helpless. She turned to go to the box. Passing the cloakroom, she stopped at one of the mirrors. A tall woman with a beautiful back, dressed in a wine-red velvet dress, stood there and adjusted her curls. Nora saw herself next to her, skinny, with bony arms, very wretched.

I'm not beautiful at all. What was I thinking of! So not beautiful. And this white gown, who wears a white gown in October!

She turned her face, went back to the box. A moment later, Arin entered and didn't apologize. His face was very strange. His look was nervous but strangely blurred. Shoshanna Bergman asked him something, but he didn't reply.

Who does he look like now? Nora had a disturbing thought. Who does he look like? And she couldn't remember, but his face scared her now, and it was no longer that happy fear that had struck her at the beginning of that evening.

In the second act, the soprano turned the singing lesson of Rosina into a little concert like most sopranos in that opera.

The audience went mad with excitement. The hall turned into a stormy sea. From the top balcony came hysterical shouts of young women amateurs. "The Nightingale!" "The Nightingale!"

And they were answered by the bass voices of rambunctious students. "The Nightingale!" "The Nightingale!"

Rosina stood leaning on the piano and with small gestures she signaled to the audience to calm down. Then a trill of bel canto came out of her mouth.

When she concluded and bowed here and there, almost like a ship bobbing in a storm, carried by the ovations, for a brief moment

Nora turned her eyes from the stage and peeped at Arin sitting behind her. Arin wasn't looking at the stage this time either, and his eyes were fixed on the same point as before.

When Nora looked in that direction, she saw clearly what he was looking at there. In the diplomats' box sat Helen dressed in black, her golden head rising proudly on her erect, white neck.

Nora lowered her head, bit her bottom lip; small mallets beat on her temples.

And I'm a fool, an idiot –

The magic of the performance faded completely. Until it ended, she couldn't listen or see anymore. Now and then she aimed a glance of dread at Arin and saw that same strange expression in him that had disturbed her and reminded her of somebody, somebody she knew very well but could not remember who.

When they left the theater after the opera ended, and Lisa kept talking excitedly in praise of the singer, there was a hard, driving rain, pelting and dancing on the pavement lighted by streetlamps hidden among the trees of the park. The small group stood in the doorway, afraid to step into the water.

Shoshanna Bergman opened her umbrella and wanted to shelter her son from the jets whipping his face.

"We have to get a cab," said Lisa, and looked at Marek. And Marek took a step into the rain, but his mother grabbed his sleeve and said, "Stand still. You were coughing last night. It's so easy to catch cold!"

Marek gladly obeyed.

"After all," said Shoshanna Bergman, "there's another man here."

But that man was no longer with them. No one saw Arin slip away or when. Everyone was looking around, gazing into the rain-soaked dark, looking for him in the crowd streaming from the theater. He wasn't anywhere.

"Very strange!" said Lisa, offended.

"Funny," said Mrs. Krieger.

They waited a little while longer, but Arin wasn't there.

"He won't come back to us," said Nora with absolute confidence, as if she were delivering a verdict.

"Crazy guy!" giggled Marek.

"You catch cold easily. Don't talk in the rain!" Nora scolded him.

Mrs. Krieger sighed. "Let's go to the bus, maybe we'll catch up to him."

They walked, and behind them voices sang in a whisper:

Good night, Don Basilio,
Good night, good night!

Good night, Nora Krieger, good night, good night.

In October, the days are heavy as metal, and the nights are long and stormy.

In October, the downpour beats on the cobblestones to awaken dead stones, but the stone is stone forever. And when the rain falls on the ground, the ground is slack and weak. All the pears dropped, all the cranes abandoned our fields, and our windows are opaque.

Heavy as metal are the days of October, and the storm at night won't raise the dead from their graves. All the rain comes down to the gray river, and the river isn't full.

Let my lot not be with those who wish for the month of death.

Days of pressure and nights of disappointment. October, October in my window.

The day after the opera, Albert Arin didn't come to apologize to the three women he had left at the door of the theater. Nor did he come the next day to beg their pardon, nor on the third day either.

On the fourth afternoon, Mrs. Krieger picked up the newspaper and folded it up again without reading it.

"What was wrong with Albert, I don't understand," she said. "Maybe he got sick after that evening?"

And since the other two women didn't reply, she added, "I think we should call him at his hotel."

Lisa pursed her lips until all the blood was drained from them, and then slowly opened her mouth, as if she were opening a rusty lock. "I've got a phone in the office. He could have called me. Or in the worst case, asked one of the hotel workers to call."

Mrs. Krieger sighed and wanted to assuage her. "It just can't be for no reason. Something happened."

Nora sat gloomily, sad, silent.

They didn't call the hotel that day, or the next day. And he didn't come.

One evening, Lisa said to Nora, "I was with Papa today. He asked me what happened to Albert. Maybe he already left? He hasn't visited him in ten days. And I didn't know what to answer him."

Nora shrugged and left the room on some pretext. There were tears in her eyes. There was something insulting about that sudden escape, but she was afraid to follow the traces of the escapee. She recalled his look, his strange face, the fair-haired woman in that box.

Nevertheless, she couldn't wait idly. In truth, Mama was right. Perhaps he had fallen ill. Perhaps he was sick and abandoned in a strange city, in a hotel, among strangers. And they, the only ones close to him, didn't think they even had to call and ask how he was. I always think only of myself. My insults and my envies. I've always been like that. Lisa's right.

The next day, she called the hotel.

"Hello! I'd like to speak with Mr. Arin."

"Who, please?"

"Mr. Arin. Albert Arin. From America."

"Mr. Arin, you said? Oh, yes. From America. One moment. Yes. Room twenty-one. The gentleman isn't here, he left."

"Maybe he left a message when he'd be back?"

"The gentleman didn't leave any message that he'd be back. He left. A week ago. Abroad."

Nora hung up. It was good that she had talked in the street, in a public phone booth. Good that no one saw her face. Good that she was alone. A week ago. Abroad. The gentleman. So, he left, escaped.

Outside, a heavy bus went by, the window panes in the phone booth shook and rattled. He left. A week ago.

A thin rain began falling, beating on the window panes of the phone booth. Left. Didn't leave any message. Didn't even write a letter. That's it. What a fool you are. But to Lisa, too, and to Mama…

She left the phone booth. Someone who came in after her scolded her as she came out. "Lady, a public phone isn't for long confessions of love. People are waiting in the rain!"

She passed by him. Didn't answer. How can she tell that news at home? How can she look in their eyes when she told them that. For some reason, she thought she had participated in his escape; she, the most deceived of all. But you don't behave like that. How will she tell?

But as soon as the three women were sitting at the table for lunch, it was Lisa and not Nora who said, "I called Albert's hotel today, and just imagine, they told me he had gone a week ago. Gone abroad and won't be back."

Mrs. Krieger glanced at her in amazement, almost fear. "It can't be."

"Fact."

"That's really…very strange." The ladle slipped out of her hand, dropped into the bowl, and she wanted to explain something to herself. "But maybe he got some news from home, some telegram."

"Back then, at the theater, when he left us all in the street, he didn't get any telegram," said Nora in a choked voice.

"And didn't leave any note? Any letter?"

"Nothing."

"You don't behave like that. You don't behave like that," said Mrs. Krieger, still immersed in her frightened astonishment. Then she picked up the ladle vigorously and poured the soup into her sister-in-law's bowl. "But in fact, he was always — even twenty-five years ago — a very strange man."

Much as Mrs. Krieger wanted to make Nora's last days of vacation pleasant, cooking her daughter's favorite dishes, inviting people she knew Nora was fond of, surprising her with tickets to movies or concerts — she failed. The atmosphere in the house, after Arin's escape, was heavier than usual. Each of the three women felt deceived. That unsolved riddle the man posed for them with his coming and his going, had offended their honor, disturbed their peace of mind, put anger in their actions. Anger, at the very least. Lisa and Nora avoided each other now even more than at first, and when they did meet, each of them wanted not to talk, for God's sake, not to talk about that one issue. But it was hard to avoid mentioning Albert Arin's name when there were strangers in the house, who would ask innocently where that American guest had disappeared to, or how he was.

And the whole city was talking now. Talking about the strange appearance of the Krieger family in the opera box, talking about the mysterious guest who came and shone and disappeared. Talking ill about Mrs. Krieger, Lisa and Nora. "The whole city is talking." That, at least, was what Shoshanna Bergman declared.

Perhaps the whole city wasn't talking, perhaps the whole city had more important things. But to Mrs. Krieger, and to Lisa and to Nora, the whole city seemed to be talking. And it was almost unbearable to meet the oblique looks that they encountered in the street from Jewish "society" who really had nothing to do with the Krieger family.

Nora walked around as if she were wounded, and more than once she fell asleep with her cheek on a pillow wet with tears.

What was it? she'd ask herself, and she knew that there are things in this life that are solved only by chance, and this chance won't necessarily happen.

But chance came. One day, when she came home from the consulate where she had to renew the visa for her trip back, at eleven o'clock in the morning, Tekla met her with a beaming face. "Young lady, my 'friend' brought a letter for you. He says the letter comes from America!"

And she replied to Nora's questioning look, "I put it on the table in your room."

Nora went into her room without taking off her coat and galoshes. From the distance, she saw the long letter on the green cloth of her desk. And she shook, pained and excited, and locked the door for some reason, even though she knew there was nobody home but Tekla.

Only then did she approach the desk and pick up the envelope. Her name and address were on it, typed. Nora turned it over before she opened it and read on the other side: Pauline Cohen, Los Angeles, California, and the name of the street and a number.

Pauline Cohen. For a moment the name was completely foreign, and despite the name of the city, she wanted to cling to the thought that the letter had nothing to do with her preoccupations. Maybe there was another envelope inside it and somebody was sending a letter to Arin and wanted her to deliver it. Maybe – but she knew at once. "Paula, my daughter."

She tore the envelope with nervous fingers. In it was a brief note, handwritten in English, in that "standard handwriting" Arin had talked about during her illness.

Nora read:

Dear Miss Nora,

Please forgive me for bothering you. My father wrote me about you very affectionately, and even gave me your address in case I needed it. And I thought I could appeal to you, even though this might be unpleasant for you. There's no one else I can turn to about this.

For a month and a half, I haven't had a letter from my father, nor has he answered any of my letters, and I'm terribly anxious about him. Perhaps you don't know that he sometimes suffers from nervous breakdowns. After the last attack, he left for Europe to recover a little, on the advice of his doctor. The only letter I got from him was quite strange.

And therefore – but YOU will understand – I'm very scared that some-thing happened to him.

    I hope this is a false alarm. And I thank you in advance for your reply.

    Regards from me and my husband to your family.

Yours,
Pauline Cohen

Nora read the letter twice, and thought she was imagining it. But everything was really as she had read it the first time. Every word was in the same place and had the same content. She put it on the desk and sat down in front of it, still wearing her coat and galoshes.

Her eyes were dry, her mouth and throat were dry. Her look was fixed on the wall across from her. Her thoughts moved heavily; her head seemed to be screeching from them.

Everything goes to the same place. The one she loved too. The whole world was mentally ill. As if everyone decided to overpower her.

And Aunt Zlata – your uncle and your cousin, too. And your beloved. You, too, therefore. Clearly, you too. Why not? They call that fate.

And you couldn't remember whose face his face looked like at the opera when he came back to the box. Like Papa, you fool, like Papa! The blurred, hard look, like that time in the dream. In the mirror. But it's not my fault. This is not my fault. What do we know about the soul of another person? It's not my fault. We don't even know a thing about our own soul. He said then, "We're healthy people, as it were." He said it then. He fooled me. He fooled himself. "I've got a certain experience in such things." He does. "I hate doctors of nerves of all kinds with a mortal hatred." You fool! But it's not my fault, God almighty, it's not.

And who told him, who told him, that it's a good deed to show them, sick people, the abyss between the boards of the bridge, so that they'd jump into it? Who told him, who? "Maybe I blurted out something stupid…" "Yes. You said stupid things." You, you told him, Break your neck. You talked to him about the fear of madness. And he sat and placated and calmed. And how he stood, facing the window… "But remember this day, Nora. Remember it well. And mainly, what I told you just now. I said life is precious. In spite of everything. Because there is no disaster and no disease of body or mind–" There is, there is, there is! Life isn't precious if that's what it is. But here, sometimes, he was happy. Really happy. Who urged her, that abominable daughter, to write me that awful letter? What do they want from me? What do they dare want from me! Why didn't she write to that Helen of hers? I, I don't want to know, I don't want to. I don't want to know the truth. I hate the truth, if that's what it is.

Nora dropped her head in her hands. But she didn't weep. Before her closed eyes, the image of the fair-haired woman appeared. Helen. And there was no point anymore, and she wasn't important anymore. It's all the same. And me, too, apparently, I don't love him. So what do I care about that?

Tekla knocked on the door. "Young lady, the mistress ordered me to light the stove today. It's cold."

Nora stood up, opened the door.

Tekla unloaded the bundle of wood at the stove, sat on the floor and fed the pieces of wood into the maw of the stove, slowly, as though counting them. Nora stood facing her and saw every single one of her movements so clearly, and counted the wood.

I'm going out of my mind. I'll go out of my mind today. Why not? After all, it's all the same if it's now or later. The little woman with no legs was folded into the bundle of wood. It's all the same.

Tekla suddenly looked up at her in amazement, then looked at her wet heels on the floor she had washed that morning. Pointing with her head, she said, "Young lady, the galoshes."

Nora obeyed, went into the hall, took off her galoshes, took off her coat, and returned to the room.

"Will the young lady watch the stove?" asked Tekla.

Nora replied automatically, "Fine."

Tekla left.

Nora lay on the sofa. Lay on her back, not moving, like a dead body.

Why did he come to my father? What did he want with him? The image of himself? The contrast? Why am I thinking about that! Isn't it all the same, isn't it all the same. They're trampling my life. Trampling, trampling my life. All of them.

The fire caught in the stove and whistled and crackled and spat. Suddenly Nora got up, picked up the letter and was about to throw it into the stove. But she stopped.

No, I have to answer her. Answer her briefly, that I don't know a thing about him.

She hid the letter in the drawer and lay down again.

So, what will she tell Mama and Lisa?

And she decided not to tell them anything.

That day was long and tiring. That day was long and annoying. Talking about everything. Silent about the dread. All day.

People came to say goodbye to Nora. The day after tomorrow she's going? Yes, the day after tomorrow she's going. She must be very glad to return to that big city? Yes, she's very glad to return to that big city. And she's not sorry to leave the family? Yes, she's sorry to leave the family. And did she enjoy her vacation? Yes, she enjoyed her vacation. And there they surely won't feed her duck fat, ha-ha? No. There, they won't feed her duck fat. And there she probably eats Vienna sausages and six rolls at Aschinger's, as students do? Yes, there she eats Vienna sausages and six rolls at Aschinger's, as students do. Six? Really six? Six. No. Only two. And Sarah Corman, who studies dentistry there, does she know her? Yes, she knows Sarah Corman who studies dentistry there. Please give her regards! Yes, she'll give her regards. And what does she think of the political developments there? What's her opinion? What's her opinion, it's hard to say. She doesn't think the situation is so bad? Yes, she thinks the situation is so bad. But if the Social-Democrats make any effort at all, it will be good? Yes, it will be good.

"Nora, come here a moment. What was wrong with you? You're so pale."

"Headache."

"Tekla told me you got some letter."

"Yes."

"From where?"

"From Antonia."

"I thought maybe the letter made you sad. There's no bad news in it?"

"No. There's no bad news in it."

"You're sure? Come on, here's Lucy."

"Just for a minute, Nora, just for a little while. I'll drop by tomorrow to say goodbye to you."

What a long day.

You're going the day after tomorrow?

Yes, I'm going the day after tomorrow.

You must be very happy to go back to that big city?

Yes, I'm very happy to go back to the big city.

And you're not sorry to leave the family?

Yes, I'm sorry to leave the family.

"Nora, some lady brought you a package of sausage for her cousin who studies in Berlin. Go talk to her."

The young lady is going the day after tomorrow?

Going the day after tomorrow.

You must be happy to go back to that big city?

Very happy to go back to the big city.

And you're not sorry to leave the family?

I'm sorry to leave the family.

"Nora, shall I get rid of them? You look like you're fainting."

"Yes. Fainting. Tell them to go, all of them. I'll go to sleep."

So, have a good and peaceful trip, goodbye –

You're going the day after tomorrow –

Yes, the day after tomorrow I'm going –

She was lying in bed. In all the other rooms, there was still movement. In the kitchen the mother's careful voice was listing for Tekla all of Nora's blouses and dresses that she had to iron tomorrow.

Nora turned out the light. Through the very narrow crack in the door, a ray of light from the corridor penetrated the room. But the room was dark. And the wind sent a downpour to the window, handfuls, rolling like peas.

The room was dark.

So, you're going the day after tomorrow?

So, I'm going the day after tomorrow.

You must be very happy to go back to that big city.

Yes, I'm very happy to go back to that big city.

And are you sorry –

I'm not sorry, I'm happy, I'm very happy. Whether you like it or not, I'm happy. There's never been a joy like mine.

Really? What is this joy about? After all, *you* will still be there. You will be there, and your past will be there, and your childhood will be with you, and your father, and me.

Shut up. Be quiet. Don't talk to me anymore. You deceived me like a bastard.

I didn't deceive you. Not I. You deceived yourself. Who told you to turn me into a high and exalted character?

You were such a character. You're like that. It's not my fault you're mentally ill.

Is it mine?

But you told me that life is precious, that life is precious in spite of everything, and that it is possible to pass over it!

Is it impossible?

But you surrounded me with abysses on all sides. It is impossible for me.

So drown yourself in the depths.

I don't want to, I don't want to. I want to live. I want to live all the many days before me, down to the last one, to the end!

Life is precious, Nora, I told you, life is precious.

(The light from the crack was extinguished. Somebody passed down the hall on tiptoe.)

Why didn't you tell me?

Why should I have told you? About my illness, what does it have to do with your life?

But my father…

That's a different story. But I told you, didn't I tell you, it doesn't pay to pick at it, it doesn't pay to be scared, trust me, I know.

But that fear will always haunt me.

So go out of your mind.

No, no, no. I don't want to. I won't go out of my mind in spite of you. In spite of you, I'll be sane, I'll be strong, I'll be very happy.

And your past? And your past? And your childhood? And the war years? And the faces of the children shouting "That's Nora Krieger's father, he's crazy"? And Aunt Zlata? And your past? And your childhood?

I don't want them. That's the end of it. I'm going beyond them. You can live without a childhood. You can pass over it. You're the person who told me you can pass over, you, the one who knows. A person can pass over even himself, his soul, his being, his own dead.

The days to come, the long string of days called life, are mine. I'll dig into them with my nails and I won't let go of them. Go wherever you want, but we, all the young people robbed of childhood, robbed of trust and calm, we're a mighty army, millions, millions of young people all over the world, we'll learn to start our lives from adulthood. And our lives will be life. In spite of all those who distort life and castrate it, in spite of all those who make history, those who torment children and murder their parents, in spite of all those who are fat and satisfied, who pass by us and say, "This is how you will be," just don't bother us –

But we, Nora, we, your father and I, we?

You? What will we do with you? They taught us to pity you,

and not to pity ourselves. You put a shaky world into our hands. You. And we will live, I will live, I will live and love this life.

Love it with its ugliness, its disease, its dread – and I won't go out of my mind. I want to live. A lot to live the life of a person who can breathe, live in the light, in the light of the days to come.

And this is the light. And this is the light that will go on shining. And this is the light.

In the morning, Nora got up early and washed her hands and face in very cold water.

After breakfast, she went to get the last signature of the consul and when she came back home at ten o'clock, Tekla met her in the corridor. "Young lady, a gentleman is waiting for you there."

Taking off her coat, Nora saw her father's cane hanging on the coat rack. A thick mahogany cane with a silver monogram, Nora remembered it from early childhood.

The last test. You can pass over it.

Nevertheless, she couldn't overcome a cold murmur of the heart. But her face was cool, almost brutal. And as she slowly entered the doorway, when she saw him, there was suddenly an unexpected calm that seemed to have come spontaneously.

He was sitting in the bay at the window and reading a newspaper. Behind the big page, she saw nothing but his high suntanned forehead and his balding head.

"Papa," Nora blurted out, almost in a whisper, as if she were afraid to wake him.

He dropped the newspaper, stood up and walked to her.

Tall, sturdy, handsome, his beard had turned all white and gave his suntanned face the look of furious and proud old age. Everything in him was serene now, almost harmonious, only the look in his clear blue eyes, like the eyes of a baby not quite shaken out of his slumber, was distant and blurred, as behind a screen of fog, even though the eyes were not dim. And Nora knew that look and that walk, and knew that he came in peace.

He came to her without a smile. Kissed the hand she held out to him, then stroked one of her shoulders.

"I planned to see you before you left. Lisa told me you're going back there tomorrow."

"Yes."

"And I'm not disturbing your travel preparations?"

"Of course not, Papa."

"Wait a moment, don't sit down. I want to look at you. You're big, but pale, as always. And tomorrow, you'll go back to school. You have to take care of your health. Your nerves, the main thing is your nerves."

"Yes, Papa."

"Come, let's sit here."

They sat down across from one another. His look lingered on her forehead, her cheeks, her mouth. And even though he wanted to examine her, to see her very well, the look was distant and blurred.

For a while they were silent. Nora didn't know how to start a conversation. Fear and regret bubbled up in her.

But he began, "Albert told me a lot about you. Have you seen him?"

"Yes."

"And he left already, most likely?"

"Yes. He left. And how are you, Papa?"

"Thank God. But the heart, the heart, you know, my heart always aches. And those stupid doctors…"

Nora knew her father's heart was strong and healthy, and much as the doctors wanted to prove to him that there was no heart healthier than his, he persisted in declaring that he had a heart condition.

She sighed for fear of annoying him.

"And how is Mama?"

They sat and engaged in small talk like old acquaintances who hadn't seen each other in many years and time had wiped out their shared memories and thoughts, and all they have to say when they meet are conventional courtesies.

About half an hour later, he got up to go.

"Perhaps you'll stay for lunch?" Nora suggested in a shaky voice, for she felt very guilty.

But when he refused, she was relieved.

She accompanied him to the stairs.

When he left, he kissed her forehead.

"May God take care of you, child. And you take good care of your health."

He patted her neck lightly. And left.

Nora left on the train that departed before sunrise. Her mother and Lisa accompanied her to the station.

A thin rain was falling and very few passengers boarded the train.

The mother entered the compartment with her and the porter, and some long-legged man there helped her put up her things.

The mother was sad and tried very hard to hide her sadness and forced herself to smile all the time.

Then the train moved, and the two lost figures stayed on the platform, until they were swallowed up by the darkness and the distance.

In Nora's compartment sat a dozing old woman, and that long-legged man was reading a French newspaper.

About half an hour later, the man began talking with Nora, and they talked and smoked to the dissatisfaction of the woman, who woke up from her doze now and then and stated with restrained anger that only by chance had she wound up in the smoking car.

"And that woman who got into the car, is she your mother?" asked the man.

"Yes. She's a teacher. She's a vocational teacher."

"And your father?"

Nora didn't answer. She turned her face back to the window.

There, an autumn dawn, veiled in gray, was rising very slowly above the fields and groves. And bare, shaking trees ran behind. And in some small station where the express train didn't stop, the light of a pale and dimmed streetlamp flickers in the gray of the new morning.

Afterword

Rereading *And This Is the Light,* Lea Goldberg's Only Novel

As mentioned in the introduction, *Vehu Ha'Or* (*And This Is the Light*) was one of the first novels published in Hebrew by a woman.[1] Stylistically and thematically ahead of its time, with its psychological, semiautobiographical qualities, fragmentary form and episodic texture, it foreshadowed later and contemporary sensibilities in Hebrew literature.

In the history of Hebrew literature, *And This Is the Light,*

1. Lea Goldberg, *Vehu Ha'Or* [*It Is the Light*] (1946; Tel Aviv, 1994). Segments of this Afterword are from "Rereading *It Is the Light*, Lea Goldberg's Only Novel," in *Prooftexts*, Vol. 17, 1997, 245–265.

written in the tradition of lyrical prose, was a swerve from the mainstream realistic and ideologically motivated writing of the 1940s. In the context of Goldberg's own writing, the novel raises myriad questions: Why did Goldberg the poet choose to publish only this novel? Why is the strategy of the novel so different from that of her poetry? Why is its narrative style so fragmented? Why did she write a psychological novel in 1946, in the midst of national trauma and a crisis in her poetry writing? In other words, where does this novel fit into her literary biography?

One may find attempts to answer some of these questions in Ofra Yaglin's analysis: "Written in midlife, *And This Is the Light* is an effort to unfold a complete scroll in prose."[2] Yaglin sees in the novel's form and texture proof of Goldberg's hesitancy in this medium. She thinks that Goldberg's prose works (*Letters from an Imaginary Journey*,[3] *And This Is the Light*, and *A Meeting with a Poet*)[4] are motivated by an autobiographical-documentary impulse. Indeed, critics who have worked on the novel have stressed this element.[5] And no wonder. Although the heroine's name is Nora, not Lea, any reader acquainted with the author's life can spot uncamouflaged details, beginning with her age and the geography of her experience, and extending all the way to her father's mental illness. Adi Zemach and Sara Ben-Re'uven have even noted that Goldberg's portrait of Arin, the narrator's love interest in the novel, is strikingly similar to that of Avraham Ben-Yitzhak, a poet whom Goldberg greatly admired and had met while writing *And This Is the Light*.[6]

---

2. Ofra Yaglin, *Yedioth Aharonoth*, 7 May 1994.
3. Lea Goldberg, *Mikhtavim Minesia Meduma* [*Letters from an Imaginary Journey*] (Tel Aviv, 1937; 1982).
4. Lea Goldberg, *Pegisha im Meshorer* [*A Meeting with a Poet*] (Tel Aviv, 1952).
5. For example, in A.B. Yoffe, *Pegishot im Lea Goldberg* [*Meetings with Lea Goldberg*] (Tel Aviv: Tserikover Press, 1984), see Oren, "The Fragments and the Whole"; Ezra Sussman, "Preface to a Struggle," pp. 41–45; and Yoffe's "Introduction," pp. 7–37. See also Hillel Barzel, "The Light and the Other Light" [Hebrew], *Haboker*, 13 November 1964.
6. Adi Zemach, "Into Reality: On the Prose of Lea Goldberg" in *Pegishot im*

The novel's autobiographical perspective is the reverse of her poetry.[7] Goldberg's early poetry usually speaks in generalities and is not personal; it is controlled, structured and universal. *And This Is the Light*, notwithstanding its slight plot and its mere 194 pages in the original, invites the reader to take a detailed tour through the *via dolorosa* of one specific girl's adolescence. But why? The will to document is there. Goldberg did, after all, leave diaries that she could have destroyed, but we must be aware that autobiographical tendencies present in personal diaries are not proof of literary motivations.[8] The contrast between the novel and the poems may be explained within Goldberg's poetics, as if she were saying, "What is permitted in prose is forbidden in poetry." Yet to return to the questions I raised above, why did the poet choose prose, and why exactly then?

Did the critic A.B. Yoffe sense this problem when he summarized Goldberg's literary activity in the 1940s in his *Meetings with Lea*

Meshoreret, ed. Ruth Kartun-Blum and Anat Weissman, Sifriat Poalim 2000, pp. 66–69; Sara Ben-Re'uven, "Who is the Night that Comes to the Owl?" *Ha'aretz*, October 8, 2010. The description of Arin can be found on p.31 of *And This Is the Light*.

7. Goldberg's theoretical writings express her views. See, for example: Lea Goldberg, "*Hamisha Prakim Biyesodot Hashira*" ["Five Chapters in the Fundamentals of Poetry"] (Jerusalem, 1957); "*He'arot La'estetika shel Hasimbolizm*" ["Remarks on the Aesthetics of Symbolism"], in *Ktavim Midor Ume'ever* [*Writings from a Generation and Beyond*], eds. T. Ruebner and Ora Koris (Tel Aviv, 1977), pp. 61–78, 242–59. See also Mati Meged, "Lea Goldberg: Theory of Poetry and Practice of Poetry" [Hebrew], Molad 13 (1970), 12–22. Meged's article points out the similarities between Goldberg's theoretical thoughts on poetry and her own writing. Goldberg's literary taste and her poetic views are also reflected in the works that she chose to translate from world literature (Petrarch and Dante, for example) and in her work "*Letters from an Imaginary Journey*" (see n.3 above).

8. Only the first notebook of her diaries was published at the original writing of this article (ages eleven and a half to fifteen, *Genazim*, Vol. 5, 1977). Segments of additional diary-notebooks are quoted in A.B. Yoffe, *Pegishot im Lea Goldberg* (see n.5 above); and Amia Lieblich, *El Lea* [*Toward Lea*] (Hakibbutz Hameuchad, 1995). The first scholarly study of the diaries is in Ofra Yeglin's doctoral dissertation at Tel Aviv University: "Perhaps with Different Eyes: Modern Classicism and Classical Modernism in Lea Goldberg's Poetry" (Hakibbutz Hameuchad, Tel Aviv University, 2002).

Goldberg?[9] He observed that she was a productive critic, editor, and translator, but wrote very few poems between the late 1930s and 1948, when her acclaimed poetry collection, *Al HaPriha* (*On the Blossom*), appeared. Yoffe does take note of *And This Is the Light*, but insists: "There is no doubt: the crisis in her creative writing in those years came following the war in Europe and the news of the Holocaust" (p. 113).

Was that the real, or only, reason for her crisis? And what was the novel's role in the poet-author's life? To answer this question, we must identify and analyze two other texts, as distant from each other as Vienna from Toledo. But first we need to know the story.

The time is summer 1931, when twenty-year-old Nora Krieger returns from the university in Berlin to her home in Lithuania. While on the train, she recalls traumatic childhood scenes centered on her father's mental illness. Nora is met at the train station by her mother and Aunt Lisa, who take her to spend the night at the home of friends. The next day, they depart for a vacation, but not before her mother reveals to Nora that she has divorced her father. On the ferry, on the way to the forest, Albert Arin, an old school friend of Nora's father who has just returned from America after many years, introduces himself to Nora. At the resort, a quasi-romantic friendship develops. Upon returning to her provincial hometown, Nora wanders about, visits friends, falls ill, attends a funeral – and mostly longs for Arin. He dallies with another woman, becomes ever more estranged from Nora and her family, and finally disappears without a trace. In the last chapter, "October," Nora says her goodbyes and leaves once more for the university.

Nora's name recalls Ibsen's *A Doll's House*. Goldberg does not leave the identification of this intertext to chance:

> "Why is your name Nora?"
>
> "At that time, Lisa was reading Ibsen," explained Nora briefly, and blushed. (p. 40)

---

9. A.B. Yoffe (see n.5 above), p. 113.

This apparent disclosure of the author's intent may actually disguise her deeper motives for the choice of the name Nora. The unmasking ploy is used for a different effect in Goldberg's first work in prose, *Letters from an Imaginary Journey*. There, "L" declares that she writes "like an actor who makes his face up on stage, in front of the audience," in other words, without pretending. In *And This Is the Light*, Goldberg's reader is implicitly led to see similar traits between the Lithuanian Nora and Ibsen's Nora. Like other critics, Ezra Sussman[10] takes the narrative ploys of the implied narrator at face value. He comments on both heroines' fear of inheriting the father's weak mental traits, their rebellion against the past, and their decision to be true to themselves even at the cost of leaving home. While Sussman does not discuss this, it is worth noting that both works also contain sharp criticism of petit-bourgeois values; a maid's subplot that parallels the main plot; and a strong feminist (as it might be called now) undercurrent. In addition, one could argue that Goldberg expresses, via Ibsen, heretical thoughts against all manner of political and social revolutions. Perhaps she shares his belief in one's need to discover one's own essence and to realize it. Like Ibsen, whose work she translated, Goldberg knows that true liberation can come only from within.[11]

However, giving a strict Ibsen interpretation to the name Nora is missing the mask beneath the mask that this unreliable narrator wears. An anonymous mask-painting, which is a recurrent motif in this novel, may even be an understated sign of the different layers of this text. In Goldberg's nuanced dialectics of masking and unmasking, taking the Nora mask off only reveals another mask, a text other than *A Doll's House*. That hidden text is never named, and I cannot extrinsically prove that Goldberg read it, even though it is most probable that she did. Yet that other text illuminates this misunderstood novel, and exposes a fateful junction in its author's creative life and inner drama.

---

10. See n.5.
11. Rolf Fjelde, foreword in Henrik Ibsen, *Four Major Plays*, vol. 1 (Signet, 2006).

Nora is Dora. Freud's Dora. "Fragment of an Analysis of a Case of Hysteria," better known as "The Case of Dora," became popular when it was reissued in 1923. Traces of Goldberg's general awareness of Freud's theory are scattered in her literary essays and letters, but the name Dora appears only in her play.[12]

"The Case of Dora" describes Feud's fragmented treatment of Ida Bauer – Dora. According to psychoanalyst Erik Erikson, this case history became the classic analysis of the structure and developmental origin of neurosis.[13] The text is also, says literary critic Steven Marcus, a literary masterpiece.[14] He has compared it to an Ibsen play in which the author is one of the characters.

Careful reading of Goldberg's novel and Freud's case history reveals surprising parallels in plot, structure, style and narrative. The fictive timeframe is the same in both: three determining months in the life of an eighteen- to twenty-year-old girl-woman. Both accounts also reach back to fragments of childhood traumas that surface, piece by

---

12. Sigmund Freud, "Fragment of an Analysis of a Case of Hysteria" (1905), better known as "The Case of Dora." All references in this paper are to *Dora: An Analysis of a Case of Hysteria*, ed. Philip Reif (1963; New York, 1993). "Dora" became the focus of an entire scholarly corpus in the medical, psychoanalytical world as well as the academic, literary one. More recently, feminist critics have contributed to the discussion – for example, Bernheimer, Charles and Claire Kahane, eds., *In Dora's Case: Freud-hysteria-feminism* (New York: Columbia University Press, 1985). Since my interest lies in Goldberg's work, I only consider references that relate directly to my reading. For Goldberg's references to Freud, see, for example, her letter to Tuvia Ruebner quoted in Lieblich (p. 255; see n.8 above). There she angrily recalls Jung's anti-Semitic attack against Freud in Germany in 1933. See also her article "Alexander Block and New Russian Poetry," *Me'asef* 3 (1962): 279–91. For Goldberg's drama, see n.15 below.

13. Erik Erikson, first part of a lecture given at the American Psychoanalytic Association, 1961, published in the *Journal of the American Psychoanalytic Association* 10 (1962): 451–74. Erikson was the first to open the discussion on Dora and adolescence.

14. Steven Marcus, "Freud and Dora: Story, History, Case History" in *Literature and Psychoanalysis*, eds. Edith Kurzweil and William Phillips (New York: Columbia University Press, 1983). First appeared in *Partisan Review* 41 (1974): 12–23, 89–108. The literary value of Dora is also discussed by H. Ellenberger, *The Discovery of the Unconscious* (New York: Basic Books, 1970), among others.

piece, in memory. Both narratives end in an arbitrary, one-sided way, before the riddle is completely solved. The essence of both stories is packed in dreams: a nightmare that haunts Nora and Dora for years and another dream toward the end of both texts. Motifs common to both are: letters and their concealment, cemeteries, funerals, maids and their dismissal, aunts, walks in resort areas and forests, railway stations, paintings, talk of suicide, self-sacrifice, devotion, and illness.

Zeitgeist and its expressions in European literature of the time may explain the recurrence and combination of these various elements in the two texts before us; but there is something more. At the core of both works lies the parallel that overdetermines this combination. What motivates plot structure and theme in both narratives is mental illness as well as the distinctive dovetailing of somatic readiness and the potential psychological benefits of illness.

Nora's fever rises and her illness returns again and again throughout the book, always after a traumatic experience. The recollection of Nora's earliest childhood illness is tied to the horrifying scene that changed Nora's family's life forever. It took place at the border crossing, in "The Year 1919," when her father was accused of espionage:

> Then they locked him up in an empty barn. And day after day, for ten straight days, they executed him, as it were. For ten days in a row, that game went on. And the man was broken, then, for the first time, Nora heard him weeping in a thin, female, sobbing voice. And the desperate pleas in the mother's voice: "For the child's sake, I beg you, for the child's sake..."
>
> [Afterward] Nora remained alone at the crossroads among fields – to watch the pile of belongings. She sat on the bundles. Alone. In the field. At the crossroads. It grew dark. It was cold. Her hands and legs were frozen. Armed soldiers passed by. They didn't touch her. Hours passed. It was absolutely clear: never would her parents come back. She would freeze here at night. And a little self-pity: she was only

eight years old, too young to die! But fear froze everything. (pp. 16–17)

Nora, haunted by nightmares, fell sick with the measles after this episode. In the years that followed, illness visited her after Hanukkah dances where she felt ignored or when children made fun of her in school. During the summer of the novel, a dying aunt whispers in her ear the verdict of madness: "It's in your blood. In the blood of the whole family" (p. 111). This is the aunt's blunt answer to the question that inwardly tortured Nora: Was the father's mental illness caused by the war or heredity? After Nora hears the aunt's verdict, her fever rises.

Nora benefits from her illness like Dora, who developed disturbing symptoms in order to regain her father's heart. The possible gains from illness can be: conservation of emotional effort, childlike dependency, escape from duties, as well as love, pity, and attention – all pleasures that good health often does not allow. The narrator's voice reflects Nora's intuitive awareness of the emotional function of illness: "Ever since Nora's recovery, Arin had changed completely and was no longer soft and friendly as during those ten good days" (p. 141).

A certain pleasure also accompanied illness in Nora's secondary-school days. She then cleaved to *David Copperfield*, her favorite of Dickens's works. Dora is the name of Copperfield's childish wife. Is the mention of Dickens's book a signal to the reader? (Marcus even suggests that Freud chose this name for his patient Ida Bauer because he loved *David Copperfield*.) Although repressed here, the name Dora finds its way into Goldberg's aforementioned drama, *The Lady of the Castle*,[15] written ten years after the novel. There, the leading male character bears a surprising resemblance to the father in the novel. His prophetic hallucinations mirror the father's insane, grandiose speech in little Nora's schoolyard. As usual, high fever follows.

Nora and Dora are both a kind of anti-Lolita: young women

---

15. Lea Goldberg, *Ba'alat Ha'armon* [*The Lady of the Castle*] (1954; Tel Aviv, 1979).

who, for one reason or another, are emotionally involved with a contemporary of their father, unable to fulfill their hearts' desires. Moreover, the men in question – Herr K. in "The Case of Dora," and Arin in the case of Nora – are both not only acquaintances of the father, but a kind of double. According to Freud's report, underlying Dora's childhood and history of illness are her father's life circumstances. In Freud's opinion, the physical and mental afflictions that had plagued her father since Dora was six years old increased her affection for him. When she was eighteen, and had become unmistakably neurotic, the father entrusted her to Freud for treatment. Freud believed that, considering her natural gifts and neurotic disposition, Dora took after her father's family, and that her difficulties were inherited. He reports that, beginning at the age of eight, she suffered nervous aches and pains and high fevers and was discontent with herself and her family. She was jealousy-possessed; her love for her father was greater than she knew or would willingly admit. In fact, she was in love with him.

Freud recorded "The Case of Dora" in 1900, shortly after treating Ida Bauer. In this work, he defined and applied one of the basic themes of his thought and of the modern mind: viewing the unconscious erotic love relations between parents and children as a revival of feelings in infancy. In analyzing Dora, he maintains: "The myth of Oedipus is probably to be regarded as a poetical rendering of what is typical in these relations – on the part of a daughter for her father, or on the part of a son for his mother" (p. 49).

Is it a coincidence, then, that Goldberg forged a character so similar to Dora? That this novel has a close intertextual relationship to the quintessential modernist text in which the narrator, Freud, unfolds and explains, as no one else before him, the plot of a love affair between a daughter and her father?

And This Is the Light and "The Case of Dora" travel along parallel axes of pain: love for a father or his substitute, accompanied by jealousy and betrayal; and the fear of having inherited the father's neurotic tendencies, blame for his having handed them down, and hatred of him for it.

Herr K. in "The Case of Dora" is, on the surface, a close family friend, but the truth is that his wife is the father's lover. Nora's Arin, in his youth, shared good times with her father, mother and aunt. In the fictive present, he is a likely candidate for attachment with Nora, her mother, or her aunt, but he betrays all three.

Dora's father brought her for treatment to Freud, for whom she developed a transference of her love-hate for her father and Herr K. It was during his treatment of Dora that Freud discovered "transference." In his report of the case, he described this new discovery: "Transferences replace some earlier person by the person of the physician" (p. 106). And then: "It was clear that I was replacing [Dora's] father in her imagination" (p. 107).

Much as in the case of Dora, the novel is replete with transference and (pseudo) therapy sessions. Arin functions as Herr K. and as Freud at once, a potential lover and a potential therapist. Throughout, Arin is in touch with Nora's father and plays, perhaps like Freud, the role of a double agent; that is, he "treats" the father and reports to Nora, "treats" Nora and reports to the father. This is evident from the father's letters to Nora and from her conversations with Arin, who insists on separating his two "patients" and suggests that Nora refrain from visiting her father. Nora is aware that Arin is the image of her father: "Suddenly his face was the face of a lad. But he is old, he could be my father. Could be my father, my father…" (p. 43). The extent to which this transference was justified is revealed to Nora only at the end:

> And you couldn't remember whose face his face looked like at the opera when he came back to the box. Like Papa, you fool, like Papa! The blurred, hard look, like that time in the dream. In the mirror. (p. 192)

The mirror-dream that Nora recalls occurred long before, but only now does she reach its depths:

> …she was standing…and combing her hair. And suddenly she

sees in the mirror that [Arin's] approaching her from behind and standing behind her back, smiling. She immediately turned her face to him, to see him, to see him and not his reflection, and he was her father. (p. 124)

Here, with the face reflected in the mirror, Goldberg captures metaphorically the essence of the term "transference," which Freud coined in "The Case of Dora."

But Nora is not the only one in the novel who knows about mirrored images and transference. Arin often thinks like Freud, or behaves like him. Freud's model of a therapeutic session reverberates in the novel's dialogues:

"Say something."
  "What?"
  "What do you like to remember?"
  [...]
  Nora didn't know why her mouth opened or why she said what she said. (p. 40)

Freud's voice echoes also thorough Arin's laconic response to the flood of sights and sounds gushing from her. All he says is: "Yes" (p. 41). Freud conceptualized this form of interchange in "The Case of Dora":

I now let the patient himself choose the subject of the day's work and in that way I start out from whatever surface his unconscious happens to be presenting to his notice at the moment. (p. 6)

On another occasion, almost at the end of the novel, there is a long, tortured conversation about Nora's terrifying dream. The interpretation suggested by Arin is patronizing and dismissive. It becomes clear that Nora has been betrayed by the mature man to whom the love for her father is being transferred, the man who identified with her mentally ill father. The same applies to the forty-two-year-old Freud, who treated young Dora while committed to her father.

Freud betrayed Dora twice: once by suggesting to her to welcome Herr K.'s approaches, and again when he did not validate her anger at the adults who raised her in a lie and manipulated her feelings for their own purposes. The sense of an adult (not only male) conspiracy against an adolescent girl is prevalent in both works.

But behind the intertextual relations of characters, materials of motifs and themes, lies another connection. In "The Case of Dora," Freud presents not only a new kind of treatment, but a new kind of narrative: "everything emerges piecemeal, woven into various contexts, and distributed over widely separated periods of time" (p. 9). This new kind of narrative that Freud introduced is Goldberg's very style in this novel. Thus, to answer one of the questions posed before, the fragmented narrative style may be a deliberate artistic choice and not hesitancy in this medium, as Yaglin suggested. The story's skeleton is linear, but its telling is winding, multitextured. It seems to move spontaneously, but it has its own inner logic. Sometimes the story turns backward in a kind of loop around itself. Freud, like the narrator in the novel, is a modernist narrator – not entirely reliable, for any analysis must advance piece by piece, examining thoughts and events, segment after segment, not in a chronological flow, always presenting a partial picture, never knowing it all.

Moreover, the weightiest material of both the novel and the case history is collected in dreams. Their meaning is, in some measure, the meaning of the text, be it the novel or the case history. Through Dora, Freud demonstrated the art of dream interpretation and how it exposes what is hidden in the inner life. The analysis of dreams, and especially of Dora's recurrent nightmare, is a tour de force of interpretation. Goldberg's Nora, on the other hand, does not confide her nightmare to anyone. Unlike Dora's case history, the novel does not offer a ready-made solution. Here, it is the reader's task to translate the language of dreams into coherent thought by collecting scraps of plot, motifs, and images and by following the recurrent nightmare's windings.

The striking similarity in the language that introduces the dreams in both Freud's and Goldberg's texts is recognizable even in translation – Freud from German, Goldberg from Hebrew. Freud says of Dora, "she reported that a few nights earlier she had once again had a dream which she had already dreamt in exactly the same way on many previous occasions" (p. 56), and in the novel: "That night, a childhood nightmare returned to her. The same dream, without any change at all, just as she had dreamed it four times, always after an interval of many years." (p. 15). In both dreams, the motif of fire and a rescue attempt dominates, and in both, a helpless feminine figure appears. Freud retells Dora's dream: "A house was on fire. My father was standing beside my bed and woke me up. I dressed myself quickly… We hurried downstairs, and as soon as I was outside I woke up" (p. 56). Freud sees here Dora's wish that her father will rescue her from falling in love with Herr K. According to his interpretation, she awakens her infantile infatuation with her father in order to escape the burning house, a symbol of her love for K.

In the novel, Nora's dream is rich in detail: Amid the firewood that Antonina the maid is carrying,

> is a dumpy Russian beggar woman. A small dark kerchief is on her head, and her arms and legs are amputated. She's short and smooth as a thick log. Nora, the four-year-old, walks behind Antonina and shouts, "Let go of the woman, Antonina, let go of the woman!" But Antonina's steps are even and calm. She goes inside. In the big living room she unloads the bundle of wood with the woman rolled up in it, then she calmly feeds it into the gaping maw of the stove. Her coarse, calm hands reach for matches in the big pocket of her apron. "Don't light it, don't light it!" Nora pleads. "Don't you see, that's the woman sitting in the little cart at the corner! She begs for alms 'for Jesus the Savior'!" And the little woman among the wood slowly

nods her wrinkled head and her thin black mouth stretches into a smile of mute agreement, pitiful to the point of tears. The tears choke Nora. She feels her legs die beneath her. Then Antonina puts the lighted match to the dry wood, and it all goes up in flames.

At that moment in the dream, Nora awoke this time too, as in all previous times. (p. 15)

Nora, when not asleep, wonders about the weird meaning of the dream, but does not come to any conclusion. My hypothesis is that the tiny woman is little Nora, a baby that needs to be carried. In a recalled childhood picture from age eight, Nora's father carries her to see a beautifully decorated store window. Does Nora, like Dora, hope the father will carry her away and rescue her from danger, just as he did when she was a baby? Does she awaken her need for him to balance her doomed attraction for Arin? The danger of fire in this context may symbolize madness,[16] passion, and love, but also death or a death wish. The pitiful beggar woman may also be a transformation of the father who pleaded for his life while his daughter looked on, her arms too short to help, and her feelings of guilt growing. The father's life was indeed saved, but he was touched by the fire of madness. His daughter continues to fear insanity and she, too, feels helpless, with no control over her fate. Freud's Dora escaped in her dream, as in reality. For Nora, within the framework of the nightmare, there is only terror and paralysis. The cure had to come from outside.

I now revisit the opening question: What is the novel's place in Goldberg's literary biography? The novel of return, which opens with the chapter "The Train Returns Home" (not "*Nora* Returns Home"), unveils a process of psychological, experiential return. This process

---

16. Using fire to describe madness is prevalent in literature as well as in the symbolic language of dreams. See, for example: Kay Redfield Jamison, *Touched with Fire: Manic-Depressive Illness and the Artistic Temperament* (New York: Free Press Paperback, 1993).

follows a Freudian recognition of the trap of childhood and a conscious effort to be free of it. Over a three-month period, Nora-Dora-Lea performs a kind of self-analysis, at times aided by the beloved, the father-substitute, but mostly on her own. She plunges into the depths of the psyche to dredge up, to reconstruct, or restructure critical details from childhood, to rework them and understand how they function in her present. If the central consciousness succeeds in this task, it may bring her personal redemption. The actual telling of the story may defeat dangerous, amorphous materials such as the embarrassing content of traumatic and partially repressed experiences. Thus, when Goldberg writes her life, she turns to prose, to a story, and she chooses the genre of the novel rather than that of poetry for this task.

Contrary to the critic A.B. Yoffe's aforementioned opinion, I suggest that Lea Goldberg's poetic silence in the 1940s was more related to a mental crisis than to the war in Europe. My thinking here gains validity mostly from a parallel thinking process that is reflected in the body of the novel. There, Goldberg poses the question of whether it was war or heredity that was the source of the father's madness. The answer given in the text is that inner causes, not external circumstances, are responsible for one's mental state. Using the text's inner logic, as well as a critical reading of it, I reach a parallel conclusion. The crisis in Goldberg's writing was internally motivated. A representative line from her 1943 diary offers some external support for my reading: "It seems, sometimes, that I'm close to a nervous breakdown" (4 September 1943).

Before she could burst forth with the beautiful poems of *On the Blossom*, published in 1948, she had to overcome her inner chaos. Like Bialik, who, according to Miron,[17] had to "take leave of the impoverished self," before he could shatter ten-year-old walls of silence, so with Goldberg. The writing of *And This Is the Light*, and its publication in 1946, was like touching fire without being consumed, staring

---

17. Dan Miron, *Hapreda min Ha'ani He'ani* [*Taking Leave of the Impoverished Self*] (Tel Aviv, 1985).

at the horror and taming it. But was it her belief in the redemptive powers of psychoanalysis that led her to choose, consciously or unconsciously, the psychoanalytical model? I think not.

"The Case of Dora" is a story of the failure of psychoanalytical treatment – Freud's failure. Dora forsook Freud almost without warning, after three months of treatment. This was her revenge against him, her father, and Herr K., all of whom had betrayed her. Freud's text serves Goldberg as a text of failure, as a model that needs to be rejected, but not before its potential is extracted.

And This Is the Light may be read as a case history told from the patient's – the angry betrayed woman's – point of view and not from the male analyst's perspective. Tables are turned, roles reversed; it is the woman telling her own story, one of the first in Hebrew fiction. In this reading, a new Lea Goldberg emerges, anti-Freudian, rebellious, subversive.

But if the journey of return ended in failure, what was the wellspring from which Goldberg drew her strength of soul? The answer seems to be flagged in the novel's title. Whereas the novel delves into the subterranean layers of the soul, its title, *And This Is the Light*, is the direct opposite of darkness.[18]

In the last pages of her novel, Goldberg slips into a Zionist interpretation of the essence of "the light" and of her linguistic choice. This has often been mistakenly read by critics[19] – Amia Lieblich claims this segment is an ideological appendix, irrelevant to the story. But as I will attempt to show, "Hebrew" and "light" hold a deep meaning, and not only an ideological one.

The title, as well as the epigraph, is from the medieval Hebrew

---

18. Zemach has also noted that although Goldberg's prose pieces are sad and often revolve around broken love, they are unfailingly optimistic: there is always a new horizon beyond the suffering. Zemach (see n.6 above), p. 70.

19. Zemach claims that the "light" is simultaneously Arin, Nora's love for him, and Nora's own life. Zemach (see n.6 above), pp. 71–72.

poet Moses ibn Ezra.[20] The epigraph reappears toward the end, followed by two more lines from the poem:

> It is the light that goes on glowing through my youth,
> And glows yet brighter as I grow old.
> It must be of the substance of God's light,
> For otherwise it would be fading
> As my years and strength decline.
>
> (Lines 8–9 in the original poem; p. 167)

One sleepless night, shortly after the final break with Arin, Nora comes upon Ibn Ezra's lines in a book near her bed. She reads the words from *A Selection of Hebrew Poetry* as though out of context: "Somewhere, in the middle of the poem, were lines that, for some reason, she didn't connect with what went before" (p. 167). In other words, Nora endows the poet's words with her own idiosyncratic meaning:

> It is the light. And thanks to it we live our lives. It is the light – and it is. And what is it? It is the light.
>
> [...]
>
> And suddenly, as if from those words, or perhaps in some connection hidden even from her, she remembered one man, not young, rather tall with a wide brow, one of her acquaintances in Berlin, Elhanan Kron, who would stand leaning on the window at the "Seminary of Semitic Languages," leafing through some book with square letters, and she heard his voice: "To choose a language as you choose a ring. That right to choose a language like a wedding ring and make a blessing over it, 'I thee wed.'"
>
> It is the light. And perhaps this is the light – (p. 168)

---

20. Quotations from the poem in this paper are from Raymond Scheindlin's beautiful and faithful translation in *Prooftexts*, Vol. 17, pp. 260–265.

This paragraph reflects Nora's quest for a creative solution to her pain. Attempts to work through her fear of madness and her love for her father were frustrated. The hope of making peace with the past by remembering and telling it had collapsed. But "the light" does appear, and the revelation of a new way is rendered in images. Finding the light means bonding with the Hebrew language, as one bonds with a beloved spouse. In the act of choosing Hebrew, Nora thus made a painful switch from a relationship with a man – who may leave her or go crazy – to a relationship with a language, which will always be there for her. This option emerges from Goldberg's original commentary on Genesis 2:24, "Therefore shall a man *leave* his father and his mother and cleave unto his wife; and they shall be one flesh." "His wife," according to the novel's interpretation, is "his language"! The Hebrew language is the instrument of liberation. Russian, Yiddish, and German are loaded with terrible memories of the recent past; therefore, *leaving* mother's and father's tongues may open a new life. The fact that Goldberg chose Hebrew, a language she did not know well, for her diaries from age eleven onward – could not have stemmed from national feelings alone. Moreover, some of her adolescent lines evoke those in the novel: "Writing not in Hebrew is for me like not writing at all" (3 September 1926), and: "it seems to me that there is something in the future. Some *lighthouse* toward which I turn. Hebrew writing [creation]" (21 October 1927; my emphasis).[21]

Psychoanalyst Roger Casement says that Samuel Beckett, who wrote in French although his mother tongue was English, did so in order to preserve his gift for creative expression and in order to sur-

---

21. Lieblich, *El Lea*, pp. 37–40; 159–62 (see n.8). Lieblich, the psychologist, misunderstands the novel's conclusion and equates "the solution, the light, Zionism, the Hebrew language" (p. 38). Later in the book she misreads the meaning of the "lighthouse" image, which she herself quotes (p. 159). Lieblich connects it again to Zionism and misses the psychological function of Hebrew, independently of its national motivation.

vive mentally.[22] Physical separation was not enough to free him of suffocating ties to his mother. The only catalyst for his inner liberation was the rejection of his mother tongue.

It seems to me that Goldberg's case bears some resemblance to Beckett's. The bond between "light" and Hebrew (or "square letters") rises from psychological depths, from the need to detach, to erase the past. Through writing in Hebrew, Goldberg writes a new self and exorcises her demons. Writing the past in Hebrew, not in the languages in which the events took place, is possible. Only thus can one look backward without being swallowed into the darkness of childhood.

Lea Goldberg went after Hebrew, to the land of Hebrew, lived inside the language, inside the light; from the language, she drew her strength to live. The work of the novel, therefore, is not memory and reconstruction, but rather, writing anew, rewriting, saying goodbye to memories in order to find her way back to composing poetry in Hebrew.

But should we follow Goldberg's implicit instructions to read the lines from Ibn Ezra, "Detached and cut off from the logical connection of the…poem" (p. 167)? I think not. Goldberg, the masking artist, almost explicitly cautions the reader against using the entire poem as a code to understanding the novel. But to ignore Goldberg's caution and to read the entire poem, "The Lamp Within," is to discover that the choice was not so random. The essence of the poem illuminates the novel. First, the exaggerated specificity in the poet's name: Rabbi Moses, son of *Jacob* son of Ezra; this poet is commonly referred to as Moses ibn Ezra, but Jacob is Nora's father's name (p. 33). Secondly, it is a poem about a struggle with (mental) slumber, and reading it that sleepless night led Nora to her new path. Moreover, this is a mystical poem, a love poem to a distant and superior

---

22. Jacqueline Amati-Mehler and Simona Argentinieri, *The Babel of the Unconscious: Mother Tongue and Foreign Languages in the Psychoanalytic Dimension* (Madison, CT: International Universities Press, 1993), pp. 176–87.

"He" who gives His light to His beloved, the mortal. The soul of the poet, God's beloved, is part of God's spirit – a divine presence in the poet's person. "For in my inert body, God has kindled, / From His radiance, a lamp."[23] The divine light in the human body grows stronger as a man grows older and is freed of earthly desires. Had the light come from an earthly source, it would have diminished with time, but since its source is divine it will continue shining forever. It is by the power of this light – which is the poet's soul connected to God – that Ibn Ezra longs for wisdom and not for the lures of this world. With the strength that God gives, the poet swims in the sea of the ancient sages' thought in order to "plunge and bring up pearls to ornament the throat of Time." The "sea" of the sages' writings serves the poet as a source for his words. The pearls, or beads, drawn from that sea, are used in the beautiful necklace he creates in his poems and rhymes. (*Haruzim* in Hebrew means both "beads" and "rhymes.") Did Goldberg also plunge into the same sea? Is Ibn Ezra's poem the cipher of the novel? The "light" then, is the creative spark, writing, and in Hebrew! Only after *And This Is the Light* was completed could Lea Goldberg return to her verse. She never wrote another novel but continued stringing lyrical beads even on her deathbed. For Goldberg, as for the hardship-laden, wandering medieval poet, writing was "the balm that soothes my pain."

---

23. See n.20 above.

About the Author

Lea Goldberg (1911–1970) was born in Königsberg, East Prussia (now Kaliningrad, Russia), and began writing Hebrew verse as a schoolgirl in Lithuania. She received a PhD in Semitic Languages from Bonn University before immigrating to Palestine in 1935. Best known as a poet, Goldberg was the author of numerous children's books, plays and essays, a theater critic, an editor, a translator, and founder of the Hebrew University of Jerusalem's Department of Comparative Literature, where she served as chairperson for nearly twenty years. Goldberg was awarded many literary prizes, including the Israel Prize for Literature, posthumously, in 1970.

The fonts used in this book are from the
Garamond and Bernhard families

The Toby Press publishes fine writing,
available at leading bookstores everywhere. For more
information, please visit www.tobypress.com